The Reaping

Annie Oldham

Copyright © 2013 by Annie Oldham

Cover design by Renée Barratt

All rights reserved, including the right of reproduction in whole or in part in any form.

While every precaution has been taken in the preparation of this book, the author and publisher assume no responsibility for errors or omissions, or for damages resulting from the use of the information contained herein.

The Reaping
ISBN-13: 978-1493564859
ISBN-10: 1493564854

*For my girls, who give me the time to write
and call me the best mom in the world.
I'm blessed.*

ONE

I wake up to the sounds of the others breathing. They found me yesterday just north of the cabin—nine nomads looking to chase down a rumor that has spread like wildfire. They emerged like shadows from behind the trees. I wasn't afraid, though. If it had been soldiers, I would have heard them coming from a mile away. Nomads have learned to be nearly silent. It's a self-preservation thing. And nomads don't scare me like they used to. When I meet a nomad, most of them ask if I've seen a girl named Terra—if I am Terra—if I'm the one that can take them to the water's edge and then deeper, down to the colony where they'll be free.

Who knew that a place I once thought was a prison could be liberating for so many?

I peer over the edge of the loft down to where they nestle against each other like a pile of newborn mice. I don't light a fire in the hearth anymore. The smoke threading through the tree tops is too risky now that the government doesn't just hunt nomads. They hunt me.

I roll over onto my back and rest my head on my hand and stare through a small hole in the roof. I've been meaning to fix it, but I've been busy. I've visited over twelve different sites along the coast. Jessa told me I've gone as far south as what used to be Oregon and as far north as Canada, though that doesn't mean a whole lot to me. It just means that the days that I spend at the cabin—my only haven—are fewer and fewer. Jessa also told me the council has discussed building another colony. I haven't brought them that many nomads yet, but they realize the potential for what I can do.

If I squint one eye closed, I can see through the hole and through the tree boughs and catch a star's light slicing through the midnight blue sky. I'm not sure why, but I think of Jack. I don't have a north star to guide me anymore. Now I just have the sense of responsibility over these people—the sense that I'm the only one who can help. It's the one thing that holds me together. Despite all the people I've come across, I feel so lonely.

In the morning the nomads and I eat food cold out of cans and then begin our three-day hike to the ocean. I haven't come this way for two months, and I haven't noticed any unusual scanner or watcher activity, so we should be safe. None of these nomads have trackers, so there's nothing to scan.

One of the nomads lopes in stride with me. He's several years younger than me, but very tall. He's all arms and legs as he stretches his limbs to meet my pace, and his arms dangle by his sides.

"Thank you for doing this."

I nod.

"Over there—" he nods toward a girl with a splash of freckles across her nose and cheeks "—that's my little sister. Agents took my mom and dad ten months ago outside of Salt Lake City. We ran as fast as we could, but I let my sister run faster. They couldn't get her that way. They got me." His face clouds over and his bottom lip trembles. He watches his sister and doesn't look me in the eyes.

I look back where she skips along with a girl about the same age. She doesn't look scarred the way he does. The sacrifice he made saved her from whatever happened to him. But he looks so haunted I doubt he'll tell me. I put a hand on his shoulder. He looks at the horizon as he wipes the back of his hand across his eyes.

"Just—thank you."

No one else says a word to me for two days. They watch me warily, and I wish I could tell them to trust me, but those words would be lost on them. We've all seen too much to trust anyone easily. They're probably waiting for me to march them into a government trap.

When we reach the beach, it's near midnight, and I sit on the cold, damp sand and watch the waves break over and over with white foam. I shouldn't sit here out in the open, exposed. I think the government knows about me and knows what I've been doing. Just three weeks ago as I hunched in the brush lining a similar beach, the helicopters came and stayed longer, taking pictures of footprints and the groove the sub dug into the sand under the shallow water. I held my breath as they sent down a line from the helicopter, and when a single soldier slipped down it and landed in the sand like a cat, I turned and bolted through the trees.

If the agents haven't quite caught on to exactly what I'm doing, they will soon. The colony can't take just the trackerless for long—there are too many citizens of New America that deserve a home there. When those with trackers start disappearing at a faster rate than they do now, the government will sit up and take notice and wonder why their citizens are vanishing off the grid.

As midnight passes and I don't see any lights beneath the water, my heart speeds up. Jessa is never late. I rake my fingers through the sand, making long furrows like the rows I tended first in the colony and then in the oca fields of the settlement. Farming was never my vocation. Neither was cooking or medicine or marine biology like my father and grandmother. I have the gift to help people in a different way. I can give them some peace.

The first hints of daylight creep over the treeline behind me, and I wonder where the sub is. We're cutting it too close, and soon we'll be too visible. Appearing out of the woods and racing for it is dangerous enough under the cover of darkness, but during the day? I shudder. The thunderheads careening over my head toward the east filter the sunlight into a bleak gray. It's a quiet morning at least. I haven't heard helicopters beating across the sky for about three days now. That means either they're just about to appear, or I'm under the radar for the moment.

The nomads wait under the trees. Their nervous energy cuts through the crisp spring air, and a few twigs snap in their anxiety. There's always that nervous energy before the sub comes. I've done this enough times now that I can wait as still as a statue for the blue lights to appear under the water. Those around me can't quite handle that. When they see the sub, they'll dash across the open space, scurrying like mice avoiding the cat. We all worry that maybe this time the agents will be there and swoop us all up and never let us go; that the colonies will be exposed as truth and not just a bedtime story. It's a bedtime story that more and more parents are telling their children—not a fairy tale, though; something to hope for. What happened at the labor camp—the agents finding Jessa's letter and my confession to Dr. Benedict—has started rumors. I began hearing about them three months ago when a group of nomads found me and begged for a way to the colony. The word is getting out. And if it's spreading among the citizens and nomads this quickly, the nagging at the back of my brain tells me what the government will do about it can't be a good thing.

I look back to the woods. I make out nine pale faces between the branches. They all have the same expression—that the one hope of peace they all have will be ripped away only twenty yards in front of them. I wish they'd calm down. The talker—the only one who said anything to me on our hike out here—meets my eyes and shrugs his shoulders up and down. I shake my head. No, I don't see the sub yet.

The knot in my stomach tells me that I share their fear. Sure, it would be calm and safe to return to the colony. I can't argue with that. But it's not for me; it never was. Sitting here with the damp from the sand seeping through my pants and the salty air on my face, in my nostrils, weaving with my hair and the wind, I know where my place is and I know what I can do best. I'm the bridge between the two worlds. I'm the peace-bringer to so many who have had nothing but pain for the past hundred years.

Then my mind wanders to Jack again, and the ache in my chest flares. I've thought about him every day for the past five months. I kept telling myself it would get easier, but I was lying. It's my fault. I figured it out, and I never told him. So many things I could regret, and that's the one that stalks me the most. I can feel his searing touch on my face, on my hands, his lips on mine, and my heart breaks more. All I can wish for now is that he's happy and well. The tears slide out before I can stop them, and I wipe them away quickly, feeling the crusty salt coating a fine layer of grit on my cheeks.

I feel the talker next to me before he even speaks.

"Are you okay? You don't have to say anything, but I just needed to talk."

I glance at him and raise my eyebrows. Is he kidding? I couldn't talk if I wanted to.

He blushes furiously. "Er, that's not what I meant. I know you can't say anything. With your—" he gestures helplessly at my face, "that is your—you know. I just meant that I needed someone to talk—"

I put a hand on his arm, and he stops talking and smiles at me with relief in his eyes. *I know*, I mouth. I can tell by the look in his eyes that he's going to let his ghosts out.

"When I joined up with them—" He nods his head toward the others in the woods—they may as well have their tongues carved out too for all they say. "I thought I'd go crazy with wanting to speak. They shushed me all the time, telling me there was always someone watching and someone listening. That's true, but sometimes you just have to say something or you'll go insane. I was in Salt Lake for so many months. Nine, I think. At that hospital, the one where they test the serums."

My head snaps up. Besides shuttling nomads, what to do about the loyalty serum has been my other preoccupation.

The talker shoves his arms close to my eyes. The skin is riddled with minute pinpricks. "I lost track of how many times they jabbed me with a needle. And there was never anyone to talk to. I was in a cell all by myself. I would see other people almost every day, but I couldn't talk to any of them. There was this old man with a red and gray beard and his eyes would glint at me as I walked by, like he was trying to tell me to hold on just a little bit longer. Only one person who ever said anything to me, though."

Something tells me I should be paying better attention to him, but I stare so hard at the water my eyes go blurry as I hope to see lights, and his endless stream of words slips past me. We all have stories like his now. I shouldn't be so easily unimpressed. I strain my eyes on the water and listen for the helicopters. It seems like they're always just beyond the treeline.

"She had silver hair, and she was the only one I ever said a word to. She was three cells down from me. She always asked about the man with the beard."

The ocean bubbles about a hundred feet beyond the tide line, and I see the lights hazy under the surface. The sub is finally here, and still the sky is quiet. I jump up and brush the sand from my clothes.

"I was just about ready to explode before we found you. They wouldn't even tell me what they were trying to accomplish with all the shots, not really."

I glance back at the tree line and hold a fist in the air. The sub needs to break the surface of the water first, and then the refugees can run. The timing is crucial. I've had a few close calls with helicopters coming just as the sub slides beneath the water.

One of these days, the timing will be everything as the soldiers descend.

"Now I'm just glad I followed them. My sister was with them. Can you believe I found her again? And I'm glad we found you." The talker's hand brushes my arm, and I nod at him.

The sub cuts above the water, and I drop my hand. The other nomads scurry from the trees, their hands clutched around a small bundle each. They are allowed one personal item. I know it's hard for people to give up their possessions, but we need speed and the sub can't handle everyone's luggage. Besides, in the colony they will have enough clothes, food, and supplies. The colony is a place of luxury compared to the Burn.

Two men, four women, two children, and the talker stand beside me just as the hatch opens and Jessa stands up. This is how I see her now. Only for the time it takes for the refugees to clamber up the ladder, but it's more than I had before. Her hair has grown down to her shoulders, and already it looks lustrous. I decided to keep my hair in a short pixie cut. Makes life easier.

Jessa smiles at me, warm and radiant, and motions the refugees to the ladder. I guide them forward and, just as I instructed them, they climb the ladder one by one, as efficient as any military unit, until they all disappear into the sub. The talker looks at me. He can't be more than twelve.

"Thank you, Terra," he says. Then he's gone. I smile. The thank you at the end makes everything worth it. I hadn't even told him my name. Somehow the nomads have been passing it along and looking for me.

I hold my hand out to Jessa in the familiar sign to show her I love her. She smiles again.

"Love you, too."

I turn to go, to melt back into the trees and lie low until I find more nomads who want a different life. I'm going to risk the cities soon. I suspect all the cities are like Seattle was—violent and cruel—and those people need a chance at happiness too. But before I can take two steps, Jessa's voice stops me.

"You can't go yet."

The pack, of course. Jessa always brings me a pack filled with supplies. I depend on her because I can't stockpile the cabin the way I'd like to. Her containers of emergency rations and silver pouches of water have saved my life more times than I can count. But Jessa's voice is filled with a smile I can't place. She's never been so happy about a pack before. As I turn to face the sub again, I freeze. Someone stands behind Jessa, his familiar brown hair wind-whipped.

Jack.

I can't move. My heart gives a lurch—it's been frozen for months and isn't used to this. My arms and legs are stuck in place. Jack has a pack in each hand—two packs, what can it mean?—and he gazes at me with such intensity that my breath catches. All I do is stand and stare, unsure what do. The last time I saw him, his eyes were so ragged with hurt that I couldn't communicate a single word. What stands between us now? Seconds stretch out to minutes between us, and I still don't know what it means until Jack swings his legs out of the hatch and climbs down the ladder. He splashes into the surf, and he crosses the distance between us in loping strides. He drops the packs when he reaches me, and after six months, my heart starts thumping to life.

Suddenly we're tangled up in each other's arms, we're both trying not to fall into the sand and water, and I'm crying. My tears burn my chapped cheeks, but the pain focuses me on this moment. I squeeze him so tightly I think I might smother him. I let go of my anchor all those months ago and set myself adrift, and now I never want to let him go, and he's holding on to me just as tightly. My heart about bursts with the words I'll never be able to say to him.

I pull back. He has to know. No more waiting—I waited too long, and that's a mistake I won't make again. I look into his hazel eyes that are more gray than brown in the dimness, look at the faint freckles over his cheeks and nose, look at his hair that he must have been growing out since escaping the labor camp. It hangs in waves down to his ears. He *has* to know how I feel; I will make him know. There's no way this chance will escape me again.

His eyes crinkle around the corners as his lips turn up.

"I know, Terra."

Does he know the right things, though? I clutch his hands. Mine are cold from waiting—waiting on the beach for the sub, but also waiting for his warmth for far too long.

He laughs—that low sound I first heard in the settlement. I was so distracted by Dave, but I remember liking his laugh even then. He tips his head toward mine, and our foreheads and noses touch. He chafes my hands with his and brings them close to his mouth, breathing warmth on them.

"I know how you feel. I love you, too."

I sigh. Now that he knows how I feel, I still don't know what his coming back means. The packs make me hopeful, but I don't dare hope for too much. I tentatively turn his hand palm up. I haven't written anything on his hands for so long I didn't even realize how much I missed it until now. The skin is smoother—the calluses earned on the Burn have faded. He must be doing medical work full time in the colony. His fingers tense as I touch his hand, but then he relaxes and they spread out as he lets me spell the words.

Are you staying?

He cups my hand in his own and traces a single word in my palm.

Yes.

He picks up the packs. I turn back and wave to Jessa one last time, and her smile flashes. She knew this was coming the whole time, no wonder she was smiling like such a goof earlier. She blows me a kiss and then closes the hatch, and Jack and I watch the sub bubble below the surface and the lights fade into the steel-gray water. We turn to the trees, and I take a pack from him and heft it onto my shoulders. He squeezes my hand once before we escape back to our woods. I wandered with him for months, and I never realized what I had right beside me. I won't forget it now.

"Where are we going?" Jack asks as he runs beside me. His breath comes shorter than mine. He would have had an hour of physical fitness every day in the colony, but that routine isn't the greatest preparation for this hike. The colony doesn't account for things like trees to dodge and hills to climb. He's out of practice, so I slow my pace. He shakes his head. "I thought I'd slip right back into this. It must be the elevation."

I laugh. *Of course.*

His fingers run down my arm and catch my hand as we jog. He raises our arms to shoulder height as we step around a tangle of brambles, just so he doesn't have to let go.

"You never told me you had an assigned vocation in the colonies. Or vocations, in your case."

We slow even more so I can write on his hand. *You never asked.*

He flinches for a moment and squints ahead. "You never offered to tell."

The words hurt, tearing into all those old pains that I've buried all this time. But he's right.

I'm sorry.

He shakes his head. "I am too. I didn't want to bring it up. I wanted all of that to be left behind."

I grab his arm and stop him. *You're right. I kept too much in. Didn't trust you enough. What do you want to know?*

He pulls me to him and his lips brush against my hair. He tugs on my hand and prods me into the lead. We break into a lope, single file this time as the woods close in around us. We follow a deer trail no more than a foot wide and the wet foliage bends in on us, streaking us with dew. Jack hasn't forgotten how to tread quietly, and all the old mannerisms return in a matter of minutes—the light footfall, the alert posture.

"I'll ask yes or no questions. Just nod or shake your head. We'll have plenty of time for writing things out later. Where are we going, anyway?"

I pause long enough to write, *Cabin.*

Jack's eyes light up. "The one where we found the sleeping bags?"

I nod.

"I liked it there. I'm glad you found it again."

A bird cackles in the distance, and I whip around to face the noise. Jessa probably would have laughed at my paranoia, but Jack's face is deadly serious.

"Is it worse than before?" He peers in the opposite direction, just like we used to scan our entire surroundings together.

I nod. *You have no idea.*

"You'd be surprised. With the number of nomads you sent to the colonies, you're probably the most hunted nomad in New America. Do you keep track of them?"

Who?

"The nomads. Do you know how many you rescued?"

I shake my head. It's the last thing on my mind.

"Four hundred thirty-two."

My jaw drops. All my time has been spent hiking to the ocean and back again and again as I found more people longing to escape. I could tell you how many days to which drop site, how many steps between scanners, but I had no idea how many people I'd sent to the ocean. Over four hundred. I must look pretty stunned because Jack grins.

"One of the nomads called you a Moses. Mr. Klein said you'd have no idea what that meant and I'd better explain it to you."

Apparently even Mr. Klein knew Jack was coming back to me. My shoulders relax and I step closer to him. His arms wrap around me. I marvel how this all comes so naturally to us. After parting the way we did and not seeing each other for months, I thought a reunion would have been awkward at best. I look up at him, and his full lips part as he catches his breath. He sees me watching and turns from my face. Well, maybe we're still a little awkward.

He runs a hand through my hair. "I like it. You look good with short hair."

Thanks.

"How far to the cabin?"

Two days.

"Your days or mine? You probably noticed I'm not used to this."

My days.

"We'd better get going then." Jack squints to the sky, looking through a break in the trees. The sky is heavy with dark clouds. "It looks like rain."

We stop for the night in a copse of young trees. There must have been a fire here a few years ago because all the giants give way for these slender pines. I don't want to light a fire, but Jack's teeth are chattering. He shakes his head when I offer to collect firewood.

"We can't light a fire. Not here."

We are. I won't relent on this. I remember how cold I was the first night I came from the colony. I wasn't used to anything colder than seventy-two degrees. Jack looks miserable as he wraps a blanket around himself and shivers.

"Well at least let me get the wood since I'm the one who can't take the cold."

The wood is wet and the fire smokes and hisses at us. Jack wraps an arm around me, and I burrow against his side, trying to give him some of my warmth. We're both snuggled down into our sleeping bags, and I pull mine up to my chin. The nights are chilly, but with summer only a month or two away, we won't need the fire much longer. Jack hums into my hair. The melody is soft and sweet. I can't place the song, but I don't want to ask him what it is and have him stop humming. The crickets croon in the background, and with the soft pat of rain falling, I'm surrounded by an orchestra that sings straight to my soul. Jack absently runs his fingers through my hair as he hums, and his head bobs once or twice against mine. I turn to him.

Sleep.

His lips turn up just at the corners, and he shakes his head. "I don't want to. I've missed you."

I know exactly how he feels, but we both need the rest if we're to reach the cabin tomorrow. We could stay this way for just a few more minutes though. I take his hand and watch the firelight flicker across his skin. His shirt sleeves are pulled up to his elbows, the edges still wet from washing in a stream. I run my fingers along his arm, and he closes his eyes and lets his head drop to his chest. He's exhausted. I'm tired, but I couldn't possibly fall asleep right away, not with Jack so close to me. Before we were imprisoned in the labor camp, I had grown so accustomed to his sounds at night—his breathing, his light snoring, the unconscious murmurs—that I couldn't sleep without them. Now I have to learn to live with him all over again. I'm not complaining. Far from it. Jack is fascinating when he sleeps. His eyes dart behind his lids. Dreaming already? I smile. He did a good job keeping up with me today and not complaining.

I look at his arm. A small line just barely lighter than the rest of his skin mars the inside of his forearm. The scar from his first tracker, the one his father cut out for him. Next to it, so slight I can barely make it out, is the scar from his second tracker—the one given to him in the labor camp. A doctor in the colony must have removed it. I slide my arm next to his. I removed my tracker just as he would have done it for me, but I only had the scalpel from Gaea and my own grit to take away the pain. My scar is jagged at one end where I didn't dip the blade in far enough on the first go, and the line is puckered in the middle where the suturing left something to be desired. It casts a faint shadow on my arm. I don't mind, though, because it means I'm free from the government. They had me once—tracked my every move, tracked my every meal, tracked my every breath it seemed like. Now I'm out in the woods again with Jack beside me.

I suck in a breath until my lungs feel like they could burst. The smell of rain, pine, and smoke fill me. This is how it should be; this is right. I turn my head to rest against Jack's chest and close my eyes. Thunder rumbles in the distance, percussion to the music still playing around us.

TWO

Another rumble of thunder stirs me, and my eyes flutter open. The night is still dark with no hints of the gray light of morning. The rain has stopped, and the occasional drip on the forest floor tells me that it was raining only a few hours ago. The smell is still fresh. I gaze between the trees and see stars piercing the blanket of dark sky. The stars are dazzling when they shine so clearly. The clouds blew off quickly, I groggily think to myself. I still haven't quite woken up yet. Thunder drums again. My brain is processing the sound. It hasn't stopped since I heard it the first time just moments ago. Why is there thunder if there are no clouds?

I sit bolt upright, my breath coming in gasps, my hands already gathering my sleeping bag as I worm out of it, my body instinctively reacting to what my brain was too groggy to realize. Jack is slower to respond. He's lived in the comfort of the colony, and isn't used to the paranoia anymore. His eyes drag open.

"What is it?"

Then he sees the look on my face and he's on his feet before I can blink, gathering his sleeping bag and crouching, ready to run. Old habits die hard.

Helicopter, I mouth.

He nods. You never forget that sound. In my stupor I had taken it to be thunder, but there's a helicopter out there. I wouldn't be as worried if it were swooping by on a scouting run. But the sound hovers just above the trees at a distance. These woods might now be riddled with soldiers.

Jack remembers the old routine flawlessly: he stomps and covers the embers of our fire, I kick leaves under our sleeping bags so the depressions in the ground vanish, he pulls branches across the path we made into the grove, I scope the distance to find a safe direction to travel. In less than one minute, our campsite looks as if we were never here and we're already running through the trees away from the sound beating relentlessly in the sky.

"They're close."

I nod.

Jack's breath shortens as we scramble on hands and feet. We're not trying to be quiet now. With that helicopter it doesn't matter much anyway. We just need to put ground between us and what waits for us. Under the sound of the beating rotors, I hear shouts in the distance. Jack grabs my arm.

"Hurry!"

My head whips side to side as I search for a tree that will hide us. We've escaped the skinny pines of our campsite and are back among the adult trees. At the top of the next rise, the dark bulk of a huge tree looms before us, and the top disappears into the night sky. I hope its branches are thick enough to hide us; there's nowhere else to go. As I jump for the lowest branch, Jack laces his fingers for my foot and hoists me up. I wrap an arm and both legs around the limb and then reach down for Jack's hand and give him the tug he needs to grip it. He's up beside me in a few seconds, and then we both look around, finding the lowest limbs and climbing, climbing, climbing until we're ten, then twenty, then thirty feet off the ground. The bark scrapes at my palms, digs into my fingers and makes me wince, but I grit my teeth and climb. When I look down, I can barely make out the forest floor beneath us through the pine needles. If I look out beyond the tips of the branches, I can see more around us.

The voices come closer, and Jack and I press ourselves against the tree trunk, trying to blend in as best we can. My lungs are screaming at me to take a deeper breath, but I can't. Not unless I want them to find us.

Through the filtered moonlight, I can make out our campsite, and three shapes come into the grove. Each one has a gun pulled up into a shoulder. I can recognize the posture even in the dark—I could recognize the posture anywhere. I've seen too many of these soldiers with their night-vision goggles and their ubiquitous weapons. They're in a triangle formation, and the figure in the lead motions the others forward. They're silent now, stalking through the woods with only the crackle of twigs to give them away. They know they're close to their prey. They know we've been here. But how? We were so careful.

One of them stops and snoops around our campsite, digging through the leaves with the muzzle of his gun. He turns around and prods some more, then looks at the leader and the glint of moonlight on his goggles tells me he's shaking his head.

Jack and I haven't lost our touch—we still flawlessly cover our tracks.

The soldiers slowly turn three hundred and sixty degrees, covering every inch of the grove. They find nothing. They don't even think to look up. I could laugh at their stupidity if we weren't in such a precarious situation. It's cold, but my hands are sweating as I cling to the tree. Jack hasn't moved an inch since we found our perch, and his lips are tight. He won't even look at me. He just stares at the soldiers below us.

One of the soldiers finally risks speaking. "Nothing, sir. There's no trace of her."

A crackling voice answers back, tinny through a walkie-talkie. "Check again. We know she's out there somewhere. She made a drop yesterday."

Jack finally looks at me, worry worn deep in his eyes.

So the government does know what I'm doing. They've figured out where the nomads are going. And they were so close to finding me, too. If I were just a few minutes slower, if the soldiers were just a bit smarter, they would have caught me.

The soldiers shrug and look around for a few seconds more before disappearing across the grove to cover more ground. The helicopter lifts into the air and flies above the forest. Our tree sways under its down draft. My foot loses its grip on the branch and I slip, my hands grappling the biting bark as my legs flail out from under me, and Jack catches my hand just in time to keep me from falling. We stay that way—me with one hand on the branch, Jack clinging to my other hand and the tree for all he's worth—until the sweat is pouring into my eyes and both of our muscles are screaming for relief.

I haven't heard the soldiers for probably five minutes, and the helicopter sounds at least two miles away. I finally let myself relax and Jack pulls me back up onto the branch, and I let my cheek rest on the bark. I close my eyes and take a deep breath.

Jack sits down on the branch, his legs dangling on either side as he leans against the trunk. "I knew it would be like this. I knew it would be. I just didn't imagine it would start so soon. That first week in the colony, I checked my back after leaving and entering every room." His shoulders slump. "It was so strange to feel safe again. Jessa teased me every time I did it." He looks at me and arches an eyebrow. "For being twins, you two are completely different. After a couple of weeks, I finally relaxed. I'm going to pick up the habit again pretty quickly."

I nod, and the tree bark scratches my cheek. I don't know if I'll ever stop checking my back.

"Think we should stay here until morning?"

I nod again.

"Alright. Well, come here."

I ease myself up onto my knees and slide next to him. He's found a spot where two branches come together in a V against the trunk and form a wide seat. It's probably the safest spot we could be in this tree. He carefully pulls out his sleeping bag, unzips it, and drapes it over us.

"You sleep. I'll watch. I'll wake you up in an hour."

I'm not drowsy. The adrenaline is still pumping through my veins and it'll be at least a few minutes until the rush starts to ebb. We sit in silence and he holds me, his head lowered against mine, and I cling to his hand for dear life. With the sound of the helicopter fading away, the other forest sounds resume. But I don't feel safe. The worry still nags at me—how did they know I made the drop yesterday? There were no helicopters, no soldiers. If there had been soldiers, they would have sprung out of the woods at the chance of capturing a group of nomads. So how did they know?

I rub Jack's hand as the thoughts race through my head over and over again.

"Relax, Terra. You're rubbing it raw." He pulls his hand away and wraps both arms around me. "We'll be okay up here."

The adrenaline is finally draining out of me, and I feel tired to my core. The thoughts of how they knew where I was are still racing through my head, but my body is too tired to think it through any more, and I can finally close my eyes and let sleep carry me away.

I wake up when the birds start singing at dawn, and I lift my head off Jack's chest and squint into the distance. My leg slips off the branch and my whole body flinches, and I gasp as I suddenly remember where I am. Jack's awake in a heartbeat.

"What's wrong?"

I smile sheepishly and point to the ground. *Forgot.*

He rubs his hands over his stubbled cheeks, and his mouth opens in a deep yawn. "Sorry I fell asleep. I should have woken you up and let you watch. I was just so tired. I think that colony of yours spoiled me."

I grin and take his hand. *Glad you liked it.* When I'm done writing, my fingers close around his and I study them for a moment.

Why did you come back?

He pulls his head away so he can see me better. "Do you really need to ask me that?"

You were safe. Never had to run again.

"Yes, but you weren't there."

I turn from him. I feel so guilty. I can't help wondering if trading the comfort and security of the colony is worth coming back here just for me. Jack must see some of that in my face.

"You're worth it, Terra."

His voice is so earnest that I turn to him again. His face is an inch from mine, our noses touch, and his eyes bore into me. He doesn't blink or turn just a fraction from me. Then he crosses the gap between us, and he's kissing me. This should have been the way our first kiss was. Not that desperate attempt at the last possible minute to show him how I felt as we were standing in the freezing water. This kiss is gentle and says more than that first kiss ever could. The kiss isn't long and is as soft as a whisper, but it scorches me so deeply I shiver. His hand touches my neck and hovers there, feeling like a wind-whisper. When my eyes flutter open, Jack is smiling. My heart races as I touch his cheek and my fingertips play with the hair curling around his ears.

The morning air is still crisp, and I realize I'm shivering. I probably have been the whole time and didn't even notice.

"We should probably get moving."

I nod and we drop our packs and the sleeping bag from the branches and make our way down the tree.

"You never told me why you left the colony. Compared to this, it seems like a paradise. I don't understand why you stayed here when you could have gone back."

We're to the bottom branch and dangle and then drop to the ground. I look past the leaves and to the slivers of blue peeking between. *I was a prisoner.*

"I can understand that. It must feel different if you grew up in it."

How are the others? I wonder if they're as at home there as Jessa is or if any of them have the same misgivings as I did.

"Kai and her little girl are so sweet. Did Jessa ever tell you Kai named her Terra?"

Sudden tears prick my eyes.

"Really, she did." He squeezes my hand. "Because of you she actually gets to enjoy her little girl. Lily is working in food prep or whatever you call it. She likes cooking. I'm glad the labor camp didn't spoil that for her. Madge is still Madge. She's a force to be reckoned with. Not very many people try to boss her around. And Jane is thriving. I don't know if you'd even recognize her. She's filled out a bit."

This makes me smile. Poor Jane with her sharp cheekbones and sharp elbows and knees. I'm glad she can let herself be happy. Then Jack falls silent and looks away from me. I lift my shoulders to ask, *What?* He rubs a hand on the back of his neck. I know who he hasn't talked about yet.

Dave?

Jack lets out a long sigh and shakes his head. "He's just not the same. After Mary died, he jumped right into his work—agriculture—and he barely said another word. I'd see him every day after my medical shift. I was lucky if I could get him to even look at me. He works harder than anyone I've ever seen, so of course people like your dad are proud of him and what he adds to the community, but he just isn't healthy." He stops walking, and I turn to look at him. "I don't know if he ever will be again."

My head droops. I tried so hard to help my friends escape the ugliness here. But Dave didn't escape, not with the glaring hole left in his life that Mary should be filling.

Jack touches my shoulder "It's not your fault, Terra. You did everything you could."

His words bring little comfort. I did everything I could? Would saying that make Dave feel any better either? I shrug Jack's arm off and scurry over a crop of rocks. I scan the forest around me—I must look like a frightened cat with my back curled up—and then break into a jog in the direction of the cabin.

"Terra!" Jack hisses as starts after me. "Wait!"

But I can't wait. Tears stream out of my eyes and I shove them away with the heel of my hand. I had ignored all of this for so long. I knew Mary died—Jessa told me months ago. But my heart was still iced over, and I shoved it aside just like I shoved my pain for Jack aside. But now he's back and my heart is thawing out, and with it comes all the heartache I've been storing up for six months.

Mary died, and from the sound of it, Dave isn't much better. Both of the casualties weigh heavy on me, dragging my feet into the ground. My feet feel detached from the rest of me as they drag through the soggy undergrowth. I'm so used to being so quiet, but I can't stop the sobs that rip out of me. My breath comes in hitches, but I keep running—away from the ocean and all the pain that lies buried beneath its surface. I need to get back to my cabin, back to the place that held me together. I need to get back there before I fall apart.

I'm just about ready to pull myself over an enormous fallen tree when Jack yanks me back.

"Terra!"

I can't look at him. I wipe my nose with my sleeve. Jack takes my face in his hands, but I train my eyes on the tree to his right, the sky above him, that bird staring at us with liquid black eyes. Anywhere but his face. I'm too ashamed for what happened to my friends—for the lives I was responsible for.

"Terra, look at me." His voice is soft but forceful. "Please."

Something in his tone compels me, and I finally meet his eyes.

"It wasn't your fault. What happened to Mary happened because there are horrible people on this earth. You are not one of those people. You brought hope back into so many lives. You're just up here where you can't see it. But when I was down in the colony, I saw it every day. I saw how happy they are. You did that."

I close my eyes, and the tears stream down my cheeks. I try to keep the whimper in my throat, but it escapes and gurgles out.

"I don't know what I can do to convince you. You are good, Terra. You can't take responsibility for all the bad that happens."

Something in his voice changes, and I open my eyes. His face is inches from mine, and though my sight is blurry from crying, I can still make out the green in his eyes. His brown hair is wild from sleep and running, and he has a faint sheen of sweat on his forehead. His lips turn down at the corners, and worry is written there and in the crease between his eyebrows.

Somehow, I'm able to put aside the pain and look just at him. With the earnestness in his eyes, I believe every word he says. In my brain, I know Jack is right. It'll just take a little longer to convince my heart. Jack leans his forehead against mine.

I clutch his hands, sure that if I let go I'll wake up from this dream and be back in the cabin, sleeping in the loft and wondering when I'll run across another desperate band of nomads; surrounded by people but all alone. But Jack clutches me back just as hard, not even considering letting go. I'm thankful for that. He still understands me so well.

We stay that way for I don't know how many minutes before I realize my fingers are going numb and I finally loosen my grip. As I turn around, I freeze, staring at the black box thirty feet in front of me.

A scanner is there—one that wasn't there before.

"What is it?" Jack follows my gaze to the scanner box. "Does that one still work?"

Oh, it's so much worse than that. *It's brand new.*

His arms drop to his sides. "You're sure?"

I nod and take two steps forward. Jack grabs my wrist.

"Don't go any closer. There's something strange about that one."

I pause, cocking my head to one side as I stare at the scanner. He's right. Most functional scanners make a faint mechanical whirring sound. This one is quiet as a grave. Only the sun reflecting off the glass at its top offers some semblance of life.

What do you think?

"Let's give it a wide berth."

It seems silly to avoid a machine that reads trackers, seeing as neither of us has one. But still, we step in a wide circle around it. It isn't until we're ninety degrees from where we started that I look at it closely again and realize what's been going on. Its glass head has been slowly pivoting to watch us. My gut clenches.

It knows we're here.

Jack looks back at it and frowns. "Is it an automatic sweep? Or is it watching us?"

I crouch down and Jack falls beside me. As we hit the ground, I watch the head keep its steady rotation until it's facing away from us.

Automatic.

Jack lets out a breath. "Okay. Hurry while it's not looking."

I don't know if it scans for anything else besides a tracker, and I don't want to stay around to find out. I jump up and lead the way through the woods. I follow a winding path between trees, hoping we're well out of sight before its head swivels back our way.

"How far to the cabin?"

Not very.

A shallow creek cuts across our path and burbles down the gentle slope south of us. I hop across the rocks in the stream, being careful not to get my shoes wet. Then I notice another of the new scanners. I stop behind a tree.

"Another one?" Jack's chest rises and falls, and he turns his head to peek out.

I nod.

"And we're going straight ahead?"

I nod again. *About a mile.*

"We're almost there."

My gut clenches when he says it. *Not coincidence.*

"What isn't?"

New scanners so close to the cabin.

His brow furrows. "Let's get to the cabin before we decide that. The scanner is turning away. Get ready."

And then he's off running through the trees again, his long legs stretching into bounding strides. I follow him, ducking under low branches and hurtling over snaring vines. When we've gone a ways, he slows to let me pass him so I can lead the way to the cabin.

We're almost there. We jog past the tree with the huge hole in its side, past the skinny tree with a ragged bird nest in the first fork, past the small clump of mushrooms I found last week. Only a minute more and we'll be to the clearing and the cabin. The light has just begun to brighten and the trees thin when I screech to a halt. Jack almost runs into me I stopped so fast.

"What is it?" He puts his hands on his knees.

I point.

Three watchers stand guard over the clearing.

THREE

"What is it?"

If you hadn't been here before, it could be easy to miss them. Two are buried in the trees, the other is mounted on the eave of the roof so it's tucked in shadow. But I know every tree and every shingle of the cabin.

Watchers. I point them out.

"I'm assuming those weren't here before, either."

I can't even move to shake my head. My clearing, my cabin, my *home*, and I don't even dare take another step closer. I'm trembling all over, shaking so hard I can't even think straight. I'm angry. Angry at the government for once again taking something that was mine, something they had no right to, something that they wouldn't even have cared about except for the fact that I had been there.

Jack prods me with his elbow, and my legs shuffle into motion, taking me to the nearest tree. We slump down behind it.

"How long have you been gone?"

Six days.

"If they knew for sure you lived here, they wouldn't have put the watchers up. They would have just camped out and waited for you to come back. They're still not sure. That's in our favor."

My head sinks into my hands. Jack the eternal optimist. *If you say so.*

"We could take them down. We could disable them somehow."

No. They'd be even more suspicious. I don't want to prove them right. I was never here.

"So where do we go?"

I peer around the clearing. One watcher is trained on the cabin's front door. The one on the roof watches the path we were about to follow to the cabin. The third is on a tree at the very edge of the clearing, watching the entire scene. But there isn't a watcher watching the back of the cabin.

We get a few supplies.

Streams of light drift down through the leaves and reflect off the watcher's lenses. The black eyes don't move. They sit passively, lurking. We stay low and keep just beyond the clearing, following the edges until we're behind the cabin. We stalk through the brush even though I'm sure the watcher can't see us here. As soon as I'm behind the cabin and I can't see a watcher's lens any longer, I creep across the few feet of open space until I'm pressed up against the wood slats. I push on the window. It groans in protest and then swings open.

Jack glances up. "Unlocked? That's not very safe."

No one lives here, remember?

"Of course."

I pull myself up, swing a leg through the window, and then drop to the cabin floor. The opposite window—the one by the door—is nothing but a thin pane of glass to keep us from the staring eyes of the watchers. The curtains hang in ragged strips on either side and the cameras can see right in. The glare of sunlight should be enough to keep them guessing for a few minutes what's inside the cabin, but it won't last for long. I keep to the floorboards and get a shirt covered in grime for my secrecy.

Jack looks around, but the cupboards are bare. "Where is everything?"

I point to the floor. I fold back a ratty rug and then pull up the floorboard that reveals the hiding space under the cabin. Jack has a look in his eyes—admiration, I think.

What?

"I admit I wondered how the government never realized you were here. But that's smart." He peers inside the hiding space. "You never stop surprising me, Terra."

I blush and reach in and pull out some freeze-dried food packs and some foil pouches of water. Two blankets, a hatchet, another first-aid kit, and a mess kit. It should all fit in our packs. We are dividing up the supplies when I hear a mechanical whir. My fingers freeze over the food, and I convince my muscles to move enough to turn my head.

A watcher perches over the cupboards in the kitchen. The gleam in its lens and the faint hum tell me it's focusing on us. How long until someone sees this feed?

Jack turns to me, sees me paralyzed over the food, and almost laughs until his eyes settle on my face. Then he follows my gaze to the small black box that hangs over us like a guillotine.

Without even speaking, we burst into action, stuffing supplies into our packs—forget carefully selecting what we need and arranging it properly—and flying out the front door in full view of the watchers. I thread my arms through the straps as my legs churn into a sprint. The food cans at the bottom of my pack thud against my back until I fasten the waist strap.

"How long?"

I can't see Jack; I'm too focused on making my way between the trees before us. I don't know what he's asking. So I make a sound that I hope he understands as, *What?*

"How long before someone sees what the watcher saw and soldiers come?"

I risk a glance back, seeing my beloved cabin—my home for the past six months—disappear behind garlands of leaves. My throat burns and my breath comes thickly, and the crash of my legs through the forest rips through my mind. I can never have a home. It's always being taken away as if it's something I'm just not meant to have. I push myself faster and I'm sweating now as the hazy afternoon light turns violet and the color in the trees washes to gray. What had I been expecting? That Jack and I could have grown old in that cabin together? The thought is laughable now because in an instant everything has changed. I'm running too fast, but the adrenaline and anger racing through me fuel my speed and I can't bring myself to slow down.

As my feet pound and my heart pounds, my mind begins to clear and I'm able to think about the past few days, my brain finding details it had been too busy to notice. I think about the moments leading up to Jack's return. I think about what the talker told me before the sub came. My heart clenches.

"Slow down!" Jack calls, and I realize his voice is too far away. I pull up.

A few moments later, Jack stumbles to a stop and puts his hands on his knees, trying to catch his breath.

"Where are we going?"

If he had asked me a minute ago, I wouldn't have been able to tell him.

Salt Lake City.

He blinks. "Why?"

The words of the talker solidify in my mind. Why didn't I hear him before?

Nell and Red.

My hand is suspended over Jack's. Can I trust the words of that kid? Surely there are dozens, maybe hundreds, of people like Nell and Red on the Burn, but the way he described them—there's no one else it could be. The odds are stacked against me, but I'm sure. I don't know why, but something tells me it's them. And they need us.

Jack clings to my hand. "How do you know they're there?"

No time. I've already pulled away from him. I turn south and start walking.

"Tell me, Terra. How do you know?"

I sigh and hitch up my pack, holding the straps as we walk. It takes a while, but I tell him about the last sub rendezvous.

"You think he was talking about Nell and Red?"

I nod, squinting into the coming darkness, ready for Jack to tell me it's a wild goose chase.

"Then we'll go."

I glance at him, and his jaw is set resolutely and his gaze focuses straight ahead. My hand slips from the strap of my pack and finds his. He looks at me out the corner of his eyes, and with that momentary gaze, I can see he trusts me implicitly.

"But why Salt Lake City?"

I laugh, and the bitterness in it echoes through the trees. *Remember the movie at the camp? The hospital.*

"Yes." Jack's voice hesitates over the word.

They test loyalty serum.

The concern on Jack's face vanishes, and the usually gentle features harden. "Then we need to hurry. If Nell and Red are there, who knows what they've gone through."

I lengthen my stride into a lope and skirt around a thick bramble of vines.

"But you can't walk all the way to Salt Lake."

I raise my eyebrows and my hands go to my hips. *Yes I can.*

Jack takes my face in his hands and laughs. I can tell he's trying hard to let go of his anger. "Stop being so stubborn. I'm not telling you not to go. I'm just telling you there's another way."

My eyes dart down. Of course I was being stubborn. I've been out here by myself for too long. I've lost the sense of depending and trusting someone else while Jack's been away from me. I need to relearn it.

Jack's lips brush across my forehead. "I've missed the way you furrow."

I smile. *How?*

"There are freight trains. That's how the government transports most of their supplies. Salt Lake is one of the largest designated cities. There's bound to be trains headed there regularly. We just need to find the tracks."

How do you know trains?

His hands fall from my face, and my cheeks still glow from his touch. We pick up the pace. "Dave and I sometimes watched the trains come into Seattle for the supply drops. And my father and I watched the trains as we traveled west. We hid, of course. There are soldiers—and sometimes agents— on the trains. Most of them have a mounted gun on the top to keep off the nomads. One night we were camping out in the prairie. It was flat and the night was clear and the moon was so bright you could see perfectly. We had passed a group of nomads during the day. We had actually risked talking to them—one of them was dehydrated and needed help. They were kind. That doesn't happen too often."

Jack's hand grabs mine, and from the urgent pressure of his fingers, I know this story does not end well. I step closer to him and touch his arm. We step over a fallen tree together.

"We stayed with them during the day, but at dusk we parted ways. They headed toward the tracks." He looks down at our clasped hands and then studies the trees stretching before us. He clears his throat. "I've seen too many nomads do too many stupid things. I think that's why I'm nervous for you, Terra."

I tilt my head.

He smiles bitterly. "I don't think you're a stupid nomad— not by any stretch of the imagination. But the government assumes nomads will try things, and so most government property is armed to the gills. That's why this rescue is so dangerous. They're planning on someone coming and trying something."

Trains? I want to keep him focused. If I let him go on about dangers and weapons and what could go wrong, then I'll start to think about what might happen to *him* if we do this. That's not something I can think about for too long.

He leans his head against mine, and we jostle together as we hike. "You just can't let yourself be distracted, can you?"

Nope.

"Can't consider the important things going on here?"

He's trying to make me rethink this again. I can't help the impish grin. *Not a chance.*

Jack sighs. "I'm not surprised. You're just lucky that I love you and Nell and Red. Otherwise you'd all be on your own."

I shudder at the thought of doing this by myself, of what my life was like just a few days ago without him. I squeeze his hand. *Trains?*

"When we had stopped with them during the day, the nomads had mentioned something about a supply train coming through that night. Food and medicine, so it was a rare one—usually they're just one or the other. Those nomads were in sorry shape. I don't know if they had just left a city and weren't used to traveling, but they were desperate. They said the train would come through around eleven. I don't know how they knew that, but they found out somehow. If a nomad has an advantage of some sort, they'll never share it with you. But they knew when that train was coming, and my father and I stayed hidden in the long grass and let them pass us by. They never even knew we were there.

"We could feel the train coming long before it reached us. It seemed to take hours. I watched the train barrel toward us and saw the shapes of the nomads as they hunched down, waiting. As soon as the train was close enough, they jumped up and ran along, trying to grab hold of one of the cars and get into it. The soldier at the gun on the top saw them. They were too close to shoot with the mounted gun, but that didn't matter. Soldiers started pouring through the doors like ants out of an anthill."

Jack looks up through trees, squinting at the fading gray clouds peeking through the leaves. His eyes glisten.

"Every single nomad—there were ten of them—was thrown from the train. Then the soldiers disappeared back inside as if they had never even been there. Dad and I watched that stretch of track for a full hour. Not a single nomad got up."

We walk for a while in silence. I have no words. Every new horror I hear of affects me just the same—I can't believe how cruel people are. You'd think I'd start getting used to it, but I'm glad I don't. I would start to be too much like *them*—the agents, the soldiers, the government, whoever they are—if I got used to this. Then I stop walking.

So why do you want to take a train?

Jack looks at me for several long moments, his hazel eyes flashing. A bird chirps off to my right, but I hardly hear it with his intense gaze on me. "Because I know you, Terra. I know you're going to do this with or without me. Honestly, I think you're better off risking the train. Hiking would take far too long. If the government is as close to unlocking the serum as you think they are, then I don't know how much time Nell and Red have left."

What do train tracks look like?

"They're two parallel metal rails with wood ties—slats—in between."

A long metal path five miles to the east of the cabin comes into focus. Sometimes I would walk along it on my way to a small lake teeming with fish. I never knew what that path was.

I always thought it strange that the leaves and other forest debris never accumulated on it. But now it makes sense. If those metal rails are train tracks and the train travels at night, then the train would have passed by and I'd never know.

I've seen some.

Jack's eyes are strange mixture of relief and disappointment. "Where?"

East of the cabin.

"Do they run north and south or east and west?"

North south.

"Then they'll head us in the right direction. I don't know if there are any direct lines, but it's a start."

We turn southeast. I just wish there was some way we could tell Nell and Red that we were coming for them, that they needed to hang on for just a little while longer.

The long shadows of trees point the way toward the tracks. We hike until the darkness under the trees hazes my vision. Just when I think I can't possibly take another step without falling asleep, we stumble into a narrow swathe of treeless land that stretches as far as I can see in either direction. The train tracks run straight through it. Finally.

"Let's rest until the train comes." Jack yawns and slumps against a tree.

But I can't sleep yet. I find a spot where I know I'm out in the open. I look up to the sky. The clouds are patchy, but the sky is mostly clear and pierced with starlight. I carefully mouth the words.

I'll need a sub. Maybe three days. I don't know where. Please just watch.

This has never felt more risky. I can't tell Gaea when or where, just that I need it. I hope that my mother can use the satellites to watch me closely enough. She hasn't failed me yet.

Jack and I bed down under a grove of slender trees. Their branches droop down around us, forming a canopy of entwined branches clothed in bright green new leaves. I try to keep my eyes open, but my head droops again and again until finally I fall asleep with Jack's arms around me.

FOUR

I wake up to rain on my face, and the sleeping bag is covered in a pattern of raindrops. All around me, I hear the soft patter of water. The woods always sound magical during the rain. All other sounds are muffled, and all you can hear is the drip, drip, drip. My breath comes out in puffs and I shiver. Jack's warmth is gone.

I panic and sit up, the sleeping bag rustling as I do. I wince. I shouldn't move so suddenly—who knows what might be out there watching me in the pale light of morning—but my heart hammers in my chest.

"Jack," I croak out, but the word is mangled.

"I wondered when you were going to wake up." Jack sits on his haunches a few feet away. He's running his hands through the leaves and then splashing the drops of water on his face. "The train didn't come last night."

My heart hasn't calmed down yet, and I can barely smile through the panic ebbing in my veins.

Jack tilts his head to look at me more closely. "What's wrong?"

I look at my hands and shrug. I pick at a thread hanging from the sleeping bag.

Jack sits next to me and leans against my shoulder. "I'm never leaving you again. You know that, right?"

If only he knew about those three days in the cabin last winter when I couldn't even move because of the hole in my heart. I haven't been able to tell him just how bad it was. It still hurts to think about it, and he doesn't need to know how I almost didn't put myself together again. Instead I chance a smile at him. He brushes his lips against mine, and the heat from his lips warms me all the way to my toes.

"Come on. Let's follow the tracks until the train comes."

He stands and grabs my hands to help me up. I shake the stiffness from my limbs and roll the sleeping bag. We munch on energy bars and sip water from a pouch for our breakfast. My mouth feels mossy, but we don't stop to brush our teeth. We keep to the trees that run along the track, always keeping it just in sight. It's an eerie feeling to see that path carved right out of the forest—knowing it's the government's road and that we're stalking along it so closely they could touch us if they wanted to. I've spent months trying to put as much distance as possible between us that it feels crazy making myself so vulnerable now.

But I'm doing this for Nell and Red.

By the time the sun is over the train tracks and shining in my eyes, the sweat trickles down my back and my mouth is dry.

Any trains during the day? I ask Jack as we pause to take a drink.

"I'm not sure. I would think not just because they'd be easier targets. Who knows? Why? Did you hear something?"

I shake my head. *Tired of waiting.*

"I am too. When you're marching to your possibly imminent demise, you don't want to wait around for it."

Too much suspense?

Jack laughs and runs a hand through his hair. "Something like that. You still haven't changed your mind?"

I zip my pack closed and keep hiking.

"I didn't think you would. Promise me, though, that you'll be careful."

I start to laugh, but then I turn to him and there's so much pain in his eyes it could go down for miles and I'd never see the end of it. His eyes remind me of the colony's trench.

Of course.

He looks away. "I don't think I could bear it if something happened to you." He speaks quietly, so quietly the faint breeze turning the leaves almost wisps the words away before I hear them.

The sun hangs low in the sky, and the tracks glow orange-black in the fading light. Fluffy pollen drifts in the breeze, glittering like snow. The sweat is drying on my back as the sun disappears altogether and the chill of night falls on us. Through the break above the tracks, the pinpricks of stars appear one by one in the sky. The crickets chirp in rhythm, hushing as we step closer and resuming their music once we've passed on.

Then suddenly all those sounds stop and all I hear is the crunch of our feet on leaves. I pause, my body quivering as I rise up on my toes, trying to decide if I should keep walking or if we need to run. Whenever the animals in the woods go silent, something big is about to happen. Jack puts a hand on my arm to steady me. Then the ground begins to vibrate under my feet. I rock back onto my heels and I've just put one foot in front of the other, ready to bolt, when Jack grips my sleeve.

"It's the train."

He puts a finger to his lips and cuts in front of me, jogging through the brush beside the tracks. He looks back over his shoulder, peering down the long scar cut through the forest. I hear the train in the distance. Not the train itself exactly, but the unmistakable stillness it creates as it creeps through the forest. The animals quiet for it, and they grow silent several miles ahead of it. It's eerie.

"They try to keep quiet," Jack says, hunched over as we peer through the bushes toward the tracks. "Trains used to whistle loudly or at least chug. These are electric trains, so all you'll hear is a hum. The government doesn't want nomads finding them. They don't even turn on their lights."

I nod, straining my eyes on the tracks that gleam in the moonlight. There are no trees and no bushes around them for about twenty feet on either side, and this strange clearing cut through the trees unnerves me. Then in the distance, I see a shape come into view and bear down on us.

"There it is." Jack tenses next to me, his long legs and arms ready to spring. I can't help thinking that he's not made out for this, but he does this for me. I want to tell him to go back and that I'll go on alone; I shouldn't put him in danger like this. But my mouth is dry and he's not looking at me. His fingers dig into the leaves underfoot, and his whole body is a live wire.

I turn my focus back to the train—it's nothing more than a phantom gliding down the tracks—and soon I hear the hum Jack was talking about. It almost sounds like summer cicadas.

My muscles twitch, wanting to run toward the train, to get this over with. Jack senses some of my anxiety and puts out an arm.

"Quiet now," he whispers.

The first car passes us, and there's nothing to hint at its passing except the hum, a few red lights along the cars that glow faintly in the dark, and the mounted gun with the soldier manning it. Even in the dark I can tell he's not relaxed like some of the soldiers I've seen. He's hunched over the gun, his arms gripping it, ready to fire. He slowly swivels three hundred and sixty degrees, taking in the woods around him. The gun is so large it looks like it could tear through the trees if it wanted to.

Only one? I write on Jack's hand. I really don't care if there's only one gun. I'm writing on his hand just to calm myself down.

Jack shrugs his shoulders. "Sometimes. It depends on the train."

I don't feel good talking. I expected the train to scream and howl as it went by. Instead it's almost as quiet as the unnaturally quiet forest. Even though we're shrouded by darkness and foliage, I feel exposed out here. I feel like the train is listening.

"Ready?"

I nod. In the direction the train came from, I can see the lighter gray of nighttime fill in the space left as the shadow passes by. We both start jogging through the brush alongside the train. It's quickly outpacing us, but we're not looking to jump on now. My eyes are trained on the top, looking for another gun, but there isn't one. This train must not be carrying medical supplies or even food. Maybe just clothing. Or maybe it's empty.

We want to catch one of the last cars, one that won't be inspected or patrolled until all the others have once we stop. Of course this is a gamble—we don't know how these trains are loaded—but it's a chance we'll take. It's the only way we'll get to Salt Lake City in time.

We're running full speed now as the last five cars come into view. We dart along the edges of the bushes. The gun is well away by now, but I don't know if the soldier wears nighttime goggles and can see us.

Then Jack hisses, "Now!" and we dash across the open space in full moonlight. The train is going much too fast. My legs churn, and I don't know how we'll make it in time. A loud pop shatters the absolute stillness, and the ground by my feet explodes in a shower of dirt.

The soldier sees us.

"Doesn't matter," Jack gasps, his breath ragged. "Keep running. Make the train and we'll hide." His legs stretch longer as his arm reaches for a handle to slide open a cargo car.

I force my legs to pound alongside the train, faster faster faster. Jack has his hand on the handle and has managed to wrench open the door just wide enough for us to squeeze through. But still the train goes too fast. The gun fires again, but we're too close to the train for it to hit us. I remember Jack's story—how the soldiers spilled out of the train like ants protecting their nest. I eye the opening warily, waiting for soldiers to pour out, but none come. There's nothing but black in there.

I'm running too fast and stumbling over my own feet trying to keep up. Jack clings to the handle with one hand and stretches out toward me with the other. My fingers fumble for his, and then I grip his hand and he holds me tight. The speed of the train starts to lift me off my feet. My arm is going to be ripped from the socket and I grit my teeth, but Jack doesn't let me go. My legs cartwheel behind me, my toes barely skimming the ground.

"Jump, Terra!" His voice strains and the veins in his neck are bulging. He can't drag me along like this for much longer. "Come on, we're almost there!"

I gasp in a breath, urge my legs faster, and launch myself toward the open door. Jack heaves me in at the same time I jump, and he falls back on the floor of the train. Only my upper body clears the train, and I land on my stomach with my feet dangling into thin air, and all the breath is slapped from me. My fingers scrabble on the smooth floor as I slip several inches out the door. I cry out.

Jack's hands clamp down around my wrists and he tugs me inch by inch onto the train. "You're lucky you're so skinny," he says between clenched teeth, and I want to laugh, but there's a fiery pain in my ribs. The absurdity of it all is not lost on me—running like maniacs for a train that by no stretch of the imagination would kill us, so we can go to the lion's den to rescue some friends that may or may not be there. Now I can't even take a breath without a hitch. The whole thing is ridiculous. And then there's Jack, trying his best to help me relax because surely he's seen what a wreck I've been all night.

Jack pulls back again, planting his feet and scooting away from the door until my thighs, then my knees, and then my feet are firmly on the train, and I'm lying alongside him, and I feel his chest hammering into my back as he struggles to catch his breath.

"We're never doing that again."

My lips turn up wryly. I haven't told him this yet, but how else does he think we're going to get to the ocean once we have Nell and Red? But then the thought stops dead in its tracks. How will Nell and Red possibly catch a train the way we just did?

I don't have time to think this through—I honestly don't want to think it through—and I try to stand, but I double over and clutch my ribs.

"Are you okay?"

I shake my head. Just touching my side sends pain shooting through me.

"Let me see."

I slowly take my hand away, and Jack reaches for me.

"I'm just going to touch your ribs."

I nod and squeeze my eyes closed. Jack's fingertips touch my side so softly I can barely feel him, and then he presses harder. I hiss in a breath.

"Sorry. Just another second."

His fingers trail from my sternum to my back bone with a constant, steady pressure, and I wince.

"I don't think they're broken. You landed pretty hard on them, though, so they're probably bruised. You'll want to be careful."

I wrap my arms around me, and it hurts at first, but then the pressure on my ribs is soothing. My legs are burning and rubbery, and I wobble on them as I look around. The soldier fired at us, and he can't be the only one to suspect we're here.

Hide? I write to Jack. He nods.

This car is practically empty. Cargo nets line the sides of the car, and one tall metal box stands in the corner.

"This way," Jack says, leading me toward the back of the car. There are only two or three cars after this one. Then there will be nowhere else to hide.

Jack pulls me to the door that leads to the next car, but I stop beside the metal container. I peer up. The light in the car is dim, and the metal container is shoved into a corner full of shadows. I can barely make out the cargo nets swaying side to side above it. Jack looks back at me, wondering why I've stopped. I point up to the metal container.

"Up there? You're sure?"

I nod. It's perfect. This dark corner is the only half-concealed place in the car. They'd never expect us to hide somewhere so open. And honestly, all I want to do is lie down.

"Well, up we go." Jack stoops down and laces his fingers together. I put a foot in the cradle, and he boosts me up. Reaching for the top of the container and clambering up makes me see stars, but I ignore the pain in my side. I can lie down in a minute, I tell myself. Just deal with it for another minute. I reach down and help Jack up. We perch for a moment on the edge of the container, and then I look back and the nest of cargo nets sways back and forth with the rhythm of the train. We start working our way into the nets. I've just dropped a net in front of me when the door on the other end of the car hisses open.

Jack and I both freeze. My fingers are woven through the mesh of the net, and I feel far too exposed. They won't look up, I have to tell myself. That's what you were banking on. Don't doubt yourself now.

A single soldier steps through the door. His rifle is up to his shoulder, and he swings it side-to-side as he searches the room. Luckily he doesn't have his night-vision goggles on. If he did, we'd be spotted for sure. I can't see his face through his mask, but by the way his shoulders relax, I know he doesn't think we're here.

His head tilts to one side as he speaks into his walkie-talkie. "They're not in this car either, sir."

"They were seen boarding the train, and they can't have disappeared." The voice on the other end is clipped and harsh. "Where are they?"

The soldier lowers his rifle and his posture sags. "I don't know, sir. It could have been a deer."

"Were you wearing your goggles?"

Silence for a moment. I can imagine the guilty expression that crosses his face. "No, sir."

"You are to search the remaining three cars and then report to command immediately. Then you're relieved of duty. Maybe you'll think twice about not wearing your goggles *when it's nighttime*. That's what they were made for, idiot."

"Yes, sir."

The soldier brings his rifle back to his shoulder and makes his way to the opposite door. When it slides shut, I take a deep breath and gingerly sink into the nets. I close my eyes. That was far too close.

"Don't relax yet," Jack whispers as he threads his way further behind the cargo nets. "He'll be back as soon as he's done."

I bury myself in the nets and when I'm finally touching the cold wall, I find a net to lie back into. Jack has found a spot just touching me, and I reach for his hand.

"Are your ribs okay?"

Barely.

"Can you get comfortable?"

Maybe. How long on the train?

He purses his lips and shakes his head. "I honestly don't know how fast these trains go. I think they're supposed to be pretty fast. Maybe a day?"

An entire day to sit here and just wait to see if they find us. I carefully unzip my bag and pull out an energy bar.

"Don't open it until that soldier comes back through here and is gone."

I nod. The last thing we need is a crinkling wrapper to give us away. They'd only believe it was a rat for so long before they figured out we were actually here.

In a few minutes the soldier returns. He looks so defeated as he skulks across the car that I almost laugh. I peer at Jack from the corner of my eyes, and he has the same grin on his face. Relief washes over me. We might actually be able to do this. For the first time in the past three days, my muscles relax.

I slump against Jack and let the gentle rocking of the train lull me to sleep.

FIVE

When I wake up, Jack runs his fingers through my hair and brushes his lips against my forehead.

"Over halfway there, I think."

Safe? I write to him.

He nods. "As safe as it ever is. They patrolled about two hours ago."

My muscles tense, even though there isn't any immediate danger. Jack strokes my arm from my shoulder down to my wrist.

"Relax. They might be doubting what they saw last night. They didn't even bother to look up. How did you know?"

I frown. *I know them too well. They never look up.*

The left side of Jack's mouth turns up. "Just like in the woods."

I nod. These flimsy nets have provided the perfect spot for us—comfy hammocks and the best hiding spot we could have found.

Do they still think we're here?

"It's hard to tell. I don't know if the patrols are routine or not. They look pretty jumpy, though, so they might. In which case, getting off may be trickier than getting on."

I hadn't thought of that. The most insurmountable task appeared to be just getting on the train. My bruised ribs are proof of that. But that was taking them by surprise. Now if they're half-expecting us, there's no way we'll get off with just a few gun shots in the dirt and a half-hearted search.

What do we do?

"Honestly, I have no idea."

The smile disappears and I take Jack's hand. This is too familiar, this helpless feeling. Just like watching Red climb down all alone among the abandoned cars to go to the med drop or surrendering myself to Dr. Benedict's loyalty serum. I focus on our goal—on Nell and Red—and try to wipe away the memory of being completely out of control. Jack squeezes my hand.

"We'll find a way."

I nod. Just as I do, the train begins to slow, and my breath comes in hitches as the panic rises in my chest.

"It's too soon."

Jack worms his way free from the netting. He dangles down to peer through the small window. I hiss at him and raise my hands.

"We're not in a train station. There's nothing out there."

Nothing? I push through the nets and grip the miniscule window sill with my fingernails and pull myself up to look. He's right. Mountains rise up to the east, and between us and the peaks is nothing but grass and scrubby brush. The tops of the mountains are still shrouded in snow, and the sky is a brilliant blue. I haven't seen a sky this clear in months. If it weren't for my heart pounding in my chest, I might actually enjoy the view.

We're hanging there by the window when the door next to us hisses open. Two soldiers appear, their guns casually slung over their shoulders. The window casts one long arc of daylight across the floor, and the corner we lurk in still stands in shadows. Only Jack's head is faintly illuminated, and he's as still as a statue.

One of the soldiers lifts his mask an inch and scratches his neck. "I don't think there's anyone aboard." His voice is raspy and deep.

The other leans up against the wall and crosses one ankle over the other. "Really?" His voice surprises me. Given his bulk, it's higher than I thought it should be, like he hasn't even hit puberty yet. "I guess nomads would be crazy to try. You heard Nolan last night. Didn't even have his goggles on."

The first soldier reaches in a pocket and takes out a cigarette. "Too bad. Would've been fun target practice."

The second soldier snorts. "Put that thing away. You'll be disciplined for sure if you're caught with that."

"And who's going to catch me? We're not in Salt Lake yet. With this stop it's going to be hours before we get there, and I'm supposed to have leave when we do. I'm itching for some time off."

My breath catches. Hours from Salt Lake. Why are we stopping?

The skinny soldier tips his mask all the way up with one finger, and I wince at the sight of his face. He has a scar running from his left temple all the way to the corner of his mouth. It twists his lip up into a horrible sneer. He takes a lighter out of his pocket and flicks a small flame in front of his face and lights the cigarette hanging from his lips.

"I don't know why you insist on doing that," the other soldier says with a squeak.

"Relax. How will they find out? There aren't any watchers."

My body moves without me even realizing it, and my eyes meet Jack's. No watchers. They put watchers everywhere else, why not on the train? My heart thumps with hope. We just might do this.

"What was that?" the second soldier says, bringing his gun halfway up.

"What? You're twitchy, you know that?" The soldier takes a long drag and then blows the smoke in his companion's face.

"Maybe no watchers," says the soldier, waving a massive hand to clear the smoke. "But there are smoke detectors." He points to a small, square box above the door. Just as he does so, an alarm shrieks and lights flash along the car. The train jerks to a stop, and the soldiers stumble. I roll forward, my hands grappling at the net to keep myself from falling off the metal container and spilling right at the soldiers' feet. Wouldn't that be a grand way to end this whole thing.

My fingers ache as they clutch so tightly to the net that my fingernails dig into my palms and I can feel the blood welling up. I close my eyes. The pain in my ribs screams at me. Jack grabs the net next to me and swings himself up onto the container. His breath comes heavy and he closes his eyes, trying to quiet his breathing. The soldiers recover themselves. The smaller one spits out his cigarette and stomps on it. Then he grabs the bigger soldier by the collar.

"It wasn't me, got it?"

The soldier nods frantically. I can't see his face, but I can imagine the panic on it. My arms shake and all I want to do is let go and clutch my side.

"It was whoever they think got on this train last night. We were doing our rounds and the alarm went off and we found this cigarette. It was them, and they were gone before we got here." He releases the bigger soldier, who falls back against the wall and shrugs his shoulders to straighten his uniform. I look up. Please hurry. I can't hang on much longer.

"You didn't have to go berserk on me, you know."

"Oh please. Stop being so sensitive."

The smaller soldier brings his gun to his shoulder and leads the way to the opposite door. Just as it starts to hiss closed, the pain in my bruised ribs bites back at me so hard I have to let go and I fall to the ground. I raise my head to see the first soldier turn back just as I hit the floor, and the shock on his face brings him to a halt and the door slides all the way closed.

Jack's face appears over the side of the container. He slips off the top and lands next to me. "We need to go now."

My feet scrape on the floor as I spring up, and we race through the opposite door to the back of the train. The soldiers shout behind us as the door closes.

The next car is lined with bunks, but there are just bed frames and mattresses—no bedding, no pillows, no personal items. It may have been used to transport soldiers or prisoners, but it's empty now and there's no place to hide. We race between the bunks down to the other door. I look back in time to see the far door open and the two soldiers both try to come through. Luckily the big soldier is too big, and they bump shoulders trying to squeeze through. The first soldier curses and has only enough time to raise his gun and fire a hurried shot. The bunk to my right explodes in a blizzard of bed stuffing. I put my hands over my head and feel the cotton rain down on me and stick to my sweaty skin.

"Out of my way!" the first soldier roars.

I don't look back; I just slip through the door after Jack as bullets pelt the metal walls around me.

Now we're in a car stacked with boxes. There are two aisles down the length of the car, and thick straps hold the pyramids of cargo in place. One of the aisles lies in darker shadow, and Jack leads the way down it, stepping past the boxes that jut out at us. I keep right on his heels, ignoring the burning running up and down my torso, making my legs go faster as I follow him. I hear the door open behind me and the scuff of heavy boots and the barked commands. A small gap between two stacks of boxes opens up on our left, and Jack darts into it, pulling me in after him. It's just wide enough for us to turn sideways and shimmy through.

The soldier's walkie-talkie crackles, and I clamp a hand over my mouth so I can hear it.

"Yes, they're here, sir," says the first soldier. "Two of them. They're headed for the back of the train."

"We're starting up again. Throw them off the train." The train lurches forward.

"You don't want to interrogate them?"

"Are you questioning me?"

"No, sir. But what if one of them is her?"

"There was a female?"

"Yes."

The walkie-talkie is silent for several moments. Jack pushes deeper into the gap and I follow him. The boxes are on a pallet, and there's barely enough space between the wall and the stack of boxes to squeeze through. We're wedged between the boxes and the wall, and I feel so squeezed I only have room to take a breath, but we're no longer visible from the aisle.

"Apprehend the female. The male is of no use to us. Kill him."

Jack's hand finds mine in the darkness. I'm not sure who he's more worried about—him or me.

"Yes, sir."

The boots tromp down the car now, one farther away in the other aisle, and one closer to us. I peer around the corner of the boxes just in time to see the muzzle of a gun appear in the aisle, and the big soldier creeps down, looking off to the right and then the left. I pull my head back in and squeeze Jack's hand.

"Anything?" comes the harsh voice of the first soldier.

"Nothing. They might have gone all the way through."

The soldier snorts. "There's nothing out there. This is the last car."

"I dunno. They could be anywhere. Think they'll make us move all this stuff?"

The first soldier curses. "I swear all the bad stuff happens to me when I'm partnered with you. This is stupid. Look, here's what we'll do. You stand guard at the door. I'll go talk to command and see what they want to do. With any luck they'll call it a wash, but I'm not betting on it. Come on."

The boots stamp back to the door. It hisses open and closed, and then everything is quiet again. I finally take a breath and look at Jack. He holds up a finger. We'll wait one minute and then we'll come out.

Jack's voice is so low next to me, I can hardly hear him. "We'll go out the back door."

Last car? I don't understand. We can't jump off the train.

"There's a platform back there. We'll have to ride it out."

It doesn't sound like much of a plan, but the soldiers will come back here, and there's nowhere else to go. Jack sidesteps behind the stack of boxes, inching his way from behind them until he can worm his way through the gap on the other side. I follow him, listening over the sound of our breathing, the creaking of the train, and the scrape of our clothes on cardboard for any signs of the soldiers coming back. But there's nothing.

We creep down the gap and to the shadowy aisle. Jack stops to look back down the aisle toward the far door, but he doesn't see anything. Then we turn the corner and a low laugh greets us.

"I wondered if you weren't really here."

I glance out the corner of my eyes, and the first soldier stands in the aisle. His gun is slung casually over his arm.

Jack pulls me behind him and steps back. I look behind us. The door is only ten feet away. There's a panel of glass, and through it I see the track stretching out behind us in an endless ribbon of metal. The brown-green grass waves as we pass, and the mountains spring up to the east. More mountains lie in haze to the west, and there's nothing else as far as I can see.

The lazy laugh grates at my ears again. "Don't know where you think you're going." The soldier settles his gun into his shoulder. "If you go that way, there's nothing but a nasty drop off the train."

"We'll keep that in mind," Jack replies, his voice carefully even. He takes another step back.

The soldier begins to sight along his gun, and Jack turns suddenly. I turn with him and we race ahead to the door. I wrench the handle and the door swings open onto a small platform, and the wind howls around us. Jack shoves me to the platform just as I hear the shots fire.

The platform is only about ten feet wide and two feet deep, and a railing with narrow spindles encloses it. In the center of the railing is a gap with nothing but a swaying chain to close it. Jack presses me into a corner against the spindles, making me as small a target as possible, and the spindles dig into my back. He hooks a foot around the swinging door to close it, but the soldier inside laughs gleefully, and suddenly the tip of his gun shows through the doorway.

"Come out, come out wherever you are."

The gun is so close to us it makes Jack go rigid. He's been away from this for too long. I forget how safe you feel in the colony, how I never once checked my back. He's frozen, but all I see is red, and I spring from the railing, pouncing like a cat. I grip the gun in both hands and pull with everything I have, using the soldier's momentum against him. The soldier isn't expecting that kind of attack, and he stumbles forward. I eye the gap in the rails, but he's regaining his feet and he's not anywhere close enough. Jack shakes his head and tumbles after him, pushing him from behind while I pull on his gun, and soon the soldier is wheeling toward the gap. He drops his gun and holds out his hands to find the railing to brace himself, but the two feet of platform doesn't give him enough time, and he hits the chain and then tumbles over it, rolling through the air and landing on the tracks in a cloud of dust as he rolls more times than I can count before coming to a stop. As the train slips away from him, I squint my eyes and watch, but he doesn't get up.

My hands are shaking and I clamp them down on the railing. My legs wobble and my heart is still racing. I close my eyes and take a deep breath to steady myself. My hands just won't stop shaking no matter how many breaths I take. All I can see is the black-haired man, Smitty, Mary, and the soldier rolling over and over again. My death count just keeps rising.

Jack's hands cover mine, and my hands feel far too icy under his.

"Come on," he whispers in my ears, trying to ease my fingers off the cold metal.

I shake my head. No. If I keep my hands here, they can't do any more damage.

"Look at me, Terra."

I shake my head. Nope, not going to do that either.

"You didn't have a choice. I know that isn't much consolation, but he was going to capture you and kill me. If he captured you, how would you save Nell and Red?"

Nell and Red. I had forgotten them in my panic as the soldier stalked us out of the cargo car. I slowly open my eyes. Nell and Red. I repeat it in my head. Nell and Red.

Jack finally opens my death-grip, and I tuck my hands against my sides where he won't have to touch them. He helps me sit against the back of the train.

"I think we should spend the rest of the trip out here. We can jump off when we start to slow down outside of Salt Lake."

My hands are still shaking, but it's under control now. I pull my knees up and look at the chain swaying innocently to the motion of the train. I look past it at the tracks stretching behind us. In the distance I can just make out a dark lump on the tracks. Anyone else might have to get closer to know what it is, but I don't have to. The dust crusts in my eyes and I can't help the tears that come.

Jack puts an arm around me, and I put my head on his shoulder. "It's okay."

It'll never be okay and he knows that, but I still appreciate him right next to me.

"I'm sorry."

What for?

"If I hadn't clamped up like that, you wouldn't have had to do that. I'm sorry."

I close my eyes again, and a tear traces its way down my nose and falls onto his shoulder. *Neither of us should have to do that.*

Jack's hair whips wildly around him, and he tries to hold it down with his other hand. "It's going to get cold tonight in this wind. You don't have your pack, do you?"

I shake my head. It's tangled in the cargo nets several cars away.

"Me neither. I don't think we should go back for them."

I shake my head. We definitely shouldn't do that. The big soldier will be wondering where his partner is. I feel so exposed out here, but I guess it's better than being in there where the soldiers have their guns and are looking for us. I just pray they won't think to look outside. Maybe it's like looking up—they just don't do it.

I shiver and Jack scoots closer to me.

"We'll have to make do for tonight. We won't have to wait much longer—I think we should get there sometime tonight."

SIX

Making do is harder than Jack made it sound. We both start off shivering, and then my teeth chatter. I try to clench my jaw closed, but the more I try to stop the chattering, the worse it becomes. Jack chafes my arms and tries to warm me, but he's just as cold as I am. The sun has begun to set behind the mountains to the west when I hear faint voices over the wind whipping around us. The voices are coming from the other side of the door we sit against. Jack's eyes meet mine in a heartbeat and without even speaking, we head for the railing.

I peer around the side of the train, and the speed of the train makes my eyes water. I blink the tears away and see just enough of a ledge that we could stand there. For how long, I don't know; it'll have to be long enough. I jerk my head that way, and Jack nods.

I swing a leg over the railing and tiptoe along the edge of the platform until my feet find the ledge. My hands don't want to let go of the railing, but I wrench them free and run my fingers over the side of the train until I find a narrow groove that I can get a surprisingly firm grip on. This has to be the way the soldiers scurried out like ants from the nest when Jack and his father saw the nomads die while they were crossing the prairie. The thought chills me. Jack inches his way toward me, and he's just come to a spot next to me when I hear the door swing open.

"Why would they be out here?" I hear the big soldier shout. His walkie-talkie crackles and then squeals as he turns it up. "Say again, sir." He has to shout to be heard.

"You tell me, soldier. Where's your partner?"

"I dunno, sir. I haven't seen him since our rounds a few hours ago."

"And did you think about reporting that?"

"Um, yes sir."

"Do you see anything out there?"

"Just a second."

I press myself even closer to the side of the train, and the cold of the metal leeches through my clothes and chills me to the bone. My fingers and forearms are screaming at me, and the wind whipping across my face pulls more tears from my eyes. My face is chapped and the tears burn as they streak across my cheeks, and it's all I can do to just close my eyes and pray. Please don't look. Please don't look.

"No, sir. They're not back here. Though the chain looks like it's been damaged."

"They could've jumped or fallen, I suppose. Report back."

"Yes, sir."

The door slams closed. Inch by inch, I follow Jack along the ledge and then swing back over the railing. I drop to my knees, and my body shakes all over. Jack leans into me, and I can feel his heart hammering against me.

"That was too close."

I nod and wipe the tears off of my face. I tuck my hands inside my shirt and cringe when my frozen fingers touch my skin, but they start to warm a fraction. I'm about ready to start thinking about getting off the train just so I can warm up, when the train starts to slow.

Buildings crop up—shadowy blocks that are mostly dark. Occasionally one gives off light through hazy windows, and shadows creep through the darkness around them, and most of the shadows have the posture of soldiers. I'm not too worried that anyone will see us. We're wedged against the platform and the train, and the sun is almost down.

"We're getting close," Jack says in my ear, and I savor the warmth of his breath on my icy skin.

We slow down even more, and then an ear-splitting shriek stabs through the night. I clap my hands over my ears. What in the world makes such an awful noise? The sound echoes in my brain and off the mountains and then stops as quickly as it started.

"The train's whistle," Jack says. He crawls to the side of the platform and peers around. His hair whips behind him. "I can make out the station." He scurries back. "Do you think we should get off here or in the station?"

I shrug. The station will be swarming with soldiers and governmental officials, but out here it's so open. Maybe the cover of darkness will be to our advantage, but I'm not sure. I'm ready to tell Jack I want to get off out here when the train passes through a gap of twenty-foot-high chain-link fence with a group of soldiers standing at attention on either side. A spotlight is trained on the opening, and the soldiers are obviously waiting for something. For us? Or just a nomad attack that may or may not happen?

Jack grabs my arm and pulls me back into the deep shadows of the corner of the platform, and we press ourselves into the train as flat as we can, hoping that we're hidden from the eyes of the soldiers. Some of them watch the wild outside of the fence, and they wear night-vision goggles. A few are turned back to watch inside, and they just wear the standard-issue masks. I close my eyes.

The train creeps along, swaying gently as we slow even more. Then we're engulfed in a huge building. The stars disappear as we're swallowed, and I grip the rails until my fingers ache. The air in here is thick and warm and smells like oil and metal. A platform appears to our left and several sets of tracks fan out to our right. Another train is stopped on one set of tracks, and it is still and empty as a discarded shell. No one is on the platform, but we haven't yet come to a stop.

"We need to get off now," Jack says, crouching next to me. "We're going to be swarmed with soldiers once this train stops."

I nod and rock forward onto my toes. I have pins and needles all up and down my feet and legs, but I set my jaw and lean forward for the gap in the railing.

Where?

Jack scopes the station. "There." He points underneath the platform to a section that cuts back and lies in darkness. I squint my eyes and just make out the glint of metal. A door? If so, to where?

"I don't know where it leads, either. But I'm sure it's safer than on top."

I glance up as we pass a soldier standing with his gun in his arms. He doesn't look our way.

Then the train hisses and lurches to a stop. The soldier looks back down the train track lazily. No one's looking for us yet, anyway.

Jack takes my hand, and he crouches in front of me at the edge of platform. The chain dangles above his head and rubs the railings with a faint clink, clink. I still it with my fingers. The last thing we need is some miniscule, errant noise to give us away. I look back up. We can't go yet; that soldier will see us. My palms start to sweat as we hover on the edge of the platform. Either that soldier will turn his gaze our way or the soldiers on this train will make their way here and find us. We're caught in the middle and my heart pounds against my ribs. My eyes flick behind us to the door of the train car that I'm sure will hiss open at any second and back to the soldier who's so bored he scuffs the heel of his boot on the platform. Then his walkie-talkie crackles.

"Be on the look out for two nomads—male and female. They are possibly still on the Seattle train."

The soldier tips his head to the mouthpiece on his shoulder. "Yes, sir." Then the soldier hefts his gun up and walks down the platform alongside our train and out of sight.

"Now," Jack whispers.

Jack slithers out the gap in the railing and down the ladder that ends two feet from the ground. I follow him, clinging to the railing and making myself as small as possible. I drop to the ground and the gravel crunches under my feet. We're surrounded by noise—announcements over a loudspeaker, the tromp of boots, the hum and creak of the trains—but the crunch of gravel is deafening. I cringe, expecting the soldier to look down at me crouched here like a cat. I must look like an animal with my wild eyes and my muscles tensed and ready to spring. I glance up and watch the soldier continue his leisurely pace down the platform toward the front of the train. The shadow beneath the platform is only ten feet away.

I wait another second but no one looks our way, and then we're up and scrambling toward the platform before I can even blink. We stay hunched over, my fingers digging through the gravel and protesting as it bites back at my flesh. Jack disappears under the opening first, and he's completely lost in darkness. I slip in behind him, crawling on one hand, reaching the other out in front of me so I don't run into him. After about five feet, I touch his shirt. My fingers fumble down his arm until I find his hand.

Where are we?

"I don't know. I think there's a door here. Come feel."

I look back out of our small hiding space. I see gravel, train tracks, and the end of our train. But no feet, no soldiers, no pursuers. For the first time in twenty-four hours, I take a deep breath. I reach out toward Jack and then past him. The gravel cuts at my knees, but I bite my lip and ignore the pain. My hands wander over a sheet of metal with a seam down the middle. Halfway down on either side of the seam are two raised pieces of metal that could be handles. Jack's right. But what's on the other side?

"I don't think it's locked."

I grip one of the handles and pull. It budges an inch and then scrapes against the gravel and shudders to a stop. I bend down and feel Jack there beside me, and we both scrape the gravel away. My hands are raw as I rake through the rock, but after a few minutes we have moved enough that the door swings open two feet and we can worm through.

On the other side of the door is a long, brick-lined tunnel lit by dim bulbs protected by wire. They line the walls every twenty feet or so. Jack pulls the door closed behind us, and the clang echoes down the passageway. I look back. On the door is a sign that reads "Track-level Access." If the door has to be labeled that way, surely there are other doors that have to be labeled too, and we could be in a system of tunnels that run underneath this entire station, maybe even farther. The gravel gives way to dusty concrete, and I crawl down the passage.

"How far do we go?"

I shrug my shoulders. I don't know how far this tunnel will take us or if it's even in the right direction.

"Can we take a minute?"

I nod, and we both sink to the floor.

"Think it's safe to sleep?"

I shake my head, but we both need the rest. We slump down to the floor. I lean against the wall, and fall half asleep while Jack takes the first watch.

After a few hours of dozing and watching, it's time to move. After fifty feet, the tunnel opens up into a corridor high enough for us to stand, though Jack is so tall he has to dip his head. I brush the grit off my palms as I look left and right. The corridor looks identical in either direction—the same bricks, the same light bulbs, and only an occasional door to punctuate the walls.

"We have to get out of here eventually. If I'm not too turned around, if we go right that will take us somewhere outside the station on the side we came in."

He's right, and there was nothing out there but train tracks and soldiers. I look the other way and then start walking. Jack catches my hand.

"We don't know if this gets patrolled regularly, so please be careful."

I touch his cheek. *I will.*

I creep along the wall, keeping close. The doorways come frequently enough that we might be able to hide in the shadows of one if someone comes.

No one does.

These tunnels are silent as a cemetery. Our footsteps swirl the dust into eddies that haze the way behind us. Every once in a while when I look down, I see the print of a soldier's boot or the exclamation point of an agent's pair of heels. I shudder as I remember the sounds of those heels clicking down the hallways of the labor camp. We see no one, but the echoes send us scrambling.

The first one happens after we pass a door marked "Electrical Access." Voices rise up before us, and I stop dead and my feet pedal back before I can even make out what the voices are saying. We press up into space partially hidden in shadows. The rough metal scrapes against my arms, and I'm wedged against Jack's arm. He's sweating and it drips on my neck. I hadn't even noticed it had gotten warm. I'm breathing so shallowly my lungs are aching. We brace ourselves as I listen to snatches of the conversation.

"Supposed to be the hottest day on record so far."

"Tell me about it. It should be snowing."

"Don't know why they don't bring some water."

"Lemonade would be better."

Laughter. "And when was the last time you had lemonade?"

"True. Sometimes I wish I were an agent."

A drop of sweat traces its way from my hairline, down my forehead, and over my eyelid. I blink as it drops through my lashes. Where are these people with their inane conversation?

After another minute Jack's arm twitches and he looks at me. He reaches for my hand.

Don't think they're coming.

Where are they?

He shakes his head and steps out of the doorway, looks up and down the corridor, and then looks up. There's an opening in the ceiling about a foot square covered with a grate.

"It's probably a ventilation shaft," he whispers. "I noticed one after we left the crawl space."

The conversation above me stops. When the voices resume, they're hushed.

"Did you hear that?"

"It's nothing. Probably another patrol. You know how the acoustics are so warped down here."

"Sure."

I grab Jack's hand. *If we hear them, they can hear us.*

He nods and we start down the corridor again, this time hurrying along as quietly as possible. The tunnel grows warmer and warmer, and my head starts to spin. My mouth is pasty. I'd do anything for a sip of water right now, but I'm surrounded by baked bricks and swirling dust. There are pipes that run along the ceiling, and even those look like they haven't seen water for months. I hold out a hand to steady myself.

"Easy, Terra." Jack takes my arm.

We've only been without water for twenty-four hours. I can do this.

We've gone another hundred feet and passed two doors—but nothing that promises water—when the most heavenly sound I've ever heard reaches my ears.

Drip, drip, drip.

I turn frantically, trying to pinpoint where the sound comes from. Please don't let it be from a ventilation shaft. Please let it be somewhere within reach.

Out the corner of my eye, I catch a sparkle on one of the walls. One of the pipes runs right up against the wall and at a seam, a slow drip of water trickles down the wall. I touch the wet on the bricks and it's warm, but who cares. I sniff it. Nothing but brick and dust. That's promising. Now to taste it.

"What are you doing, Terra?"

Just going to taste the wall. I just shrug and turn back to the bricks.

"Are you sure? Who knows what goes through those pipes."

Better idea?

Jack takes a deep breath, eyes the wall, and licks his lips. "None at all. Go for it."

I carefully touch just the tip of my bottom lip and let a drop flow in.

Tasteless.

Jack puts his hand against the bricks and rubs his fingertips together. "Oh, who cares. It looks and feels and tastes like water, and I'm too thirsty to worry about it. Drink up."

I try to laugh, but it gets caught in my dry throat. I put my lips on the wall and want to cry. There's so little water that actually makes it into my mouth, but the few precious drops that do make it to my throat make me feel like I could walk another hundred feet. That's something, anyway.

"Oh this is killing me."

I know.

But we stay there for another ten minutes, trying to slake our thirst. When I've finally slurped in what might amount to a cup, I pull myself away and Jack follows.

Up ahead, the tunnel ends in a metal grate. There are no tunnels branching off to either side. When we reach the grate I notice a sign so dusty I took it to be part of the grate. I pull down my sleeve and wipe it off. Words finally appear.

Hospital Access Restricted.

I peer through the holes of the grate and see the tunnel continue on away from us. We're finally here, and here we stop? I bang a fist against the grate and growl.

Jack puts a hand on my shoulder and points up. A faint circle of daylight traces the edges of a round metal door. The door is set into a round access hole, and a rusty ladder hangs down several feet above Jack's head.

Safe?

"That's a moot point by now."

True. I point to the ladder.

"I'll boost you up. I think you can reach it."

Jack laces his fingers together and I step into his hands. My fingers grip the first rung and I heave myself up. Jack keeps his hands braced under my foot, and I use his strength to pull myself up the ladder. I reach for the door and it's almost hot to the touch. It must be in direct sunlight. I look around, but there's no sign telling me where this leads. I cling to the ladder with one hand and push against the door with the other, but it doesn't budge.

"Do you need both hands?"

I nod.

"Okay, just a second." Jack centers himself under the access hole. "Stand on my shoulders."

Jack guides my foot to his shoulder, and I stand on him, my arms reaching the diameter of the access hole to brace myself.

"Steady?"

I nod again.

"Okay, I'm ready." He holds my ankles and plants his legs.

My shoes dig into Jack's shoulders, and I put all my strength against the round metal cover. It lifts a mere few inches, but enough so the dust spills in and I can peer out. The sun dazzles my eyes, and I blink, trying to force my eyes open against the brightness. Tears stream out of my eyes, washing out the grit. Finally my eyes adjust, and a chain-link fence comes into focus. The fence is twenty feet high, and it's topped with a snarl of barbed wire. Beyond the fence are small squatty buildings and then the huge white block of the hospital. We're almost there, but that barbed-wire fence makes me nervous. If there's a fence like that, there's bound to be additional security out there. I squint and make out guard towers in the corners of the compound. As I turn to look behind me, I realize the metal cover is in the middle of a swathe of concrete. A road. I look behind me and make out the sprawling train station. Then a shape wavers into focus through the heat haze, and I watch it for a moment as it rumbles toward me. I gasp and drop the metal cover as a truck rumbles overhead. When the rumble stops, I brace my shoulder against the cover and heave it open one last time. About twenty feet on the other side of the fence is another round cover. I crouch down and slip off Jack's soldiers.

"What was that?"

Truck.

"Are we by a road?"

Right under.

"Close to the hospital?"

I nod.

"How does it look?"

Barbed wire. Chain link. Guard towers.

Jack wipes the sweat off his forehead and licks his lips. They're chapped and cracking. If we don't get more water soon, we won't last much longer. "The fence won't work, not if there's trucks driving by."

I nod. *Another hole.*

"Like this one?"

Building close by.

"Look up again. Are there any more trucks?"

Jack grunts as I step onto his shoulders and heft the cover open. I look back toward the train station. The dust from the previous truck is settling into eddies on the concrete, and nothing else is headed this way. I look toward the hospital. The chain link fence is rattling closed over the road. I totally missed the fact that the fence over the road is an enormous gate. The truck bounces in the distance, and there's still ten feet of gate open. If we hurry, we can make it through before it closes. I have a split second to decide.

I follow the perimeter of the fence with my eyes to the far guard tower maybe two hundred feet away. I can't see anything in it. I turn the other way. Nothing there, either. That doesn't mean there aren't soldiers slouched down, ready to pounce, but it's a chance I'm willing to take. I slide the cover onto the concrete and then go down a few rungs and offer my hand to Jack.

"What are you doing?"

There's no time for any kind of explanations, not when I can hear the gate slowly closing off our immediate chance to get closer to Nell and Red.

I thrust my hand to him again, his eyes meet mine with an intensity that burns me, and then he jumps and grips me. He almost wrenches my arm out of its socket, as he dangles and reaches for the bottom rung. I clench my jaw and my biceps are burning as I try to pull him up a fraction of an inch. Jack grunts and then wraps his fingers around the rung.

"Got it," he says through clenched teeth. "Go."

I scurry up as he pulls his feet up to the rungs and then I'm sprawled on my belly on the hot concrete as I leave the hole and head for the gate. Only five feet open. I cry out as the concrete burns my palms and my arms, and I hurry across it like a lizard with as little contact as possible. The dust coats my eyelashes and makes my eyes gritty. I cough and keep crawling, hoping that Jack is right behind me, because there's only three more feet open.

I slip through and collapse on the other side. Jack's hands are there beside me, and then his shoulders, and the gate keeps creaking closed, falls silent, and then he gasps.

"My ankle!"

I look back and his ankle is caught in the few inches of space where the gate doesn't quite meet the fence. His ankle is twisted and he pulls on it gingerly. I put out a hand to him.

"No, it's fine; it's just stuck." He pulls and the chain link rattles, but his foot doesn't budge.

I give his leg a small tug, and Jack can't hide his wince.

"Okay, that might start to hurt."

I twist his ankle the other direction and give it another tug.

"No good."

I sit down and put a hand to my forehead and study his leg and foot—how in the world am I going to do this?—when a movement catches my eye. It's the faint waver of a truck leaving the train station. I sit up and motion to Jack.

"No." He turns back and yanks on his leg and manages to jerk it free just another inch. "They'll be able to see us soon."

I crawl to his other side and pull on the gate in the direction it opens. Maybe, just maybe I can move it another inch. I brace my feet on the stationary side and wrap my fingers through the chain link of the side that moves, and then I stretch out as hard as I can. The chain link digs into my fingers and I groan, but I push even more. The fence gives the smallest fraction.

"I'm out!" Jack scrambles toward the building twenty feet away. Jack stands and cups his hands to his eyes as he looks into a window on one of the outbuildings. "It's a storage shed," he says, putting a hand to the door handle.

I grab his arm and shake my head.

"And it's empty," he says. He pulls open the door and steps inside. I follow him.

With my trembling muscles, I manage to stumble to my knees. Jack takes a few limping steps, and we huddle on the ground as the gate begins to creak open again and the truck rumbles over the road next to us. Dust swirls up outside the window above us.

After a few minutes we dare to move.

The walls of the shed are lined with shelves. Bags of fertilizer and potting soil, spades, clay pots in stacks, and gardening gloves surround me. Dust motes drift through the sunlight filtering in through the windows. This is the kind of place Nell would love. I have to remind myself, though, that it's for *them* and someone like me or Nell would have no place here.

Jack rummages through the supplies and comes up with a couple of dirty water bottles. I snatch one out of his hand before he even has time to offer it to me. I pour the water down my throat and it crackles on the way down, burning for a moment before settling in and filling me up. I close my eyes and savor it.

"Water never tasted so good. Much better than your drink of choice off the tunnel walls."

I can finally smile again.

Jack digs through a box and pulls up a pair of coveralls. "Think we could use these?"

I shake my head. I don't think a gardener would walk right into the hospital. *Too out of place,* I write on his hand. He carefully puts the clothes back the way he found them. I turn back to the shelves I was examining, when a gleam in the back corner catches my eye.

In the corner is a metal grate. It is clean—almost too much so for such an earthy place—and two words are raised on the surface: Tunnel Access. I beckon Jack over. He scratches his cheek.

"I wonder if all these buildings and the hospital are connected. They're like ants burrowing around down there."

Only one way to find out. I brace myself to pull hard at the grate, but it swings open without even a squeak. I fall back and Jack catches me. He smiles.

"I expected it to give you a bit more of a fight, too."

I walk to the edge of the square opening and peer down. Concrete steps lead down to a narrow hallway. Bulbs set inside protective covers line the hall as far as I can see. Just bricks and dim light. Nothing more, just like the tunnel we came from.

Should we?

Jack nods. "It's our best bet. It will be easier than scurrying across the open like mice. And it will be easy to hear people coming."

Which means they'll hear us too.

"True." Jack pulls me close and buries his face in my hair. "But I know you'll plunge down there anyway, so I'm not going to think about whether or not anyone can hear us."

I hold him close, suddenly aware what he just realized—we're going into the lion's den. *What do we do?*

Jack holds my face in his hands, his eyes searching mine for fear. He'll find it in spades, but that doesn't matter now. Nell and Red are right in front of us, and we have to save them.

"You mean once we're inside?"

I nod.

Jack turns to look down the tunnel, still keeping a hand on my cheek. "Find a doctor's uniform, I think. Scrubs or a doctor's coat. Anything to make it look like we belong there. I know enough about medicine that I'm sure I can play the part. You could be a patient. That way no one will expect you to say a word."

I bristle at the insinuation—that patients are nonentities—but it's true, the way the government sees us. We're commodities, nothing more. The only thing we're good for is slave labor and experimentation. Jack sees the look in my eyes.

"Don't waste that energy on me. You'll need it later."

I suck in a breath and close my eyes. He's right. I'll need all my energy for what's ahead of us. I put my foot on the first step. Jack touches my arm.

"Let me go first."

I roll my eyes. I love the chivalrous side of him, but if one of us is going to get captured—or heaven forbid, killed—it should be me. Jack is too good and kind.

He laughs. "I know, I know. You're not going to listen to me. It was worth a try, though."

I squeeze his hand and take another step and head down into the tunnel.

SEVEN

I trail my fingers along the bricks as we go down, and I feel like I'm in a cave. The lights flicker every so often and cast long, wavering shadows down the corridor. There is nothing but red bricks on all sides of us and other brick corridors that lead away into darkness. I cling to the side of the passage. I feel like a rat in a maze down here, sniffing my way to the reward. Jack follows me so closely his breath is warm on my neck. I've been so used to treading lightly in the forest that the *scuff scuff* my shoes make on the floor hammers in my ears. Up ahead two tunnels fork off from this one, and I slow down. All the way from the train station, we never came across an intersection of tunnels, and the fact that I can't see what lies around the corner unnerves me. My fingers creep along the wall toward the corner, and I'm ready to peek around and down the passage next to us, when Jack grabs my arm and yanks me back. He puts a finger to his lips.

I hear voices.

A man and a woman, but I can't make out their words. They speak just above a whisper, and their voices float toward us from the tunnel I almost looked down. Jack and I flatten against the wall and I barely breathe. Another sound comes—the creak of wheels. The man raises his voice.

"I told them he couldn't withstand much more. We may have an unlimited supply of test subjects, but if we seriously damage each one just at the verge of a breakthrough, we'll never succeed. The schedule is too rigorous; surely the president can see that."

The woman snorts. "And do you want to go to the government island and tell her?"

The footsteps and wheels stop. The man clears his throat. "Please don't tell anyone I said anything."

"You honestly think I would? Why do you think I prefer the tunnels? I don't like my every word recorded by a watcher." The wheels and footsteps resume. "I don't know how I ever got myself into this mess."

The woman's voice is close now. I turn my head, expecting to see her at any moment. There's a click and a soft whoosh, and the tunnels are silent.

Where? I ask Jack. His eyebrows turn down and he shakes his head. I wriggle free from his grasp and inch my head around the corner. All I see is a tunnel identical to this one.

Gone, I tell him, and he creeps around me and stands in the open.

"They can't have disappeared."

I narrow my eyes and study the corridor. The walls are perfectly uniform except for there, just past the wire-caged light. A slight bump stands out. I touch it, and Jack comes over to look.

"A door?"

I nod. There's nothing else it could be. I dig my fingers around all the edges, but I can't see how to open it.

"Are you sure you want to go in there? Those people could be in there and we'd have nowhere to go."

But I do want to get in. I need to see what's inside. A door with no handle and no obvious way in just begs to be opened. Jack knows I'm not going to relent, and he joins me, his long fingers tracing the wall on either side, looking for a button or keypad. He puts a hand on the back of his neck.

"I don't know, Terra. Maybe it only opens from the inside."

How did they get in? I shake my head. There has to be another way. I push on the door with both hands and all my weight when it starts to slide left-to-right under my palms and a blast of warm air that smells like burning meat hits my cheeks. I jerk back and stare as the door slips away and I'm standing face-to-face with a man in a doctor's coat. His mouth drops and his face pales, and he looks as surprised to see me as I am to see him.

The closest I've come to a confrontation like this was with Smitty all those months ago in a mountain forest. I can still see his angular face rippling with shadows, and I can still feel the weight of the gun in my hands. I can never forget those things. I can never forget the small *o* of surprise on his mouth when I killed him. I want to close my eyes and shake the image from my mind, but my eyes are so dry right now as they're riveted on the doctor that I don't think they'll ever close again.

Then the same reflexes that pulled my finger tight around the trigger fly into action as my fingers curl into a fist and slam across his jaw. My knuckles feel like I just pummeled a rock, and both the doctor and I stagger back, but then he slumps to the floor and holds his face. Jack rushes in behind me and stands over the doctor. My eyes move to the woman just a few feet behind them. Then my eyes widen even more.

The woman stands before a huge metal furnace. Her fingers have just closed a door and her other hand is frozen in the act of pushing hair away from her face. The heat has put roses in her cheeks. Her eyes stare at me, unblinking, like she's not even sure I'm there. Her mouth slips open and she gapes.

"Who are you?" Her voice is no more than a whisper.

I'm so used to the agents, the soldiers, the people like Dr. Benedict who take so much pleasure in hurting us. The fear that riddles this woman's entire posture is such a surprise to me that I can't move. Jack steps forward.

"We need his doctor's coat." He nods to the doctor on the floor. The doctor still whimpers and doesn't move.

The woman's hand moves from the door. I notice a gurney beside her. A rumpled sheet drapes half of it, and there's an impression on the thin mattress still. A human shape. My eyes flick to the furnace. Then a howl escapes my lips.

"What?" Jack asks.

I point to the gurney and to the furnace, and the gears click into place for him. His eyes narrow on the woman.

"What is the furnace for?"

She shifts her weight and looks at the floor. Her shoulders slump. "For the patients."

"Please tell me they're dead first."

She looks up at him, and her eyes are shining with tears. "Of course they're dead. I would never. . . . I could never do such a thing. They may all be monsters up there. You might think I'm a monster, and maybe you're right." She puts a hand out and limps to the wall, bracing herself there. She looks like a breeze could knock her over. "I'm no better than any of them."

I glance at Jack. *Who?*

"Who are you?" he asks.

"Just a physician's assistant. I'm no one important. Of course I'm no one important. That's why they gave me this job." Her voice wavers over the last two words, and she puts a hand to her mouth. All the color has drained out of her. "I went to school to learn how to heal people. Not to do this."

"Who's he?" Jack looks down at the doctor.

"The doctor I'm assigned to. To make sure this gets done."

The man finally stirs. "Shut up!" he snaps at the woman. He points a finger at her. "You don't even know who they are. Nomads by the look of them." His eyes rake all over me as he rubs his jaw. "And you just asked for trouble. Did you really think you could get into the hospital? And what's your plan this time? A bomb? A raid? Kill the chief medical official? You nomads are all the same. Pathetic, weak, and shortsighted. And you all end up the same way. Burned to ash."

It may be the heat from the furnace or it may be the man's words, but I fly into such a fury that I don't even realize what I'm doing until Jack's voice is in my ear and his hands are on my arms pulling me back. I look down, and the doctor moans once and then loses consciousness. My knuckles are bleeding. I fold my arms, burying my fists, and lean against Jack.

The woman sags against the wall. "Please don't hurt me," she begs. "I want to help."

The funny thing is, I believe her. Her eyes are tired and her mouth frowns like it's been a long time since it's done anything else. She looks like she never asked for any of this. Jack nods.

"I need his doctor's coat."

The woman's face clears, and she stumbles from the wall and onto her knees next to the doctor. She grunts as she pulls one arm out of the coat, flops him over, and pulls out the other.

Jack goes to the gurney and straightens the sheet. "How do you access the hospital? Does he have a keycard?"

She yanks the coat out from under the doctor and stumbles backward. Then she hands it to Jack. "That name badge on the front has a code on it that is automatically scanned at every door. He has clearance to the whole hospital except high-level security areas. Those are marked with red doors. Stay away from those."

I narrow my eyes and grab her hand. She flinches. *Why are you helping?*

"Because this—all of this—is wrong. I went into medicine hoping to help people. Hoping I could help the citizens and even the nomads. Instead I was put here where all I do every day is watch people lose their minds and then watch their bodies shut down under the stress of it all. And what do I do to help? I burn them to make room for more." She closes her eyes and tears slide down her cheeks.

"We need to find someone," Jack says, slipping his arms into the coat. The sleeves are too short, but it'll have to do.

"Please don't tell me what you're going to do because I don't want to be able to tell anyone." She straightens the badge over his left pocket. "All I'll tell you is that if you're looking for a patient, they will be on levels two or three. If you're looking for the medical officials, they'll be on level eight."

I drop her hand and turn to Jack.

"Lie on the gurney," he says.

I sit and swing my legs up. The woman shakes her head. "That will never work." She reaches into a drawer below the bed and pulls out a hospital gown. "No one will believe you're a patient wearing outside clothes."

Jack turns his back as I slip out of my pants and shirt and pull on the gown. I grab the woman's hand again. *How do we get there?*

"This room is on the main tunnel. Go left. Follow that past two more intersections. There will be a gray door at the end of the tunnel. That door is the hospital's freight elevator. Take that to wherever you need to go."

I lie down and Jack pulls the sheet over me. The woman grabs my shoulder.

"How are you getting out?"

Jack's hands freeze and the sheet hangs half over me. "What do you mean?"

"If you are here for a patient, you should know they will hardly be able to walk."

I look up and feel the tears coming to my eyes. The closer I get to the hospital, the more scared I am to actually find Nell and Red.

The woman looks down at her hand and slowly draws it away. "I'm so sorry. Truly. But if you want me to, I can help you get out."

Jack and I look long at each other. My heart wants to trust her, but my head is screaming at me to stop being so stupid, to remember what happened the last time I trusted someone on "their" side. Jack gives a slight shake of his head, but I turn back to her and nod.

Yes.

"I'm scheduled to help with a medical shipment in one hour. If you take the freight elevator to the loading dock, I can get you on a supply truck. You'll need to figure out the rest."

Thank you.

"One hour. If you're not there, I can't stay around to help you. We're watched so closely, and if I do anything out of the ordinary—" Her eyes dash around the room like she's waiting for someone to snatch her and take her away.

"We understand," Jack says. "Open the door, please."

She jumps up and presses a button I hadn't noticed on the brick, and the door slides open. "Be careful. And here."

She reaches to her hip, and I tense. Then she hands me a Taser.

"Most of the staff is equipped with them. Don't ask me why. Most of the patients can't do a thing. But take it. You'll need it more than I will."

I take the Taser from her and slip it next to me beneath the sheet. Jack pushes the gurney, and I watch the bricks on the ceiling go by. We pass two intersections and then the gray door greets us at the end of the corridor. Jack presses the up button, it illuminates red, and we wait. Behind the door, the elevator creaks and rattles and it sets my fingers twitching anxiously. Jack grabs my hand to still it.

What if there's someone on it?

"Then you're the patient and I'm the doctor," he replies, his voice steady and calm. Too calm. I can tell he's trying to convince himself that this is foolproof.

Patients don't come back from down here.

He frowns. "That's probably true."

Maybe I came back to life? Yup, my stupid humor to the rescue.

His frown relaxes. "Maybe. But let me do the talking. You're a patient and have who-knows-what running through you."

Of course. I need to be silent. I probably also need to look sick or crazy, too. I let my head loll to one side and close my eyes halfway.

"Just don't over do it," Jack says, hiding the laugh in his voice.

I smile, then return to being sickly.

The elevator dings and the door scrapes open, but no one comes off. Small miracles. Jack wheels me on.

Two.

Jack nods. "Two or three, if that woman can be trusted."

She can.

Jack presses the button. "I think you're right. In which case we have less than an hour to find Nell and Red and get to the loading dock."

The elevator rocks side-to-side as we ascend, and that combined with my nerves, the harsh light, and the antiseptic smell, I don't need to do much pretending to be sick. By the time the door slides open again, I feel pale and woozy.

I lie on the stretcher, my shoulder blades and hips digging into the scarce padding beneath me. The thin sheet stretches over me, and even though I'm fully covered, I feel exposed with just the sheet and a hospital gown over me. I hope I'll be able to grab my clothes on the way out of here, but with Red and Nell in tow, who knows what might happen.

Jack stands behind me, pulls a surgical mask over his face, and pushes me along the hallway. I squint against the fluorescent lights and turn my head to the side. Doors slip by. 231, 233, 235. We slow as we pass each one, and Jack glances through the windows. Soldiers line the hall every so often, and Jack doesn't look at them. He just dips his head condescendingly as he passes by. He could have graduated from the Dr. Benedict Class of Bedside Manner. Only I who can read his eyes so well sees more than just feigned coldness in them. He glances about, taking in all our surroundings, counting the soldiers, looking for exits. I do the same as my fingers tighten over the Taser next to my hip. I hope the soldiers can't see any trace of it under the sheet that is barely more than a piece of paper. Goosebumps raise on my legs and my toes are cold. This whole building is cold. I shiver and close my eyes.

"Just two more doors until the end of the hall," Jack whispers. I can hear how clenched his teeth are. "Then we'll have to go up again if Nell's not here." He grips the bars on either side of my head more tightly, and his knuckles turn white. I want to reach up and touch his hands, soothe him, but that would be out of the question. Any move like that and the soldiers would be on us in a moment to stop a nomad from attacking a precious cog in their system. I clench my fists to keep my hands still. My palms are still sore from crawling through gravel. I take a deep breath and slowly let it out.

Jack stops the gurney outside room 241. The sign next to the door says, "Female, age 67." My eyes open wide. This might be her. But where is Red?

"We'll find him, Terra," Jack says so softly I can barely hear him. "Let's worry about Nell for now."

I nod. One thing at a time.

Jack turns the door handle with a soft click. He looks up and down the hallway, but the soldiers ignore him, and he pushes open the door and wheels me in. As soon as the door closes behind us, I push aside the sheet and jump off the gurney. The tile freezes my feet, but I shove the sensation aside and clutch my Taser, surveying the room for any threats.

The only thing I see is a single bed with a single occupant and dozens of tubes and wires plugged into so many machines with so many blinking lights and beeps it makes me dizzy. The woman lying in the bed has gray hair that used to be glistening silver, long fingers that used to plant hydrangeas just for a touch of beauty, and a sunken face that still radiates kindness despite what the doctors have done to her. Tears flood my eyes as I run to her and fall next to her on the bed.

"Nell," I sob, but of course it doesn't come out right. I'm afraid I might crush her. She wasn't more than a waif at the settlement, but now she's more of a wraith. She stirs next to me, and her eyes flutter open.

"Terra? That sounded like Terra."

I half-laugh, half-cry and wipe my nose with the back of my hand. Jack rushes to my side and takes stock of the machines Nell's hooked up to.

"Yes, Nell. It's Terra and Jack. We've come for you."

She turns her head to stare at Jack, and it takes a second for her eyes to focus on him. "Who?" He pulls down his mask and smiles at her. Her head sinks back into the pillow. "Bless you both. I haven't seen anyone from the settlement for months. Are they all right?"

I close my eyes and more tears fall out.

"We're not sure. We're still looking." Jack puts a finger to his mouth and his brows furrow as he traces the lines of tubing from the machines to Nell's arm, figuring out which tube belongs to which machine.

Nell reaches a hand for mine, and I grip hers tightly. Her fingers are cold. I rub them, bringing warmth to her. I bend over and kiss her forehead, then slip off her bed. Nell smiles at me.

"Are you a patient here?"

I manage a half-smile. I'd be all smiles if I weren't still terrified that we were going to be found out at any moment. It was one thing to just have Jack with me. Now I'll have Nell, and the responsibility presses down on me. I put a hand to her cheek, and she leans into it.

"Is Jack your doctor?"

I shake my head. She should know what's going on here, and her confusion worries me.

She looks to Jack, who has meticulously started unplugging her. "I think I need those machines, Jack dear. The doctors explained it all to me."

Jack's fingers stop moving along the tubes and he turns inch-by-inch to face her. "Nell, we'd like you to come with us." He speaks slowly, like he's explaining it to a child. The frown on his face brings one to my own. "Can you do that?"

Nell smiles sweetly and folds her hands on her lap. "I couldn't possibly do that. Not when the doctors have taken such good care of me."

My heart falls and I feel empty inside. Not Nell. Not my dear, dear Nell.

EIGHT

"I'm sure they could patch you up, too, Terra. That scratch on your arm doesn't look good." Nell traces her fingers along the cut so lightly I barely feel her. I pull my arm to my chest.

I'm fine. Fine except that I'm numb all over.

When her lips turn up into a smile, her eyes don't sparkle the way they used to. "Best not to risk infection. My Red would tell you that. Have you seen him here?" Her eyes roam the room and she cranes her head around me. "I haven't seen him for so long. The doctors told me that he's in intensive care because his health was failing. But I know if anyone can save Red, it's them."

"Nell, we're not sure where he is." Jack wheels the gurney closer. "Would you like to find him with us? Then you can make sure he's all right."

Nell beams. "That's a wonderful idea. The doctors tell me I should stay here, and I'd like to listen to them, but they really shouldn't keep me from him, you know. It would be better for my recovery to see him. And if Red's not doing so well, it wouldn't hurt for him to see me either."

I glance at Jack and he nods. He wheels the cart with the machines and tubes along as I help Nell swing her legs to the side of her bed. She is as thin as a sapling, and I'm scared she'll break under my touch.

"Now give me just a moment to collect myself, Terra." She puts a hand on my shoulder. "I'm not used to being up and about, and I don't want Red to see me exhausted."

I smile and hope she sees how much I want to help her. I also hope she doesn't guess what form that help will take. With the loyalty serum wreaking havoc on her, I have no idea how she'll react when she finds out just where we're going to take her.

She lies down on the gurney and smooths her hospital gown. She shivers. I pull the sheet up over her. Her knees and elbows cut sharp angles that are visible through the sheet, and my heart aches. She shivers again, and I open cupboards until I find a blanket. I pull it up around her chin.

"Thank you, Terra. The doctors said the medicine they gave me might make me cold. They weren't joking."

Jack frowns as he studies the liquid dripping into her veins. He rubs the scruff on his chin. "Can I unplug any of this, Nell? Would that help?" He tries to say it with a casual concern, but I know him too well, and I can hear the stress surging below it all. We're going to have to unhook her eventually, and she may have been lucid enough through all the testing to know what does what. But Nell shakes her head.

"No, dear. I'm afraid I need all of them. The doctors said so. They're such nice people. Haven't you met any of them yet?"

I've had enough. I shake my head and make for the door when Jack grabs my arm.

"You're still in a hospital gown."

I was too caught up and almost walked out of here in just a gown. And how would that look to the soldiers in the hall?

"Stay here," Jack says. "I'll find you something."

He opens the door and slips out. I lie down on Nell's bed so that if anyone looks in, there will be two patients.

"Are you not feeling well, Terra? I can page the doctors if you need me to."

I sit up and shake my head. Not that. I smile, trying to wipe the worry off my face. I squeeze Nell's hand. Hurry Jack, I think. Please just hurry.

I look at the clock on the wall and watch the second hand stagger forward until five minutes have passed. We only have thirty-five minutes until we meet the physician's assistant at the loading dock.

I hold my breath as a soldier marches past the door, but he doesn't even glance in here. I close my eyes.

"You're sure you don't want me to page them?"

I try to smile. It doesn't work.

Then Jack opens the door. He opens his doctor's coat and pulls out a white bundle. He shakes it out. Scrubs.

"It's what the nurses wear. There's a laundry drop at the end of the hall. Sorry if they're dirty."

Jack turns as I rip off the gown and pull on the scrubs. Nell frowns.

"Why do you have that uniform?"

Please don't put it all together, I beg her silently. I smile as sweetly as I can and push her toward the door. Jack opens it.

"Please, Nell. You need your rest. Let's go find Red."

Her troubled gaze lingers on me, but she draws the blanket up closer to her face. Her lips rise up at the corners, and I can tell she's thinking about Red. Jack looks up and down the hall. A sign next to the elevator door says, *Intensive Care 4th Floor*.

"Fourth floor," Jack says. He leads the way as I push Nell.

"You look nice in a doctor's coat, Jack. So handsome. I'm glad you finally made your way here. I was so worried for you when you left the settlement. When you both did. But life went on like it always does." Nell hesitates on the words, and a strange look flashes across her face. "Then the helicopters came. Everyone was screaming and running. I'm not sure why. All the soldiers wanted to do was help." She stumbles over her words for a moment and then continues. "And then an agent came out of a truck. He was such a nice—" She puts a hand to her head as if it's hurting her. "But that can't be right."

A timer on the machine next to her starts beeping. It's slow and steady, and after three beeps, one of the tubes fills with pale lavender liquid. It creeps toward the needle in Nell's left hand.

I hiss at Jack. Nell is so befuddled she doesn't notice a thing I'm doing, but Jack turns back to me. I point to the trail of fluid evacuating the tube for Nell's veins.

"What is it?" he asks, studying the tube.

The serum.

"You're sure?"

The liquid reaches the needle, and Nell's eyes begin to cloud over and she smiles at us. "And you haven't met the nice doctors yet?"

I nod to Jack.

We get on the elevator and Jack presses the button. The doors take several moments to close and we wait. The car still hasn't lurched upward.

"Nell, can I adjust one of your IVs for you?"

Nell smiles. "Of course. Did I tell you how handsome you look in that doctor's coat?"

Jack gives her a half-smile. "You did, Nell. Thank you. Let's get this adjusted and then after we see Red, we'll talk to your doctor about it."

"You've always been so concerned about me, Jack; about everyone. It's no wonder you and Terra became fast friends. You're alike." Nell gives me a fond look, and I hold her other hand.

Jack takes her left hand. "I'm just going to remove this from your IV. You'll still have the needle in when the doctor wants to administer your medicine again, but I'm a little worried about the dosage."

"Of course, Jack dear. You know, I'm so glad you made your way here. You fit right in with all the other nice doctors."

The elevator finally starts moving and slowly lumbers upward. Jack removes the tube and carefully coils it up and sets it beside the machine.

How long?

He shakes his head. "How often do they administer that medication, Nell?"

Nell squints at the ceiling. "Maybe every day or so. It's easy to lose track of time."

"Of course. Yes, I think that might be too frequently. I'll be sure to note it in your chart."

The elevator lurches to a stop, and I put a hand on the wall to steady myself. The doors start to slide and I peer through the growing opening.

The intensive care unit is a large square space dominated by a station in the center with monitors and computers and shelves of equipment. Doorways lead off the open space into small rooms each with a large window. Every room has at least two beds, and most of the beds are occupied. The lights are dim, and I can't make out any of the occupant's faces from here.

I brace myself for the doctors, the staff, the looks. I brace myself for the questions that will surely be asked of an unfamiliar doctor and nurse. Why would someone from the second floor be moved here? Why is her monitor beeping? When did you two get transferred here? My muscles are twitchy and I'm ready to run. The doors squeal as they stop.

The open space is empty.

I'm not sure which is worse—facing the doctors, or the eerie silence that creeps into my ears.

The sound of the gurney's wheels creaking echoes through the space. Nothing but the beep of machinery and the occasional wheezy breath greets us. The room is full of shadows.

Nell tries to sit up as she looks around. "Are you sure Red's here? He should be somewhere with more medical attention. The doctors told me he would receive the finest care."

Jack puts a hand on her shoulder. "I'm sure, Nell."

He paces forward, peering through doorways until he pauses in one and his hands fall to his sides. My heart clenches at the defeat sagging his body. Nell grips my hand.

"Jack? Is he there?" Her voice quavers. All Jack can do is nod.

I can't do this—the suspense. I push ahead and cross the threshold.

Red lies on a bed, a sheet pulled up over his chest. His arms rest on top of the thin fabric. The lean, sinewy muscle I remember from the settlement has withered and his arms are nothing more than skin and bones. White hairs cross over the wrinkled skin. His beard is more gray than red. His eyes are closed and his breathing is shallow. If the machines weren't persistent in their regular beeps, I would have thought he was dead.

"Red?" Jack whispers.

Red's eyes move beneath the lids, but he doesn't open them. I wheel Nell in so her gurney is next to the bed. Nell sucks in a breath as she looks him over. Then she reaches for his hand, and he flinches under her touch.

"Red." Her voice is stern. It surprises me after seeing her so docile.

His eyes open a fraction. His voice comes out as a croak. "What do you want now?"

"Red, you open your eyes this instant." Nell sounds positively peeved.

Red's eyes flutter open, and he drags his head to the side to look at us. His eyes widen and his eyebrows rise. Not much, but they go up. His lips are chapped and they stick together as he closes his mouth to swallow.

"Nell? Is that you?" He raises his head an inch off the pillow.

A smile plays across her lips. "Who did you think it was? The queen?"

"I wish we had a queen. It would be better than the president."

"Now Red . . ." Nell's disapproving tone slices my heart.

Jack peers down the hall. Still no movement. He leans over Red. "Red, it's Jack. Are you getting good medical treatment?"

Red squints. "Good medical treatment? *Good?* Have you been living under a rock?"

Jack smiles. "Thank you. That's all I needed to know."

I'm so relieved I could cry. I wrap my arms around Red and he groans.

"Easy there, sweetheart." He pauses and looks at me. "Terra?"

I nod.

"I knew we hadn't seen the last of you." Red touches my hair. "You got a hair cut."

I look away. Jack clears his throat.

"We were in a camp."

Red's eyes turn flinty. "A labor camp?"

Nell glances from one of us to another. "Don't be ridiculous. There's no such thing. We always told those stories at the settlement, but you shouldn't go believing it and spreading rumors."

Red finally looks at Nell—really looks at her—and frowns. "What did they do to you, Nell?"

She looks puzzled. "They've been taking very good care of me. But I don't understand why they aren't doing the same for you."

Jack leans in to Red and whispers in his ear. Tears well up in Red's eyes, and I don't have to hear Jack's words to know what he just told him. Red's hands clench the sheet and his lips tremble. He turns his gaze to Nell, and the tears spill out.

"Why Red, whatever's the matter?" Nell squeezes his arm and leans closer. She brushes her lips against his hand. "Should I call for a doctor?"

He closes his eyes and takes a deep breath. "No, dear, no need. It'll all be fine. This'll pass."

"Can I unhook you, Red?" Jack asks.

Red shakes his head and glances at Nell, worry creasing his forehead. "Not sure. I think everyone who's a little more *resistant* ends up here. I don't know what'd happen if you took those things out of me. Any guesses what these infernal things do?"

"A few," Jack says, moving one of the carts next to the gurney. "I've noticed a few prisoners being moved, and most of them have these two machines with them." He points to a monitor that shows heartbeat and temperature, and another machine with a frosty window with a small vial inside. A tube leads from the machine to an IV in Red's arm. "The problem is that I'm not sure what's in that vial. Nell's wasn't like this. I don't know if it's something important or just the loyalty serum. If it's the loyalty serum, I want to take it out and just tape the tube to your IV so it just looks like it's still hooked up. But if it's something else, I don't know if it's safe to take it out or not." He frowns and rubs the bridge of his nose.

"Just take it out," Red says. His face is serious.

"I don't know if I can do that," Jack says, studying the vial.

"I've been hooked up to too many machines for too long. Take it out, and let's get my Nell somewhere safe."

Jack lets out a long breath and then nods. He reaches for Red's IV, but Nell puts a hand on him.

"What are you doing, Jack? The doctors treating Red think he needs that."

Jack gently puts his hands on her shoulders. "Does it look like there are any doctors treating Red?"

Nell looks around and her eyes are pained. "I.... I don't know. They took such good care of me. Why would they do this to Red?" She looks out the window and across the way where another man lies in bed in much the same condition. "Why would they do this to anyone here?"

My heart hurts for her, and I hug her and then take her hand. *We'll talk about it later.*

She nods.

"I'm ready, Jack."

Jack carefully takes the tube out. He rummages through a supply cupboard, finds some medical tape, and fastens the tube in place.

"Are you feeling okay?" he asks Red.

Red flexes his arm. "Yes. Better, actually."

Jack rubs his chin. "It might have been a sedative."

Red manages a smile, and it takes up his too-thin face. "They would need to sedate me, you know? The only way to keep me from fighting back."

Nell sits up. "Why would you want to fight back, Red? None of this makes any sense."

I soothe Nell back down, and Red lies back down in his bed. He clasps Nell's hand, and his fingers are so bony he looks like a skeleton. "There'll be plenty of time for making sense of it soon, Nellie girl. Just wait." He brings her hand to his lips. A smile spreads across Nell's face that could warm this entire building.

"You take Nell, Terra. I'll get Red."

I pull the gurney out into the open space, and Jack follows.

"Where are we going?" Red asks.

I'm not sure how wise it is to reveal our plans in front of Nell. What happens if we're caught? With the loyalty serum still in full effect, she would betray us in a heartbeat and not even realize she was turning us in.

I shake my head at Jack. He nods.

"I'm going to talk to someone about a hospital transfer. One where they could take better care of you both. I know the top official in this hospital, and I think she might agree with me."

"That's sure sweet of you taking care of us like that, Jack."

I pat Nell's shoulder. The sooner we get out of here, the better. If she was getting a dose of the loyalty serum every day, it'll be a little less than twenty-four hours until it wears off.

"I scheduled an appointment downstairs. If the official agrees with me, there's a truck we can get on right away."

"Where would we go?" Red asks, glancing out the corner of his eye at Nell. His lips are turned down in worry.

Jack presses the elevator button. "Somewhere on the west coast, I think."

Nell closes her eyes and takes a deep breath. "It would be nice to be by the ocean. I haven't seen the ocean in so many months."

I smirk. Oh, the irony.

NINE

The elevator jostles us as we descend to the loading dock. My shoulder bumps up against Jack's, and his eyes are hard when he looks at me. Things just got a hundred times more complicated now that we have Nell and Red with us. My fingers tighten around the metal bars of the gurney, but Nell just smiles up at me. She folds her hands, and she looks so serene. If only she could feel what I do—the way my stomach clenches with every jolt of the elevator, the way my heart pounds with dread because we're getting closer and closer to the loading dock. Will the physician's assistant be there? Will she be able to get us on the truck?

Jack leans closer. "Relax."

Right. Relax. It was one thing when it was just me and Jack—we can turn and run. Now we have two invalids—two invalids that I would never let anything happen to.

Can't.

"I know." He looks up at the lights that wash his face out.

The elevator rumbles to a stop and the doors open. We stand on the edge of a huge hangar. Three enormous trucks are lined up next to a door. The sun glares through it, silhouetting them and putting the rest of the loading dock into shadow. The space is filled with the smell of gasoline and exhaust. Workers scurry from stacks of pallets to the trucks while an agent marks their progress on a tablet. They're loading small cardboard boxes that I recognize from the med drop I went on with Red. That seems like ages ago. Then I look closer to us. Two soldiers stand on either side of the elevator. I glance around, but I don't see the physician's assistant.

Jack stares at them. He shifts his weight to one foot. "Excuse me," he finally says. He tries to put authority into his voice, but I hear the quaver running through it.

For a moment, I'm afraid the soldiers aren't going to move. I wish I could see their expressions, but they're hidden behind the black masks. Then one nods to the other and they both stand aside. Jack wheels Red out and I follow with Nell. I'm just about passed them when one clears his throat.

"Sir? Where are you going with the patients? They aren't allowed on the loading dock."

Jack keeps walking. "Special transfer."

One of the soldiers leaves his post and the scuff of his boots on the concrete follows us. The hairs on the back of my neck stand on end. Please leave us alone.

"That's against established protocol, sir. Do you have authorization?"

Jack quickens his pace. There are three huge trucks a hundred feet from us. One of those is the one we need. Jack changes direction toward the far one—the one farthest from the agent—

and doesn't look back. "Yes. This is a special case. A containment issue. We didn't want these two exposing other patients."

Nell opens her mouth like she's ready to say something, but Red shakes his head. She frowns but lies back down.

"Yes, sir, of course. But I'm still going to need to see your authorization."

Jack nods. "I have it with me. Let's just get to the truck."

"Yes, sir."

The soldier follows us, but his posture is still relaxed—he doesn't suspect anything. Not yet, anyway. I tighten my grip on the gurney to keep my hands from shaking. I don't know if it will help because surely the soldier can hear my knees knocking together. I try to take even breaths, but my heart is pounding too hard. It's scorching hot in here, and the sweat is already beading on my forehead and trickling down my skin. I blink a drop of it out of my eyes. I stand up straighter and try to look the part.

"It's too hot out here," Jack says, his tone offhand.

"Yes, sir. Can't believe how hot it is for April."

I look out the corner of my eye, but the agent is still counting boxes as the workers load them onto the truck, and she doesn't notice us. We're to the front of the truck, and Jack slips around the side where we won't be exposed to anyone else in the loading dock.

"I have the authorization here in my pocket. Let's just get to the rear doors. Do they give you enough to drink down here?"

I smile. Sweet, charming Jack. Just like him to keep the soldier off his guard.

"Probably, though it never feels like enough on a day like today."

"Just pay attention to how you're feeling. If you're dizzy or nauseated or have a persistent headache, you need to let someone know."

"Thank you, sir."

Jack's eyes dart to the oxygen tank on the bottom shelf of Nell's gurney. It's small, just the right size to heft. I nod. Jack keeps talking to the soldier, and he turns his back on us. Careful not to make a single sound, I bend down and undo the strap holding the tank in place. It's heavier than it looks with the compressed oxygen inside, but not too heavy for me lift it up over my head. I grip it hard, focus on the back of the soldier's head. I've ready to swing it down when a voice makes me pull up sharp.

"What are you doing?"

I fumble with the tank and clutch it to me awkwardly so it won't clang to the floor. All the blood has drained from my face, and even though it's unearthly hot in here, my fingers feel cold. No. We've come so close to be caught now. Red reaches across the small gap between him and Nell and grips her hand hard.

"I thought I told you to bring the patients to the truck bound for San Diego."

The voice is familiar. I look up and see the physician's assistant. She's shed her lab coat and is wearing the black suit of an agent, and her hair is scraped back into the too-tight bun. She even wears the haughty eyes and sneering mouth. I hardly recognize her.

"Yes, of course. My apologies." Jack smiles a we're-in-this-together-right? kind-of smile to the soldier, and the soldier tips his head.

"This way." She flicks two fingers and turns on her heel.

Jack and I gratefully follow her. The soldier hangs back, unsure what to do. The woman turns around.

"You are not needed, soldier. Return to your post."

"Yes, ma'am." He salutes and hurries back to the elevator doors.

The physician's assistant sweeps back a thin strand of hair that has escaped her bun. "I thought you were never coming," she murmurs. "I didn't know how much longer I could keep this up."

"Sorry. It took us a few extra minutes to get our friends." Jack pats Red's shoulder.

Her eyes lower to the floor for a brief moment. All I can hear are the shuffle of cardboard boxes and the click of her heels on the concrete. "I never knew how they felt about the agents until I was one. I hate the way they look at me—the way they're afraid."

The workers ahead of us look away as soon as we get past the truck. They don't want to make eye contact with the woman. They hurry to load their cargo.

"It won't be much longer," Jack says.

"Thank goodness." She turns to the workers. "All of you. Wait over there." She points to the opposite wall.

The workers shuffle away.

"The truck is almost loaded. Get in with your friends. You won't be able to take the beds, so they'll have to walk—I'm sorry, ma'am, sir. Stay up as close to the front of the truck as you can. You'll be better hidden that way. There shouldn't be too many stops or inspections, but stay up there the whole time, just in case. I've put a pouch of food for the two of you," she looks at me and Jack. "I didn't know there would be two more, though. It might be able to last you if you ration it. Once you get to San Diego, you're on your own."

I clutch her hand. *Thank you. Come with us?*

Then she does something surprising. She smiles. Her face loses the sadness and fear and becomes beautiful. "No. I'm not that brave."

I want to take her hand. I want to say, "You are one of the bravest people I've met up here; you just can't see that." I want to tell her, but there's no time to spell the words. Instead I take both her hands and hope my eyes tell her what my fingers cannot.

I help Nell off the gurney. She stumbles as she plants her feet, but then she manages to get her footing, and she climbs up into the truck.

"But I don't understand, Jack. How will this provide me better treatment? It doesn't make any sense."

Jack puts a hand to her cheek. "I'm just asking you to trust me, Nell. Let's just get to San Diego and then we'll explain everything. I promise."

Nell puts her hand on top of his and studies him for a moment. Then her clouded expression clears. "Alright, Jack. San Diego." She wags a finger at him. "And then you'd better explain everything, and I mean everything. Do you understand, young man?"

Jack smiles. "Yes, ma'am."

Red is a little trickier. He tries to stand, but his legs buckle underneath him. Jack and I have to carry him—and I'm disturbed at how light he is—onto the truck. We guide him to the back where Nell has already found a spot behind a stack of boxes. She's half in shadow and disappears even further into the corner as we approach.

"Lay him here, Terra." She indicates a spot on the floor where she's put down the blanket from her gurney.

We lower him down and he mutters curses the entire time. I knew Red had some colorful vocabulary, but I haven't ever heard quite this many expletives used in one long, run-on sentence. Nell gives him a stern look.

"You clean that mouth up right this second, Red." She looks at me. "I'm sorry you had to hear that, Terra."

"I've just never been so helpless in my life," Red says, his breath coming short. He lays his head down, and Nell runs her hand down his cheek.

"That's why Jack and Terra are here. We'll get you to San Diego and get you the help you need."

Red looks at us, a probing look that says, "You *are* aren't you?"

I nod and take his hand. *Going somewhere safe.*

He raises an eyebrow. He looks skeptical, and I don't blame him. We'll see how it goes when I actually tell him where we're going.

I turn back to the doors, and the physician's assistant closes one side. She gives me one last smile and then closes the other door, and we're lost in darkness. The truck's engine rumbles to life, but then the shouting begins.

"Who are you?"

Jack has been molded into my side, but now he sits up stick-straight.

"Why are you wearing an agent's uniform?"

The woman's voice is muffled, but I catch the pleading edge to it. She starts begging. I don't need to hear the words to know this is going to go terribly, terribly wrong.

Jack's feet scrape on the floor of the truck as he presses himself as far as he can against the wall.

"Why were you overseeing the loading of this truck?" The agent's high-pitched, nasally voice slices through every sound around me.

"They're going to open it," Jack whispers, and we crouch down as close as we can to Nell and Red. I can't see anything in the darkness, and I feel like I'm breathing so loudly the agents can hear me all the way out there.

The woman is pleading again, and I hear scraping against the doors of the truck like she's trying to stop them from opening it. Then a dull thud and she doesn't say anything more.

The doors rattle and then a shaft of light breaks the darkness and swings wider. I pull my legs up to my chest. All I can see are the boxes stacked in front of me all the way across the truck. Please don't search it. Please don't search it.

"Everything looks in order, ma'am." It's the same soldier who walked us over here.

"Get in there and take a closer look," the agent snarls.

"Yes, ma'am."

Red's breath catches in his throat and he starts to cough. Jack clamps a hand over his mouth.

"What was that?"

"Not sure, ma'am. I'm checking it out."

There's a thump of boots as the soldier clambers in, and I close my eyes and listen to the slow pacing as he searches the truck, making his way back to where we hide.

"Anything?"

"Not yet, ma'am. It's too dark in here to see much."

"Well take off your mask, idiot."

Scuff, scuff, scuff. He comes closer, and I press myself over Nell and try to shield her. She seemed so happy in the hospital. Granted, it was an obscene, false happiness, but she doesn't know that. I can't let her die this way.

Finally, inch by inch, the soldier steps into view. He looks behind the boxes across from us, and then his head swings our way and he freezes.

It's dark back here, but not that dark. I know he can see us.

I have seen only one other soldier without a mask on. That time I had been surprised at how young the soldier was. This time, I'm surprised at the kind face looking back at mine. I can't see what color his eyes are in the dimness, but I see he's a middle-aged man. He could be a father. He could have a daughter my age; he could have a son Jack's age. Nell and Red could be his parents. I'm not sure what thoughts are running through his head, but his face isn't anything I ever expected. It belies the rigid posture and the gun held up to his shoulder. He keeps the perfect soldier's stance, but his face is soft.

"What did you find?" The agent's voice makes me jump, and I hold my breath as I stare at the soldier. Two long, interminable seconds pass—it could be a thousand years.

"Nothing, ma'am."

I let out my breath, and I hear two sighs beside me. Jack and Red were holding their breath too. Nell is probably just so confused she has no idea what's going on.

"Then get out of there."

"Yes, ma'am."

I realize there are tears in my eyes as the soldier backs away. I hear the thump as he jumps from the truck. The doors close and encase us in darkness again. The truck's engine groans and then we're moving—bumping and swaying as we drive away.

My heart aches that I'll never know what happened to the physician's assistant. Half of me hopes she isn't killed for her disobedience. Half of me hopes she is so she's spared any misery. And I hope the soldier gets to go home to a family.

I never imagined I'd find people who work for the government who are truly kind.

TEN

The truck jostles us along for hours, with nothing but fuel stops to punctuate the time. The rear door never opens to let in time-telling daylight. My eyes adjust, though, and with the slivers of sunlight that creep in through a nook here and a cranny there, I make out the shadowed outlines of Jack, Nell, and Red. In the darkness, my fingers find a few water bottles and a few plastic packages of food. Jack and I have an unspoken arrangement that most of this will be for Nell and Red.

"Come on, Terra. You need a drink too," Red rasps.

I take a miniscule sip just to appease him. Nell was weakened in the hospital, but after a good drink and some food in her, she perks right up. Red, on the other hand, can barely sit up.

"Good, Red," Jack says, and another food wrapper crinkles. "Now see if you can take another bite."

"I don't understand why he's so weak. The doctors told me he was in intensive care because they could take better care of him there."

"When was her last dose?" Red says.

Jack sighs. "Probably twelve hours ago. She still won't believe us."

"What are you two talking about?"

I can just imagine Nell's hands on her hips. I close my eyes and smile. Then I take her hand and squeeze it once.

"You two are talking in riddles, and now Terra's holding my hand like I'm a feeble old woman who needs some reassurance. Will one of you please just speak up?"

"Red?" Jack says. He's right. If someone is to tell her, it should probably be Red.

Red tries to speak, but the words get caught in his throat. He coughs. "Nell, there's no easy way to tell you, dear."

"Oh, stop it, Red. Whatever you have to say stop hemming and hawing."

"It's the loyalty serum."

"What about it? You know that's just lies and rumors the nomads told to make us afraid. We don't need to be afraid."

Faint rustling, and the dark shape of Red's arm moves from where he's lying and onto her arm. "The serum is real, Nellie girl. That's why we were in the hospital. That's where they test it." His voice is getting creakier as he continues, and I fumble a bottle of water into his other hand. He stops to take a drink. Nell waits patiently for him. "They got it to work on you."

"That's impossible, Red, and you know it. They took such good care of me there."

Red sighs. "What did you think when we were in the settlement?"

"What everyone thought. That the government was out to get us."

"Did they ever prove you wrong?"

"Well, no, but—"

"And when did you start changing your mind?"

"In the hospital, after they took good care of me."

"When *exactly* did you start changing your mind?"

There's a pause, and the only sound is the creak and rattle of the truck as we rumble along. I wipe the sweat off my forehead.

"I . . . I'm not sure. I can't remember my first week in the hospital very clearly. After I got off the truck—I remember there were so many nomads on it—they put me in a room and took so many tests and drew so much blood, but they said they just wanted to make sure I didn't have diseases."

I remember what Dr. Benedict told me about making sure I wasn't going to make any of the other inmates at the labor camp sick. Of course I bought into it. They can be so convincing when they need to be.

"After that, they told me I had a blood disorder they were going to treat. They brought in machine after machine and ran test after test. After another week, they finally brought in a machine with my medicine. After the first dose, I felt so much better. I could see that they were helping me. I could see—" She stops speaking. Then I hear a quaver in her voice. "It's not true, is it?"

"No, Nellie girl. It isn't." Red's voice is so low and gravelly I can hardly understand the words.

Nell's voice breaks on a sob. "I desperately wanted it to be true. I still feel like it should be. Whenever I think about the doctors or the government or the agents, I think how misunderstood they are. How we made villains out of all of them. But when I stop and try to reason through it, then all the pieces don't fit into place."

"You were given a dose every twenty-four hours," Jack says. "So you might be confused for the next few hours. I'm not sure how long it takes to completely leave your system."

Nell's breath slows. "I'm sorry if I make this difficult for you."

"Aw, Nell." Red wraps his arms around her.

"You don't have the strength for that kind of hug, Red," Nell says, and I can hear the laughter underlining her words. Then anger blazes into its place. "I don't want to know what they did to you. And the entire time I just sat back and thought they were helping. They *were* helping, weren't they? Those doctors are such nice people."

I pat Nell's hand. The serum can't wear off soon enough.

We exhausted our water supply hours ago, and with the heat, I've sweated out every drop of moisture. The next time the truck stops, Jack scurries toward the doors. I grab his arm and hiss.

"Don't worry. I just want to see where we are. We can't go much longer in this heat."

But I do worry. What if those doors just happen to be opened when he's trying to see? I can't see him, but then his hand is pressed against my cheek. His skin is hot and dry. He should be sweating, but he hasn't drunk enough for that. I nod against his palm.

"I'll be fast."

His silhouette cuts across the line of silver moonlight that creeps through the crack between the two doors. He presses his face against that crack.

"We're in the city. Some of the buildings are lit up. We're not at a fuel station. Maybe we're nearing a security checkpoint."

"Which means they'll search the truck."

I whip to Red's direction. *What?*

"They'll search the truck to make sure what the drivers tell them is on the truck is actually on the truck. I saw it enough times at the Seattle supply drops."

"Then we need to get off."

"Thought you'd never ask," Red says as he stretches his legs toward me. He groans.

"Oh, Red, you can't walk like that. Why aren't we closer to a hospital? You said they'd give him better treatment, Jack." Then Nell pauses, and I can tell she's trying to fit the pieces back together again. "We're not going to a hospital, are we?"

"No, Nell, we're not."

She sighs. "Then we have to move. Jack can help you; can't you, Jack?"

Jack is at her side in a flash. "Yes, but we have to hurry and we have to be quiet." Red groans as Jack helps him up. "Terra, you help Nell."

"Oh, don't worry about me. I think I can manage now."

"Nell—" Jack says, but Nell stops him.

"Don't you 'Nell' me. I'll tell Terra if I need help. But Red's worse off."

Jack and I each slip one of Red's arms over our shoulders and we crab-step down the aisle between boxes to the doors.

"There anyone behind the truck?" Red asks.

"Not that I could see."

"For now, anyway." Red coughs. "Listen, Jack. I'm going to do my best, but if I'm too slow—"

"You won't be too slow."

"If I'm too slow, you leave me, you hear? Leave me and get my Nell safe."

I shift uncomfortably in the stuffy silence.

"It won't come to that, Red."

"Safe, you understand?"

Jack waits another long second before answering. "I promise, Red."

"Now you quit talking that way, Red," Nell says as she comes up behind us to stand by the door. "We're all going together."

"Love you, Nell. Always have, sweetheart."

"And don't you dare go saying good-bye to me, either. Don't you dare."

"Yes, ma'am."

Jack peers through the crack again. "Still no one. Here's what we're going to do. I think we've made it through the perimeter fence, so we're almost to the inhabited part of the city. I'll open the door, we get off, and it looks like there's an abandoned building just to the right. We make for that. We find a place to hide there, and then we think through the next step."

I nod. One step at a time.

"Ready?" Jack says.

"Yes," Red and Nell say together.

Jack unlatches the door and catches it before it swings open. He peers outside. "No one. I'll jump down. Then we'll get you off of here, Red."

He jumps from the truck and then turns to Red. I help Red sit down, and Jack and I help him slip from the truck. I turn to help Nell when the truck rumbles to life.

"Hurry!" Jack hisses.

I lower Nell down and Jack grasps her hand. Nell's feet have just touched asphalt when the truck lurches forward. I cling to the door and watch Jack slip away from me. He waves me to him.

"Jump, Terra!"

I grip the door with both hands and focus on the ground rolling out behind me. Jack takes a step forward. "Hurry!" He doesn't care now about people hearing us.

The truck speeds past the buildings, and they're all dark. The windows in some are shattered. It's eerily quiet, like a ghost town. I thought Seattle was an anomaly—that a designated city would be bursting through the seams with people. But San Diego is just like Seattle. The outlying streets are vacant and looted, and the people must just be further in.

I close my eyes, imagining all the stupid things I've done over the past year, and leap from the truck. I hit the ground and roll. The asphalt rips the shoulder of my shirt open, dirt sticks to my sweaty arms, and gravel digs into my skin. I gasp as rocks bite through my shirt. I roll to the side of the road and somehow manage to come to a stop in a crouch, and I watch the truck continuing on its way, the doors swinging open.

I turn back and Jack is waving his arm for me. I stumble to my feet and run for the shadowy space along the sidewalk right next to the building. The night is silent, my feet slap along the pavement, and the sound echoes against the bricks and shards of glass. Surely someone will hear me.

Hot blood trickles down my arm, and I press my opposite hand to my shoulder. The wound throbs under the pressure, but I ignore it. I'm almost to Jack.

"Are you okay?"

I nod, and incline my head to my shoulder.

"Let me see."

I move my hand, and it comes away wet. Jack leans closer.

"I think it's just a really good scrape. Let's get off the street and I'll take a closer look."

We each take one of Red's arms and limp into the nearest doorway. Nell hobbles after us. How in the world are we ever going to get to the water like this? We'll be lucky if we make it to the next building in one piece.

Jack pulls aside the rusted metal sheet that hangs askew from two of its hinges. We slip through the opening into the musty smell of the building. There are remnants of carpet that has been torn from the floor, and some of the walls have holes in them. The holes expose the bones of the building, and I can see pipes running through it. There's a steady drip, drip, drip somewhere in the building.

Water, I tell Jack.

He nods. "We can hope, anyway. Let's get settled and then we'll look."

We sink to the floor, and I'm still panting. Red's breaths are coming out in rasps.

He okay?

Jack nods. "I think so. He just tires easily, which is understandable with how he was treated. He should be fine, though."

Nell crawls over next to Red and puts his head in her lap. "I love you, foolish man. Don't ever talk like you did on that truck again, you hear me? We're in this together."

The moonlight filtering in through the windows illuminates Red's smile. "I promise." Then his eyes flutter closed and his breathing deepens.

"Let him rest for a while. We need to decide where we go next."

Water first. We won't get far without it, and Jack and I have been depriving ourselves for too long now.

"Alright. I'll go. You stay with them."

Nell strokes Red's hair. "Nonsense. You'll both go." Jack opens his mouth, but Nell holds up a hand. "There's nothing either one of you would be able to do for us if you stayed. If you go together you'll be safer and probably find water quicker. You know I'm right, so both of you just go." She sighs and puts her hand to her forehead.

"Nell?"

She shakes her head. "I'm fine. I'm just starting to get a headache. Maybe it's from the serum."

"You remember our conversation?" Jack asks.

"Of course I remember."

Red peeks out of one eye. "Now don't get snippy, Nell."

Nell sighs. "I'm sorry, Jack. I just feel like I've been hijacked for so many months. I get so angry every time I think about it. You two just go. We'll be fine."

I glance at Jack, and he shrugs his shoulders. We both stand and make our way across the room.

"We'll be back in twenty minutes. Maybe sooner."

"Go," Nell says, shooing us away.

ELEVEN

The building moans as the breeze sweeps through the holes and windows. We pick our way through crumbling walls, patchy floors, and smashed furniture. We find a stairwell and climb up a flight. Still I hear the incessant drip, but I can't place where it's coming from.

Place gives me the creeps, I write to Jack when he takes my hand halfway down another shadowy hallway.

"I know. And I can't figure out where the water's coming from."

We turn a corner when my feet stop dead. *Hear that?*

What? Jack writes back, seeing the serious look on my face and knowing we need to be silent.

Whispers. I could swear that's what I heard. Yes, there's the moaning of the decrepit building, the drip that's just about to drive me insane, but something else that I heard for just a moment.

Sure?

I nod.

Careful.

We come up to another corner, but the room it leads to is so shrouded in darkness, I can't make out any shapes. I'm just about to turn back when I hear the scuff of a foot on the floor, but I have no time to react before something hits me from behind and I stagger forward.

"Hey!" Jack shouts, and he's on the ground.

I whirl around to see our attackers, and two hands shove me so hard I fall down next to Jack. I should be scared, but I'm not. If it were government agents, this wouldn't be a shoving match. If it were dangerous nomads, I think this would be a little more cruel. I can't place what in the world this is. Not until a light flares up and illuminates the faces of a man and a woman not much older than we are. The man has a dirty bandage wrapped haphazardly around his head, and the woman's hands are balled into fists. Jack rubs the back of his head and sits up.

"Don't move," the woman commands in a squeaky voice.

I could almost laugh if I weren't sitting on the floor with them over me, and I have no idea if there are more of them.

"Who are you?" the man says.

Jack holds up his hands. "My name is Jack. This is Terra."

At the sound of my name, both of them flinch and their eyes meet. Weird.

"What are you doing here?"

Jack glances at me, and his expression asks me if we can trust them, if we should tell them, if we're being idiots for telling them just our names. Ifs, ifs, ifs. I'm tired of ifs. I jump up and grab the woman's hand in one swift movement, and the man is ready to pummel me.

"Stop!" Jack says. "She's not going to hurt you."

The woman's fist is clenched so tightly her fingernails dig into her skin. I hold her wrist gently and look into her eyes. In the light from the man's flashlight, her eyes are green and scream at me with such defiance that I like her already. I meet her gaze and our eyes lock. Slowly she uncurls her fingers.

We're helping friends escape.

"Where did you come from?" she whispers.

Salt Lake.

Her eyes widen. "So far?"

I nod. *On a truck. We're headed for water.*

"Are you *Terra*?" She says my name like it's something more than a name, and it makes me uncomfortable.

Just Terra.

"That's not what I mean. Are you the Terra that takes people to the ocean?"

I had no idea they would have heard of me so far south. I just nod.

Her whole posture relaxes and she chances a smile at her companion. Then she gathers me up in her arms and squeezes me.

"We're helping you, you know," she whispers fiercely.

I pull back. *What?*

"We help people escape too. Then we send them in the right direction."

I'm speechless. All those nomads I found in my woods, some of them could have been sent from these two people.

"Come with us," the man says.

"Wait," Jack says. "Our friends, they're downstairs. They're both older, and one of them is very weak."

The man whistles, and three figures separate from the shadows. "Go bring their friends." The shadows melt back into the darkness.

The woman looks us up and down. I put a hand to my chapped lips. I must look horrible.

"Are you hungry? Thirsty?"

I nod.

"Come on." She inclines her head to a doorway I can just make out in the dark.

We follow the man and the woman through hallways and over debris. The building creaks around us. We enter a hallway of windows and the man turns off his flashlight.

"Stick to the wall," he says.

I press myself into the shadows, and as we make our way down the hall, through what's left of the windows, I see lights flickering in the distance. Another building several blocks away is all lit up.

"That's the town center. The agents and soldiers are there, along with any medical care—whatever that is these days. We have to be careful they don't see us at night. It's illegal to live in this part of the city."

It reminds me of the settlement—the way we'd meticulously cover all the windows at night and wouldn't burn fires during the day. Glass crunches under my shoes, and we turn a corner and go up another flight of stairs, and then we open up onto a wide-open room and the murmur of voices. I see stars in my eyes until they can finally squint open and I can see. All the windows are boarded up so no light escapes.

There's a fire in the center of the room with a makeshift chimney that vents out one of the windows. About ten to fifteen people huddle around the fire. They pass around cans of food and granola bars—it's all government issued—and as soon as we come into view, their hands freeze, and the murmuring stops and everyone is dead silent.

"Don't worry; they're safe," the man says. He slings a gun off his shoulder. I never noticed it before.

"So who are they? And what are they doing jumping off the transport at night?"

Jack and I exchange glances. I had no idea we were being watched so closely.

The woman steps forward. "This is Terra."

The murmurs start up again.

"Says who? Her?"

The man raises his hands. "Yes, she says her name is Terra. This is her friend Jack. She has two others with her downstairs. They're being brought up. They're trying to get to the ocean."

A short blond woman. "So what is she doing down south? I thought she was up in Washington."

The man looks at me expectantly. Jack clears his throat.

"Where we lived before, it was an old school by the Puget Sound. It was a lot like here—the government didn't know we were there. Terra and I left. Then the settlement was raided and our friends were taken. They were sent to Salt Lake to the hospital where they were serum-tested."

Someone whistles. Jack ignores it.

"We made our way to Salt Lake and got them out and escaped on the truck here. Now we're hoping there's a sub waiting for us."

A tall man. "When?"

"Tomorrow night."

A freckled kid. "Why isn't she talking?"

"She can't." Jack's voice is flat. He doesn't like this part of my story any more than I do.

The woman steps next to me and takes my hand. "So it's true."

I nod.

"There were always rumors about that, but you never know quite what to believe. I'm so sorry—that's horrible what the agents did to you."

I laugh. Rumors are funny things. I take her hand and write, *They didn't do it.*

"Oh. But I always thought that must have been.... Then who did?"

And the story just got a whole lot more complicated. *I did it to keep the colonies safe.*

The freckled kid. "Did what?" An older kid next to him nudges him to keep quiet, but the freckled kid pulls away. "Why can't you talk?"

I walk over to them and squat down. The fire is warm, and their cheeks are rosy with the heat. I touch the freckled kid's hand. *You really want to know?*

He nods.

I sigh and then open my mouth.

He falls back. "Gross! That's disgusting."

The older kid starts laughing and teasing him. I smile and wink.

There's a scuffle from the stairwell door, and then Nell and Red come in with three others.

"Here're your friends." Red is propped up between two of them. "This one needs some help."

The man and woman rush to his side and help carry him to a spot by the fire. He groans when they set him down, and Nell sits at his side and holds his hand.

"Let's get them some food," the man says, and he motions us over.

We're presented with canned chili and granola bars, and I tear into them like I've never eaten before. Someone gives me a bottle of water, and I down it before I even taste it on my lips. I can still feel the eyes of just about everyone in the room on me. I slow down and clear my throat. After another moment, the woman speaks.

"Do you know how to get to the ocean?"

I shake my head and turn to Jack. He shrugs his shoulders.

"I've never been here."

"If you come with us to the supply drop tomorrow, you might be able to get close." The woman takes a stick and pokes at the fire. Sparks fly up in a flurry. "The drop spot is near the bay. Can your sub get in the bay?"

Probably.

The spoonful of chili freezes in Nell's hand on the way to Red's mouth. "Why are you talking about the ocean and subs, Terra?"

I study her a moment, and the glazed look is completely gone from her eyes. I think she's free from the last dose of loyalty serum. I look at my hands clasping my granola bar wrapper. I squeeze my fingers into a fist and crumple the wrapper. I don't know how many times I'm going to have to tell people that I'm from the colony—how many times I'm going to have to admit that I lied. My chest tightens. Jack puts a hand on my knee.

"Terra's not from Arizona," he says. He squeezes my knee once.

Nell narrows her eyes. "So just where are you from?"

I reach forward to take her hand, but Jack speaks. "She's from a colony. She's a colonist."

There used to be a time when it sounded like a dirty word coming from his mouth, but now he's unapologetic about it.

Nell's jaw drops and the color drains from her cheeks. Red turns to face us.

"You're from where?" he croaks.

"One of the ocean colonies," Jack says.

"So that morning we found you," Red says, laying his head back down on the folded blanket, "you had just come from your colony?"

I nod my head. Then I grab his hand. *The day Dave was in the boat. He almost drowned. I saved him.*

Red shakes his head. "I wondered about that."

Nell's hands are trembling, but she's keeping her voice steady. "Why didn't you tell us?"

I'm about to write again, but Jack jumps in. "Why do you think she didn't tell us? Everyone who finds out is angry at her." His eyes find mine, and they're filled with apologies. He was one of them. "She doesn't deserve that, not for where she grew up."

Nell raises an eyebrow. "And how do you know so much about it?"

Jack looks at his hand on my knee. "I've been there."

Red really does sit up now, even though he strains to do it. "When?"

"I lived there for six months. I came back about a week ago."

Red looks at the woman at my side, at the people around the fire, and back at my face. "You're who they were talking about."

Who?

"The agents in the hospital. Of course they didn't know I was listening in, but I was. What else is there to do when you're lying in a hospital bed waiting to die?"

Nell closes her eyes.

"Sorry, Nell. It's true." Red turns back to me. "They talked about someone who was sending nomads to the ocean. To the colonies. I always thought it was a load of hooey, but now I'm starting to rethink that opinion."

I reach for him, and he holds his hand out to me. *I want to take you there.*

"Me and Nell?"

Yes.

"She'd be safe?"

Yes.

He takes his hand away and folds his arms over his chest. "Right then. We'll go."

Nell frowns. "Now don't you go making decisions for me, Red."

I can see the conflict in her eyes—it's written all over the way she wants to look at me but can't quite do it. She's trying hard, trying not to be one of the people Jack was talking about, but she just can't reconcile what she thought she knew about me with this new information.

"What would we even do there? They wouldn't have a place for people like us."

I laugh and take her hand. *You could plant hydrangeas.*

She smiles and shakes her head. "Why would they need hydrangeas a million miles under the sea?"

They appreciate something beautiful. And not just the flowers. They would love having someone like Nell there. They'd love her the way I love her.

She eyes me skeptically. "They really grow flowers?"

Jack leans forward. "It's amazing, Nell. They have fields of crops. There's a flower garden. They have an enormous bakery, they have beehives. The only difference between here and there is it's under the water, and there are no soldiers or agents."

Nell settles back into Red. "So why did you leave? Why did you both leave?"

I felt trapped.

Nell considers my answer, her eyes filled with questions. She doesn't ask them, though. She just sits and watches me. I shift under her gaze, but I keep my eyes on her. Then her eyes crinkle around the edges as she smiles, and she pats my hand.

"Jack?"

Jack turns to me and touches my face. "I love Terra."

He says it like it's the most logical answer in the world. And Nell leans forward and pinches Jack's cheek.

"Good for you, Jack. It's about time."

And then the subject of the colony is dropped and the tightness in my chest eases, and we laugh with these strangers and all fall asleep in each other's arms.

TWELVE

When the first light of morning trickles through the cracks in the windows, I'm stiff and sore from being cooped up in trains and trucks and lying woven with the others on the floor. Jack's eyes flitter underneath his eyelids, and then slowly he stretches and yawns and finally opens them. He draws his arms around me and kisses my forehead.

"How did you sleep?"

Good.

"Mmm. Me too."

I'm not ready for today. I feel his breath in my hair. It pauses for a second before resuming its rhythm.

"Me neither."

I'm scared for them. Nell and Red are by my feet. She's already awake, and she strokes through Red's gray hair.

Jack's whispered voice drops even quieter, and I have to strain to hear him. "I don't know if Red can make it."

He's said it, the thing I feared: that one of us is incapable of meeting the sub. My heart speeds up, and it feels like a panicked bird trying to escape my chest. Jack holds me tighter.

"But don't worry about it yet. We're not there."

We will be soon.

Jack lets out a breath and it ruffles through my hair. "I know. I've been trying not to think about it." He burrows his head closer against me. "I don't know what I'd do if we lost one of them."

I grip his hand tightly in mine. I don't know what I'd do either. I watch Nell playing with Red's hair. I watch his eyes open and watch the smile spread across his face as he focuses on her. She leans down and kisses him gently on the lips, and he snatches the ends of her silver hair to keep her there longer. She laughs against his mouth and bats his hand away.

I don't know what they would do if they lost each other.

I won't let it happen.

"I know you, Terra. And I know that's true." He hesitates. "But there's only so much you can do."

In a few minutes everyone around us is waking up. The woman steps over a few still-sleeping bodies and crouches down next to us.

"Come on over. We'll walk you through what's going to happen today."

We help Red to his feet. His coloring looks a lot better than it was, and having enough to eat and drink for just a day has already started to fill in his cheeks. He's still too frail though, all jutting bones. He's a twig that could snap at any second. I exchange glances with Jack, but neither of us says anything.

There's nothing to say. We *are* going to try this impossible thing. I don't think Nell and Red would have it any other way.

We sit down with the man and the woman. They give us more granola bars and water.

"Lana and I are going to the med drop. Everyone in the city will start making their way to the med drop this morning. Five others are going with us—all of us with trackers. We want to bring back as many supplies as we can. I think that'll be enough of us that you can fall in with us. Having Red there might even help. No one will question bringing him to the med drop. People might think he's going to the free clinic."

The man takes out a faded, worn map of the city. He smooths it open, careful not to tug on the edges. It's so thin along the folds that it looks like it will fall apart if you breathe on it too hard.

"The supply drops happen here." He points to a round blob on the map. "It's a baseball stadium. You can see the water is close. It's an industrial area—most of this has been converted into work places."

"Will we be closely watched?"

The man frowns. "I don't know. We've always just worried about the drop part of it. We've never tried to go to the water. I don't think very many people go over that way at the time of the drop, so you might stick out."

"They could pretend to be workers," Lana says, chewing on a strand of hair.

"Maybe."

"There isn't any other option that will get them to the water if someone sees them." Lana looks at me, and her eyes are shining. "It's so dangerous. Are you sure you want to do this?"

Nell looks at Red and then squeezes my hand. I nod. There's no other choice. Jack hasn't said so, but I really don't think Red can get better on his own, not with the way things are now. He doesn't stand a chance.

"Yes," Red says in a raspy voice. He turns to me. "I trust you, Terra. I've trusted you since you first came to us. That's not going to stop now."

Tears fill my eyes. I've hurt so many people because of the lies I've had to tell on the Burn. But Nell and Red don't care about where I come from. They just care about *me*.

Thank you.

"What time is your sub coming?"

No idea. Dread fills my gut. I have no idea. I look at my hands. *Usually comes at midnight.*

"You'll have to find a place to hole away. The supply drop starts at noon and lasts until four or five. You can't wait around after that, or the agents will take you into custody for loitering."

Is there anything they don't take you into custody for? But of course I don't ask it. I don't have to—they're probably all thinking the exact same thing.

Nell smoothes her hair back away from her face and twists it into a neat bun at the nape of her neck. "Then we should probably go. Are you ready, Red?"

"As ready as I'll ever be, I'm afraid."

"We're going to slow you down," Jack says to the man. He puts a hand on the back of his neck as he watches the man and Nell lift Red up. "If anything goes wrong, I don't want to be the one who got you into it."

"Don't be ridiculous," the man says, patting Red on the back. "We're all in this together."

We make our way through the building. Sunlight filters in through the windows and glints off the shards of glass littering the floor. The whole building seems to sparkle. How could something so run down seem so beautiful? I linger at a window and look over the city. Out there, though, the sun shines harshly and there's litter in the street. People are starting to trickle out of the buildings. They look around them and scurry away like rats. The man said it was illegal to live in these buildings, so anyone in this part of the city must fear the agents.

When we make it to the bottom floor, the man opens the door, and the warm breeze sweeps over me. I can smell the ocean on it. I stand on tip-toe, waiting until he motions us out, and then we creep from the cover of the building and we're back on the street. I feel exposed out here with all the windows watching us.

We inch along, and Red stumbles with us. He curses as he tries to get his legs moving one after another, step by step.

"What did you say?" Nell asks. She has a stern look on her face, and Red knows he's in for a scolding.

"I said this is never going to work."

"So help me, Red, if you say something like that again—"

He grips her hand. "I know, I know. I won't."

But I'm not convinced. I can see the round bowl of the stadium ahead of us. We're not even halfway there yet, and his limbs are already trembling with exertion.

We come to an enormous metal fence topped with curls of barbed wire.

"It's the border between where *they* want us to live and where *we* want to live," the man says.

"Is it guarded?" Jack says.

"Not usually. Only when there's been some kind of infraction and they want to make a point of it. Then we're cut off from the rest of the city until it eases up a bit."

"How long does that last?"

"Depends on the infraction. A month was the longest it's ever gone." The man looks down. "We lost a few of the old ones then. They gave up their rations to the kids."

"If they know you're here why even bother with the fence?" Jack asks. His face is troubled.

"I couldn't tell you how many times I've asked myself that. They don't really see us as a threat, and I think they just like to see us suffer."

Yup, sounds about right.

We near the fence, and the group in front of us stoops through a hole cut through the wire. All of us bunch up here, waiting our turn to funnel through. We come through in a steady stream, filing down the wide street. On this side of the fence, more people pour from the buildings. The difference in the buildings on this side of the fence is drastic. The windows are all intact, trees line the streets, and only an occasional scrap of trash skitters down the concrete on the breeze. The people are entirely different, too.

Most of them look like empty shells.

Every single person that we stayed with last night had determined faces and fierce eyes. But everyone filling in the gaps around us look like they're on autopilot.

Loyalty serum? I ask Jack.

He shakes his head. "I have no idea." He turns to the man. "Are they all like this?"

The man frowns and adjusts Red's arm over his shoulder. Red opens his mouth to curse, but Nell glares at him.

"No, not all of them. But it seems like after a while they all get this way."

"Why?"

Lana shrugs her shoulders. "All of these people work for the government. Nothing glamorous, of course. No 'normal' citizen gets a glamorous job. They're street sweepers or shelf stockers or janitors or cafeteria workers. In exchange they get barely enough food at supply drops and an apartment the size of a postage stamp. They're told their jobs are essential to the city and that they're doing their country a great service. They either lap it up or completely snap. You can guess which ones these are."

Lappers?

She nods. "I've seen a few completely snap. I've never seen them again."

Jack looks askance at an older woman next to him whose eyes stare straight ahead. Her hair is combed stick-straight and her clothes are neatly pressed. She actually looks like she could be right at home in the colony. Except for the blank expression on her face. At least in the colony everyone looked alive.

"I wonder if they have the loyalty serum here?" Jack whispers.

Nell's eyes harden. "If they're subjecting these poor people to that awful stuff. . ." She pauses for a long moment. "I don't know if I can go to the sub with you, Terra."

What? I'm sure she can see the shock all over my face.

"What are you saying, Nell?" Red says, straining to lean toward her.

"Look at them all." She waves her hand at them. "We can't just run away. We have to help them."

We will help them, I write to her. *Let's get to the colony first.*

"So you're coming with us?"

I hadn't really thought about it. In my mind I had only gotten as far as the sub. What happens after that is nebulous. I just assumed it would be what happened after any other sub rendezvous: the nomads get on, and I disappear again. But the more I do think about it, the more it's the only way for this to work. Nell's right—we have to help these people, and to do that, we have to get rid of the serum. But that's not something I can do by myself. I don't know if it's something this man or this woman can do.

I don't think a handful of nomads would have the resources I need—but the colony might. I think I have to ask my father for help. The idea makes my stomach churn. I shake my head to clear the fear away. My mouth is dry.

"Will you come with us?" Nell asks again.

I can feel Jack's eyes on me. He has a vested interest in my decision. I know he'll follow me, and that's not something I take lightly. Taking him back to the colony would keep him safer. But then when I come back to the Burn—because I will come back to the Burn, there's no question about that—I'll be throwing him right back into it again. I have a headache coming on.

"Terra?"

Finally, I nod. My decision takes away a burden but adds a hundred more.

"I'm glad for that," Nell says, looking forward again. We're almost to the stadium. "I don't know if I could go down to this colony of yours if you weren't coming with us."

Red chuckles. "An odd thought, isn't it? Going to an ocean colony? If we had ever had children, Nellie girl, that would have been one bedtime story I would have loved to tell."

Nell has a wistful look on her face. "We'll see."

We're still half a block away, and now there are people pressing in on us from all sides. Most of them have the ghost look, but some of them have watchful eyes. When our eyes meet, they linger and then flick away, always wary. There are soldiers standing at attention around the stadium, and an agent with a scanner. He waves the machine over people's forearms as they come in. As I watch, the agent scans someone's arm. The scanner lights up red. The agent motions, and two soldiers pounce on a middle-aged man. He kicks and screams as they drag him to an unmarked black truck.

"We can't go that way," Jack says.

"No trackers?" Lana asks.

I shake my head. Not a chance.

"What about them?" the man asks, nodding to Nell and Red.

"Yes," they both say in unison. Of course. That would have been one of the first things the government did when they were captured.

"That makes it trickier. There's scanners and soldiers all over this place. We could cut them out."

"We don't have the right supplies," Jack says.

"Don't need to," the man says, and Jack makes a horrified face.

"We'll make it work," Jack says. He drifts to the edge of the surge of bodies, so slowly no one would notice it. We're pressed up against the front of a building. A red-and-white-striped awning shades us, and the window is crystal clear. There are books lined up inside. Every book is exactly the same, but still—a bookstore? I had no idea such a thing existed here.

The man cranes his head. "There's an alley that runs between this building and the next. It leads to the next street over and we can bypass the stadium that way. It might be watched, though, so we'll need to be careful."

Lana looks over her shoulder. "They're not looking this way," she whispers.

We move as quickly as we can into the alley. Red's jaw is set and I see the pain in his eyes. He clenches Jack's hand until his knuckles are white. I can't imagine how hard this is for him. Sweat drips down his face and his cheeks are pale, but still he doesn't say a word.

The alley is half in sunlight and half in shadow. Doorways lead off on either side, and a few windows sparkle further up the sides of the buildings. There's nothing else here but us, and the flash of glass on a black scanner at the other end of the alley. Jack hisses in a breath.

How far to water? I ask Lana.

"Two blocks."

I look at Jack, and he knows what I'm thinking. How much time do we have until those scanners relay their information back to someone who will do something about it? The hospital knows by now that Nell and Red are gone. I doubt they think they're in San Diego, but once someone figures it out, when will the soldiers leave the stadium and come after us instead?

How long to midnight?

Lana frowns and checks her watch. "It's only twelve o'clock right now. You still have a long time."

This is never going to work. There are too many scanners, too many soldiers, and too many things that could go wrong. I feel Nell's and Red's eyes on me, and I'd like nothing more than to crawl into a hole. Taking those nomads I had never even met before to the sub was so different from this. I feel the weight of this pressing on my shoulders, because these are people I love. They're family. I close my eyes and put my fingertips to my temples. The headache that's been threatening is coming on hard now.

Nell puts a hand to my cheek. "Terra."

I can't look at her. If I look at her, I'm afraid all I'm going to see is death.

"Look at me, dear." She gently pries my hands from my face. "You're so young. Sometimes I forget that. How old are you? Seventeen, eighteen?"

Seventeen.

Nell smiles and wraps her arms around me. I lean into her, into the comfort she offers me. "I don't want you to feel responsible for Red and me."

I laugh, and it's choked.

"I mean it, Terra. You've done so much already just getting us out of that hospital, letting me see Red again when those . . . people . . . might have taken him away forever."

I glance over at Red, and his chest is heaving. Nell gently turns my face back.

"I love you. You should know that. I know that makes things both easier and harder. But you should also know that because I love you, I know you'll do your best, and anything bad that happens won't be your fault, and I won't blame you."

Nell looks at me expectantly, but I'm not sure what she wants me to say. The alleyway feels much too stuffy for this conversation. Sweat pours into my eyes and I brush it away.

"I won't blame you," Nell whispers again, and she starts walking toward the scanner.

"Nell!" Red hisses, and the man, Jack, and Red start after her. "What are you doing?"

"Someone had to get started. Poor Terra feels the weight of the world on her shoulders, and all the rest of you can do is stand around and stare."

We're halfway down the alley, and I can already hear the faint whir of machinery in the scanner. It makes me cold all over. It'll be able to scan Nell's and Red's trackers soon.

"Where do we go once we're out of the alley?" Jack asks.

"We either go to the high-rise just south of us, or we go to the industrial area," the man says, eyeing the scanner. Its glass face glints as it rotates toward us. "I say you get as close as you can to the water and hide."

"You're not coming?" Jack says.

The man shakes his head. "Lana and I still have trackers too. And if our tracker info is sent along with your friends' here, the government will probably assume we were together, and I don't want to be caught with some escapees. They'll hunt us down and there'll be no way we can help anyone else find you again."

I nod.

"Thanks, Terra," Lana says. She shakes my hand.

I try to smile, but I'm shaking so hard it probably looks warped on my face. Then Lana and the man turn abruptly and follow the alley, disappearing around the corner. The four of us stand still for a moment. Then Red reaches for me, and he drapes his other arm over my shoulder.

"Might as well get it over with," he says.

I laugh loudly, and this time the laugh booms out of me, and all of my worry is expressed with it. It feels like a relief to let it out.

"Let's go," Jack says.

We make our way down the alley, and our progress is painfully slow. Each step toward the scanner makes my stomach lurch, but Nell steps in beside me, and with Nell, Red, and Jack surrounding me, I feel like we just might be able to do this. It seems improbable with Nell's and Red's medical condition, but I don't pause to dwell on that.

We're twenty feet from the scanner when I hear the faint beep of a tracker being scanned. Then another.

"Now we hurry," Jack says.

We shuffle along, turn the corner, and I blink to keep the sun out of my eyes. We're out in the open, the wide expanse of street leading the way past a tall building on our right and toward the industrial area. It's a series of low buildings, and on either side of each one, I see a patch of blue. We're so close. I keep expecting to hear the pounding of boots on the pavement, the bark of a soldier's command, or the snide laughter of an agent, but there's nothing but the blazing sun and the occasional call of a seagull.

Our feet scrape against the concrete, and Red is getting heavier and heavier on my shoulder.

"Do you need to stop, Terra?" he asks. He breath comes out ragged.

I shake my head, forcing my legs to keep plowing ahead.

"We need to get as close to water as we can," Jack says.

"Not at the expense of all of us," Nell says, worry written all over her face.

"Keep going." Jack puts one foot in front of the other, and Red's feet are dragging, but he moves them and tries to keep up.

We pass the high-rise and cross another street toward one of the work buildings. There's no one around, and the streets are eerie in their silence. We come to a gate that's been left open as everyone has made their way to the stadium for the med drop. A beep to the left stops me dead in my tracks. Another scanner.

"Now they know we've been here, too. Keep going." Jack leads us through the gate.

"We can't hide inside, Jack," Nell says. "Not when they know we've been through this gate."

"We're not going to hide inside."

He pulls, and Red and I follow him around the building. Nell is close behind, her hands fluttering and her face turned away, watching our backs. Still nothing but the sound of our feet on pavement. Nothing but footsteps, seagulls, and the ripple of water. The lack of sound is pressing on me, and soon I can hear my heartbeat thrumming and the sound beats down on me. The tall buildings loom a block away, and all the reflecting windows are watchful eyes, and I'm sure there's someone in there telling an agent exactly where we're going. My palms are sweating, but there's nothing to be done for it now.

"Where are we going?" Red asks in a croak. His lips are dry and he licks them, but it doesn't help.

Jack grunts. "To the water."

"We can't stay there all day long, can we?" Nell asks. She puts a hand on my back as she once more turns over her shoulder. "I thought I saw something."

I look back, but the sweat drips into my eyes, and I can't be sure of anything I see. There's still no sound, and everything behind us looks the same.

"I don't think we'll have to. Keep moving."

Jack sounds so sure of himself, and it almost brings me up short. Of course we'll have to wait all day. The sub comes at midnight. On a few occasions, Jessa has even been late. A few of those times it was a close call, but most of the time it didn't matter—we weren't backed right up against a city full of government officials peering down at us from towering buildings. I try to swallow, but my throat is dry.

"I saw it again," Nell says, and her hands clutch at my shirt and tug on it until I feel like I'm dragging Red and her.

I look back again, and Nell points. There, at the alleyway we came from, are two soldiers. They're looking around.

That answers the question about how long it would take all that information to be relayed—ten minutes tops. Which means they're going to find out what the scanner at the gate learned in just a few more seconds.

One of the soldiers puts a hand to his ear; he must have an earpiece. He lingers in that posture for a few more seconds, and then he looks up at the industrial area, and I swear we lock eyes. My legs start churning forward before I can even tell anyone else what I've seen.

"What is it?" Jack asks, bewildered.

Nell saw the whole thing. "Soldiers. They see us."

I grip Red more tightly around the waist, and we try to pick up the pace, but my legs are so tired and the sun is so hot, and I feel like I'm walking through mud.

"Just leave me, all of you," Red croaks, and his legs stiffen.

"Stop it, Red! I warned you!" Nell tries to be stern, but her voice is full of tears, and she's trying to grab him too and carry him along, but her muscles aren't strong enough after months of lying in a hospital bed.

Jack looks back, and we both see the soldiers trotting toward us, their eyes wary and their guns half-raised. Jack pulls Red toward him, sets his legs, and then purses his lips as he hefts Red up and slings him across his shoulders. The veins on his neck stand out and his face is red, but he starts trotting along.

"Come on," he gasps out.

I grab Nell around the waist and help support her as we race toward the water. We turn the corner and now I see the ocean stretching out before us. Cracked sidewalks lie along the path before us, and old metal docks float ragged on the water. It's a ruin. The government must not have wanted anyone to have ocean access.

But where will we hide?

I glance behind, and the soldiers have closed the gap, and my pulse quickens even faster when I see two more cutting toward us at a diagonal. Now we have to step over chunks of concrete and debris, and Jack's legs quiver with each step. He keeps his pace, but I don't know how much longer he can last. Nell's face is hard, but her eyes are streaming tears, and she grips my arm so tightly I want to wrench it away, but I can't. Not now when these people trust me, and where am I taking them? There's nothing but ocean before us.

I squint at it. The sun glares down at us and reflects off every facet of every wave, and it hurts my eyes, but I can't look away. It wasn't supposed to end like this. The ocean was supposed to be a refuge, and now it's just going to be a brick wall up against our backs as the soldiers press in on us.

"Jack?" Nell says, and her voice is so quiet it's almost lost in the pounding of footsteps.

Jack can't answer; his mouth is clamped shut.

"Where are we going?"

"The water," he manages to get out.

But where? I want to scream. There's nowhere to go. There's not a pier we can hide under, no boats, no cover of any sort.

The soldiers stalk closer, and one of them is raising his gun.

We're finally to the water, and we creep onto a jagged piece of metal that once was a dock. It bobs precariously under our feet. We stop right at the edge, and I can see down into the depths, at the spindly stilts that float askew in the water. Seagulls bob on the surface and cock their heads to look at us. We must look insane to them, our small group of terrified nomads worn way too thin. Jack's face is frantic as he swivels his head left and right, then left and right again up and down the stretch of water in front of us.

"It can't be," he pants, and his legs are wobbling so badly, I'm sure he's going to drop Red. "I thought it would be here."

I manage to grab his hand. *What?*

His face is full of despair. "The sub. I thought for sure it would be here."

The soldiers have just reached the broken sidewalks. "Stop there. Hands behind your heads."

Why?

"It's the way Gaea is. She'd be watching you the whole time. She would be ready. I know it."

"Hands behind your heads!" I turn back and the soldiers stalk toward us, their guns raised.

Nell and I slowly raise our hands, but Jack goes stick-straight.

"There!" He points a hundred feet to our left, and there in a surge of sea foam against the decaying dock, I see the lights of the sub. "Run!"

I grab Nell's hand and drag her after me. Jack's footsteps pound behind us, and Red's breath comes out in heavy gasps as he thuds against Jack.

"Stop or we'll shoot!"

The sub surfaces, and the water is still pouring off the hatch when it opens and Jessa's face appears. I've never been so happy to see her in my life. The dock groans under our weight and wobbles. I almost lose my footing, and I cling to Nell to keep her from going down. I glance back, and Jack staggers under Red's weight.

"Keep going!" he shouts.

Then a shot sounds.

I freeze, expecting to feel a bullet ripping through me, but there's nothing and my legs are surging again. I skid to a stop in front of the sub, and Jessa's face is terrified as she reaches for Nell. Nell grasps her hands and takes a quavering step from the dock to the rim of the hatch, and then she's disappearing down into the hole.

Another shot sounds, and it dings off the hull of the sub. There's a pock in the metal, but it's superficial.

Jack stops behind me, and together we lower Red off Jack's back and lean him toward the hatch. His arms cartwheel for a moment until he can reach Jessa's, and then she almost collapses under his weight as she maneuvers him down the ladder.

Another shot fired, and Jack screams.

I look down, and he clutches his leg. There's a dark red stain spreading across the leg of his pants, and his face is contorted. I shove him toward the sub, and he leaps awkwardly to the hatch. Then I follow him down with the pounding of boots and bullets in my ears.

"Stop or we will kill you all!" one of the soldiers yells.

Jessa shoves passed me on the ladder and yanks the hatch closed. There's a flurry of bullets on the other side. The sub lurches and descends faster than I thought possible, and I tumble down the rest of the ladder and land in a heap on top of Jessa and Jack, and cling to them for all I'm worth, tears pouring down my cheeks.

THIRTEEN

The sub shudders as it docks, and creaks and clicks echo all through the metal. Nell grips Red's arm. Her eyes whirl around like she's expecting a monster to rip its way through the hull at any second. Red encircles her protectively and gives me a long look.

Safe, I say. *I promise.*

"You'll be fine," Jack says. He's lying down on a bunk built into the hull, and his left leg is elevated. The bullet grazed his thigh. It took a good chunk of flesh with it, but the bleeding has stopped and the doctors in the colony will be able to patch him up in no time. He's in a lot of pain, though. He grits his teeth every time he shifts his weight. "The people are kind. Different, but kind. It definitely takes some getting used to. Dave's still here." Jack hesitates over the words, but I don't think Nell or Red notice. "You'll be able to see him."

"He's here too?" Nell's eyes brighten. "I've missed that boy. I was so worried about him."

All I've been worried about is getting Red to medical so they can put him on an IV and a tailored diet and get him back to health. We've tried to get as many protein bars and sips of water into him as we can, but he's so exhausted he doesn't even want to spend the energy on that. His arm around Nell looks like a skeleton's, and I'm worried he's too brittle to even step out of the sub onto the platform.

The sub comes to a stop, and I take a deep breath. Jessa sits next to me.

"Are you ready?"

I nod, and she squeezes my arm.

"Dad's probably up there right now. He knows you're coming home." She sees the look on my face. "Coming back."

I study my hands. There's nothing for it—I can't put this off forever. I stand up and rub my palms on the legs of my pants. Why do my hands always sweat so much?

How many others know?

"I don't know." She half-smiles at me. "I doubt Dad got on the intercom and told everyone the prodigal was coming back."

The hatch hisses open and light floods the sub. Jessa is up in a flash, scurrying up the ladder. I hear her talking to the sub techs.

"There are four more down there."

"How many from the Burn?"

Jessa stumbles over her words. "Well, Jack has come back. You remember Jack?"

A few words I can't make out.

"And an elderly man and woman."

"Elderly my foot," Red mutters.

155

The sub tech speaks, and he sounds too impatient for my taste. "That's only three. Who's the fourth?"

"My sister, Terra. But she's not from the Burn. She's from here."

If only it were that easy.

"Don't get worked up, Jessa. We just need to ask for quarantine purposes. Terra will have to go into quarantine just like the rest of them."

I've had enough of this listening in on the conversation. I want to see who's out there. I climb the ladder and as soon as my eyes clear the metal rim, I see them. Three figures all dressed in biohazard suits: two sub techs and my father. My stomach drops out from under me. I knew this was coming. I knew I'd have to see him eventually, but I honestly didn't think he'd see me off the boat. It's too . . . personal.

He doesn't realize I'm watching him. He's looking over the tech's shoulder, watching him press the buttons on his tablet. His hair is grayer around the temples, and the skin around his eyes looks thin and papery. He looks worn out. A pang of guilt strikes me. I'm probably the cause of the extra wrinkles. The guilt doesn't last long, though, before it's replaced by a flare of anger. Dad's wearing his speaker's sash over his suit—how arrogant. Does he really think the people coming from the Burn will care? That I care? But his philosophy was always to let people know who was in charge so they knew who they could talk to. After the Burn, though, I'm a little more cynical about such displays of authority. I'm so caught between guilt and anger that I'm not sure what to do with my face. My features harden the longer I watch him. He finally looks up, our eyes lock, and his eyes cloud over as he studies my face. Then after a few moments, they clear.

"Terra? Is that you?"

Does my own father really not recognize me? But I need to be kind. If any of this is to work, I need to be kind. I left abruptly, I remind myself. Even if ours wasn't a perfect relationship, judging by the way he looks now, it still gave him at least a moment of heartache. I try to soften my eyes.

He offers a small smile. "It is you. I almost didn't believe Jessa when she told me you were coming back."

He opens his arms wide for me, but I can't just run to him. I stand up and swing my legs out of the hatch and stand before him, my arms stiff at my side. Dad lowers his arms and puts his hands behind his back. When he speaks, his voice is more formal.

"Welcome home."

I close my eyes, willing myself not to explode. Jack is suddenly there beside me, his hand in mine, his warm fingers grounding me, helping to ease the anger that has reached its boiling point. I step an inch closer to him, letting his calm wash over me. I can open my eyes again.

Thanks.

I don't care if Dad can read my lips or not. I turn away and watch two medical staff help Red into a wheelchair. His face is set into a grimace, and the meds handle him as gently as they can. They try to help Nell into a chair, but she swats her hands away. Jack laughs.

"You probably should, Nell."

She eyes him but finally concedes, though she does it all on her own and refuses the meds' offered hands. Nell reaches over and pats Red's arm. Her eyes are shining.

Dad turns to Jack. "It's good to see you well, Jack."

"Thank you, sir."

Jessa takes Dad's arm and lets loose a torrent of chatter about anything and nothing as she leads our group away. Dad has no choice but to be swept up in it. She tosses her hair over her shoulder and her brows are furrowed when she looks back at me. *You okay?* she mouths.

I shake my head. I'm anything but. There's nothing to do about it now, though. Jack squeezes my hand and bends down to whisper in my ear.

"You knew it would be hard."

I nod. I did know. I try to stand straighter.

One of the meds offers Jack a crutch, and then we walk out of the sub dock and down a corridor to the nearest transport. The halls are sterile white and the lights are harsher than I remember. I've lived in sunlight, and that must be the difference. Every few moments Dad's head twitches to the right as if he's going to look back at me, but changes his mind. My chest is getting tight just watching him decide whether or not to ignore me. Guilt, anger, and now what? Heartache? Heartache that my own father doesn't know what to do with me. I hadn't expected that to come with this reunion. I had expected the anger, and I was ready to face that. Even the guilt wasn't a complete stretch. But not sadness. My heart is racing, and I'm trying as hard as I can to keep the tears from my eyes. We're the last in line, and no one has noticed we've stopped. The others disappear around a bend, and Jack and I are alone. I grip Jack's sleeve and stop dead in my tracks.

"Do you need to sit down?" Jack asks. He's frowning and leaning in to hold me up.

I put a hand on his chest to stop him and shake my head. I breathe deeply, hoping to keep the panic from rising up my throat. Now my throat feels too thick. I put my hands on my knees and lower my head, trying to calm my breathing and my heart. I can do this, I tell myself. I've fought, I've been a slave, I've starved, I've hiked miles through the forest, I've survived a summer and a winter without climate control, I've dodged so many bullets I've lost count. Surely I can face the colony and my own father. When I squeeze my eyes closed, the tears slip out and run down my cheeks.

Jack puts a hand on my back. "You don't have to do this today, you know. It can wait. It all can wait until you're ready. This is a lot to ask of anyone."

Jack is just bending down to look in my face when Nell and the man pushing her wheelchair come back into view. She takes one look at me and brushes his hands off the handles.

"You wait right there, young man."

He makes a move to step forward, but she shoos him away. Jessa peers around the corner followed by my father.

Nell's eyes narrow. "All of you please give us a little privacy."

Jessa smiles at me and Nell—she can guess some of what I'm going through just by looking at me—and disappears around the corner. But my dad hovers there, a question on his face, that same twitchiness in him like he's not sure if he should come comfort me or if he should follow my sister. He stays that way until Nell clears her throat.

"You too." Nell raises an eyebrow at him, and he shuffles away. Then she wheels herself over to us. She props her elbows on the arms of her chair and leans toward me.

"Family is never easy, Terra. Even for those of us who had decent families."

I wipe my nose and look at her. Her eyes crinkle at the edges as she smiles at me. Not a happy smile, but an encouraging one. I told her a fraction of what my life was like here, and I shouldn't be by now, but I'm always amazed at how perceptive Nell is.

"I can read your father like a book, and you probably could too if you're willing. His heart has just about broken into so many pieces he's not even sure what to feel anymore. Your sister has done what she can to hold him together, but there's only so much one person can do. You need to help him."

I take her gnarled hand. *It's not just me.*

Nell sighs and puts her other hand on my cheek. "It usually isn't just one person. I don't know what's happened to your family, and it's probably none of my business, but I do know that when he looks at you, he loves you. He's just scared to admit that to himself. And he's probably scared to admit it to you, too."

I look away, but Nell gently tugs my chin toward her. "Just try, Terra. That's all anyone can do. And listen to Jack. He's right—it doesn't have to be today because it won't all come at once. It'll take time to fit the pieces back together. But you'll be glad if you do. Knowing you could have made it better but didn't will just eat away at you until there's nothing left."

She gently pats my cheek then clears her throat again. "Young man?" She cranes her neck around. "Young man! I know you're there eavesdropping, so don't pretend like you're not."

The medical assistant comes back around the corner, his cheeks flaming red.

"I'm ready to keep going," Nell tells him as she folds her hands in her lap. She smiles at me and then they disappear around the corner.

Jack takes my hands from my knees, holding mine in both of his. He traces his fingers through my hair. "Are you ready?"

I take a deep breath and nod. Quarantine, here I come.

We make our way to the transport. Nell and Red both flinch when the door slides open to let us on, and Red grips the arms of his wheelchair tighter than I thought he'd be able to. Nell and Red find spots next to the windows, and then we fly out in the transport tube over the ocean. Red blinks and shrinks back into his wheelchair. He puts a hand on Nell's shoulder, and she grips his hand. Both their eyes are wide as they watch the black ocean fly by the glass.

"How far down are we?" Red asks, his voice hushed.

My father stands with his hands behind his back, gazing serenely out the window. "A couple of miles."

Red whistles, but stays firmly rooted. Nell rests her head on his arm. "It's kind of pretty in its own way. Are there any fish out there?"

Jessa sits down next to her, and my sister's face lights up and her hands start going as she describes some of the fish that live down here. Nell laughs when Jessa wiggles a finger in front of her face as she describes the fish with glowing danglers.

I'm glad Nell likes it. I've seen the way she glows in the sunlight, the way she loves having her hands in the dirt. I was so worried she'd suffocate down here. Maybe she still could eventually, but for now her hands are resting on her lap, and her face is turned into a smile, and Red sits right beside her, and everything looks just the way it should be. I even feel my muscles relaxing a bit.

"Arriving at the medical quarter," the indifferent female voice tells us. The transport slows and then the door opens. We get off. I just noticed no one else is on the transport, and I haven't seen anyone else beside our small group in the corridors either.

Where is everyone? I write to Jack.

He leans close to my ear. "It's quarantine, remember? All the corridors we used were sealed off and UV scanners disinfected them after we left—same with this transport. They had to create some kind of standard procedure with all the nomads you've sent here. The hallways should be reopened by now, and there are probably lots of other people in those hallways now."

But still my father came with us. *Did my father greet the others?*

"The others from New America?"

I nod.

"No. Just the medical staff greets the new ones, along with one of the other nomads who has been here for a while. We figured it would make them feel more at home, being met by someone who knows what they are going through."

So my father is willing to go through quarantine to see me. I bite my lip and roll the thought around in my head for a while. Still all I see of him is the back of his head and his speaker's sash crossing his back. His hands twitch behind him, like he knows I'm watching him. I look past him down the corridor.

We arrive at the main entrance of the medical area—a set of double glass sliding doors illuminated with cool blue light—but step past them to a single sliding door that is all solid metal and no windows. The words *Quarantine (Please check in at the medical desk)* shout at me in bright red lettering. I don't remember this door being here before.

New? I point to the door.

Jessa laughs once. "Yes and no. I watched them put the words on it. It was a series of supply rooms before, and you probably never noticed it."

So the people who come down to the colonies are relegated to a supply room. Jack notices the cloud that comes over my face and squeezes my shoulder.

"Wait and see. It's not what you think."

One of the medical staff presses his hand to the scanner next to the door, and after a second the metal panel slides open. We step through, and I am surprised. There's a small desk on one side of the door. A medical attendant sits there, and she beams at us as we walk in. Three white chairs with cream cushions are on the other side of the door. Two doors lead off of this room. In one of them are two white tables with chairs. I recognize the food port on one wall. In the other room are two cream-colored sofas with brown and green cushions. A screen hangs on one wall, and a shelf is on the other. There are tablets on the shelf for reading and playing games. A plant stands in the corner, its wispy, ferny leaves leaning into the room.

The medical attendant aligns her tablet with the corner of her desk and smooths her pants as she stands. "Mr. Speaker, Jessa, please report to the medical area for detox. The rest of you all must be exhausted. Please follow me."

She leads the way through the room with the sofas and through another door. Bunks line the walls. There are probably ten beds all together. The crisp white pillows and soft green blankets are so inviting, I want to fall into one and cover my head and not come out for three days. A closed door in one of the walls says *Bathroom*.

"Please each of you choose a bed. You'll notice there are boxes under each bunk. You can put any of your belongings in those. Your boxes will be collected and everything inside will be sanitized using an ultraviolet light." Red raises an eyebrow. The medical attendant smiles. "Don't worry—it won't hurt anything. After you've put your things away, go into the bathroom and wash and choose a set of clothes. You'll see them in the cubbies, labeled by size. Put your others in the laundry chute, and they'll be washed and returned to you."

Red motions to the bunk in the far corner. "That one over there." His attendant starts to wheel him over. "Think you'll fit in there with me, Nellie girl?"

Nell laughs and I swear she blushes. I haven't seen her blush since I've known her. With the way her eyes are sparkling, she could be ten years younger. "I'll just take the one right next to you. It's closer than we've slept in months."

The medical attendant grins. "I'm sorry we don't have anything bigger. When you're assigned your own quarters, of course you'll be given a bed for two. For the rest of you leaving quarantine, remember the procedure. Go through the decontamination chamber."

Red looks up from his box. "How long are we in here, anyway?"

Jessa and my father leave the room. The attendant is already at the door, but turns around. "Two days. Then your new life here can start."

Jack showers first, then he sits on the bed while I go into the bathroom, choose a shower stall, scrub myself until I'm pink, and return wearing clothes I chose from the cubbies. I sit next to him and watch the medical attendant finish bandaging his leg. After the med leaves, Jack wraps an arm around my shoulder and leans down into my hair.

"You smell good."

I snort. *No B.O.*

"It will take some getting used to. Are you hungry? It's lunch time."

Famished.

We go into the dining room and find Nell and Red already at a table, steaming bowls of soup and crusty bread in front of them. Nell sits in one of the white dining chairs, and Red is still in his wheelchair. He has a fluid bag on a stand next to him, and an IV is taped to his hand.

Nell waves as we step in. "That pretty young lady at the desk told us to press a button on that machine over there, wait a minute, and something from the kitchen will come up."

Red dips a crust of bread in his soup, and a few drops land on his beard. "Beats a government supply drop any day." I don't know if it's the IV or the warm food, but he looks more alive already.

Jack puts a hand on the small of my back and guides me to the table. Then he gets our food from the port. My bowl of soup is bigger than I ever would have gotten when I lived here before. Everyone else's portions look larger as well. I am so used to hollow cheeks and hunger pangs that I forgot how skinny we all look. Nell closes her eyes.

"I haven't had a warm meal in far too long."

"Not even in the hospital?" Jack asks between bites.

"Not even then." She holds her bowl between both hands, enjoying the warmth. She doesn't meet our eyes. I reach to her, brushing her fingers with my own. She looks up at me and closes her eyes. Tears streak down her wrinkled cheeks. I raise my eyebrows, asking what's wrong. She slowly brushes the tears away.

"You okay, Nell?" Red asks, leaning closer to her.

"I know what you'll all say if I tell you what's bothering me. So it won't do me much good to tell." She keeps her hand under mine.

I squeeze her fingers and look long at her, hoping she knows how much I love her.

"Oh, Terra. You're so persuasive without saying a single word."

I smile and take a bite of my soup.

"I feel like I should have known what was going on the whole time. With that loyalty serum, I mean. I should have seen the difference between what was real and what wasn't. This place here, this colony, it's like a dream. There's warm food at the push of a button, and a nice lady to make sure we're all right, and my friends are here. I wonder when I'm going to wake up. That hospital—with people who want to stick you with more needles just to get your brain wrapped around their way of thinking—I thought that was the center of the universe. I feel so confused some times."

Nell leans against Red and he wraps an arm around her shoulder then presses his lips to her silver hair. "Shh, my girl. There's time to work through all of that."

Jack sets his spoon in his soup. "And it may be the serum just needs time to work its way out of your system. There are some medicines that can stay in the body for weeks. Maybe the serum isn't completely gone yet and it's still affecting you somehow."

Nell half-smiles, one side of her mouth turning up while the other side frowns. "Even down here, they still control me."

Red takes her face in both his hands. "Don't you ever say that, Nell."

Nell tries to pull away from him, but he holds firm.

"You listen to me. We're gone from all that. It's behind us and we're part of something new here. So what if that serum is still in you somehow? It won't be that way forever, and you're still you. You're the strongest, bravest woman I ever met, and you've beaten them in the end. You're still my Nell."

Her half-smile turns into a radiant full smile, her teeth showing, her soft cheeks turned up, and her eyes glistening. She leans her forehead against Red's. "Thank you."

Even though we're miles below the crushing water where sunlight can't possibly reach us and we're surrounded by plastic and metal, I feel like we're back in the settlement again—I can almost imagine the hazy summer sun filtering in through the cafeteria windows. I watch Nell and Red together—the way they should always be—and I settle into my chair. The colony feels more like home than it ever has before.

FOURTEEN

Jack's eyebrows furrow in concentration as he reads a book on a tablet. My legs are curled under me as I sit on the opposite end of the sofa. I have a tablet in my own hands and my fingers have been sliding across the screen, but I've only caught about a third of the words. Jack is fascinating to watch as he reads; his mouth twitches and his eyes are so expressive as he tracks the words. Right now his lips are puckered just slightly, and his other hand is running through his hair and I don't think he even knows it. Jack finally grins at his screen and turns to me.

"What?"

I look down, trying to find my place in the text.

"I know you were watching me."

I shrug my shoulders and show him my own tablet.

Jack leans in closer. "Hmm. I believe you were on page thirteen ten minutes ago."

I laugh and raise my hands. *Caught me.*

Jack slides closer and gives me his hand when I reach for it.

What were you reading?

Jack shows me the tablet. There's an image of the human nervous system. "I was reading about how drugs affect the mind."

Thinking of the serum?

"Yes. I really didn't think a drug could be so powerful, but seeing Nell the way she was changed my mind." Jack sets the tablet aside and looks at his hands. I trace the long, slender fingers and linger on the calluses. He's such a contrast in so many ways—the strong hands that are tough from hard work; the gentleness of them when they treat a wound. I look in his eyes and see the concern laced in the brown and green, but also the anger burning just below the surface. I put a hand to his cheek, and he presses against my palm.

"I never thought Nell could be that way. She was always too strong for that. She's an old woman, but she's a force, you know? Like old Mayan ruins or an ancient Greek temple that would always stand the test of time. But the serum—it turned her into a child again. She had no thought of her own in her head."

Can we do anything?

"I don't know. If I studied long and deep enough, I could find a way to reverse it, I'm sure. But that won't stop the government from creating new and more powerful versions of the serum." He taps the tablet. "The resources here seem endless. It's like a dream come true for me. I could spend years reading through it all."

I try to keep my face still, keep the same serene look there, but my left eye twitches and the corners of my lips turn down for a fraction of a second. I turn aside and scratch my nose to cover it, but I'm sure Jack saw.

He turns back to his tablet. "Not *years*, of course. But I could become a real doctor here."

And there it is—what I've been dreading about coming back to the colony. I know Jack is happy here, and why shouldn't he be? He could become a real doctor here, just like he says. He could probably be the best doctor the colony has ever seen. And where would that leave me? I won't be here long, I know that. I don't know how long I can last, but it's not years. I don't know if it's even weeks. And I can't ask Jack to always come with me; it's not fair to him. The gnawing in my stomach returns, and it's not hunger. It's the beginning of the panic that sets in when I think about either being alone on the Burn or being trapped here forever. My fingers flick too fast across the screen of my tablet.

Jack stills my hand with his own. "We don't have to talk about it now if you don't want to."

Then when? This will be the elephant in the room until we do.

"How about when we know more? You still need to meet with your father."

Don't remind me.

"The council could offer us help about what to do with the serum."

But the idea of sitting down and having a meeting with my dad leaves me cold.

Jack kisses my forehead, his lips lingering on my skin, his next words whispered into my hair. "You can do anything, Terra. You're just as strong as Nell. Maybe stronger."

I don't feel strong.

"That's because you're caught in the middle of it. But I see you—really see you—and you're amazing."

I lay my head on his shoulder, wishing we could stay this way forever, but knowing it won't last. Even the peace we have with just the four of us in quarantine won't last. It will end after one more day, and then I will probably prove Jack wrong. I'll face my father, and we'll see how strong—or weak—I really am.

FIFTEEN

"It's time for your scheduled evaluation, Terra." The medical assistant smiles her white teeth at me, and her eyebrows are raised expectantly. She gestures for the door next to her desk that reads *Medical Area Access*. Nell and Red came back from their evaluations half an hour ago.

"I've never seen so much gadgetry in all my life," Red said, huffing as he sat down to lunch.

Nell patted his arm and *tsked* him. "Don't let your temper get the best of you."

Red shook his head. "They examined every inch of me, let me tell you. I have no secrets anymore."

Jack frowned. "They were professional, though, weren't they? It wasn't humiliating or offensive like in the Salt Lake hospital?"

Red took a bite of his sandwich. "Doesn't need to be humiliating to be too personal." He chewed for a minute and then sighed. "No, they were very professional. As professional as a professional doctor should be, I guess—I've never had a real doctor's appointment in my whole life. But let me tell you one thing. I asked the doctor about the nomads who've come here, and you know what he said? Not a one of them has brought any kind of illness. So why are we in quarantine?"

"Oh, hush now, Red," Nell said. "They're just protecting everyone who lives here. It may not seem necessary, but I think it shows they care. And it's not bad at all here where we are." She lowered her voice. "And we get to have our own place tomorrow morning."

Red's face unwrinkled as he kissed Nell's hand. "And it's just not coming fast enough."

Now here I am, waiting for my own exam. I have a light gown on, and I clutch it to me, closing up the open back. The lights are bright and almost warm. The door from the quarantine room is closed, but the door into the rest of the medical area hangs open a fraction of an inch. They must be getting more lax in their quarantine procedures. I expected this room to be zipped up tight. Through the crack, I see the white scrubs of the doctor approaching.

"Terra." He extends his hand and I reach mine to shake it, all the while being careful to keep my gown clenched closed with my other. "It's nice having you back again."

I nod.

He reviews his tablet. "Since we have your exam results from a year ago, we'll just take a few tests and then compare the results to see how you're doing. This shouldn't take too long."

He places the tablet on the counter and pulls on exam gloves. I sit through the poking, prodding, and blood draws with stoic toleration. The doctor chats as he works, and his blue eyes reflect his patience and attention to detail as he works. It's so nice to be able to read his eyes, unlike a certain pair of black eyes belonging to a certain doctor at a certain labor camp.

"Relax," the doctor says as he hits my knee to check my reflexes.

Sorry, I mouth. I didn't realize thinking about the good doctor had quite that effect on me. I take a deep breath and give him a watered-down smile.

My exam is over, and the doctor is about to leave the room so I can get dressed and return to quarantine when he pauses at the door and turns back to me. "I'm working on something for your communication problem. We'll discuss it tomorrow when you're ready to leave quarantine." Then he's gone.

Funny, I didn't realize I had a problem.

I lie in my bunk, listening to the sounds of snoring—Nell's soft rasp and Red's deep bullfrog. It might keep anyone else up, but it's comforting to me. I'm curled on my side, enjoying the unfamiliar softness of the mattress and gazing at the empty bunk across the aisle from me. The last time I slept on a bunk, I shivered all night long and listened to much worse things that snoring. My blanket is pulled up tight around my chin, and I'm trying to trick myself into thinking about how perfectly comfortable I am. I should be able to close my eyes and fall asleep in a heartbeat, but my eyes are glued open and all I can do is stare. I need to meet with my father; I need to ask the council for help with the loyalty serum; I need to talk to Jack about how long I'm going to stay in the colony. The pit in my stomach is growing by the second.

Jack leans his head over the top bunk. "Are you still awake?" he whispers.

I peer up at him, and his eyes gleam in the faint reflections of light filtering under the door. I nod.

He climbs down. "Do you mind?"

I scoot closer to the wall and fling the covers over both of us. He grabs my hand, leaving the palm up and starts writing on it. His touch tingles through the calloused skin of my hand all the way to my toes.

Nervous?

Yes.

Shouldn't be.

I know. Can't help it.

Jack leans his head against mine, and I feel his cheeks turning up with his smile. His finger hovers over my hand before he decides to write.

You'll be fine.

Don't know. Apparently I have a communication problem.

You saw a psychologist?

I bump his shoulder. *Not that kind. The doctor said.*

Your tongue?

I guess.

Jack presses his lips to my forehead before writing again. *You're beautiful.* I nudge him in the ribs, but he holds my hand still. *I'm serious.*

I know he is. And the thought that he thinks I'm beautiful warms me and even helps shrink the pit in my stomach. If only my father could see the good things in me the way Jack can.

Jack lets go of my hand and traces a finger down my cheek to the corner of my mouth. Then he presses his lips to mine so softly I could just be imagining it. I fall asleep with his warm breath in my hair and his fingers laced through mine.

Nell, Red, Jack, and I sit in the chairs by the medical attendant's desk. Nell and Red have both left their wheelchairs behind. It's amazing what two days of decent food, rest, and no loyalty serum will do for your health. Nell's eyes are sharp, the way they were the first time I met her in the settlement, and Red has already started filling out.

We each hold our set of clothes we were wearing from the Burn, and the medical attendant is going through the checkout procedure on her tablet.

"Item three. The keypads next to the door of your quarters have already been programmed to recognize your handprints," she says, pausing to look up and smile at us. I wonder if she has a quota of smiles she has to meet each day. I shouldn't think it—she's been nothing but kind to us—but her demeanor is just such a contrast to what I'm used to. Funny how I was accustomed to this not even a year ago, and now it's foreign all over again.

Her sweet voice continues until Red clears his throat. "Miss?"

She keeps going.

"Miss?"

Her eyes take a second to focus on him. She smiles. "Yes, Red?"

"How many more of these items are there?"

She scans her tablet. "There are ten items total. Did you need something or shall I keep going?"

Red sighs and leans back in his chair, and Nell pats his knee. "No, no. Keep going."

The medical attendant turns her eyes on all of us one at a time, her lips turning higher. Her singsong voice continues, and Red folds and unfolds his hands. Then he crosses his legs and a minute later recrosses them. He checks the clock on the opposite wall. I understand his fidgeting. He wants nothing more than to be out of limbo and into a real life. I think another day of this would have driven him insane.

"Terra?"

My head snaps up. How many times has she been saying my name? Jack chuckles behind his hand.

"As soon as you're released from quarantine, you're to report to the medical area for a last exam."

My communication problem, no doubt. I shake my head.

"Is it a problem, Terra?" The medical attendant checks her tablet. "I can reschedule the appointment if necessary."

I wave my hand. No, it's not a problem. That's the whole point.

She drones on for another minute, and then we're free. Red stands, stretching his legs and his arms like he's waking up from hibernation. Nell's eyes are shining as she watches the medical attendant open the door. It slides back with a hiss, and outside, people are coming and going. A few glance over as they pass by, and Nell clutches Red's hand.

"Is it possible?" she whispers. She takes a hesitant step.

Red stoops to kiss her cheek. "Let's go. I feel like we're on that honeymoon we never got to have."

"Would you like help finding your quarters?" the medical assistant asks, hugging her tablet to her chest and smiling. Looking at Nell and Red, I can't help smiling either.

"No, no. I think Terra could show us around."

I nod. I'd like nothing more than to spend a few hours with them outside of these few rooms. We walk out the door.

"Terra!"

Mr. Klein's rich, warm voice greets me as I step outside quarantine. He's leaning against the opposite wall and stands as soon as he sees me, running his hands to smooth the creases in his pant legs. I rush to hug him.

It's an awkward moment as I clasp his back and he pats mine. Before I never would have dreamt of hugging a teacher. But he got me to the Burn. I always thought of Gaea as the one getting me there, giving me the supplies and the sub and the directions. But I never would have found Gaea if Mr. Klein hadn't pointed me in the right direction. He fed my love of the Burn. I never really realized how grateful I am to him.

He pulls back and grips my shoulders, holding me at arms' length. His eyes look deep into mine, and I'm not sure what he's looking for. I hold my own, afraid to blink. Finally he lets me go and nods.

"You're happy." It's not a question.

I nod. In a strange way, I am. If someone were to look back on the turn my life has taken, they might seriously doubt my sanity to consider me happy. But I am.

His voice drops. "Gaea told me the price you had to pay. I've told her it was too much. I'm sorry. And I think she is too, every day."

I look at my feet. I still haven't wrapped my head around the whole idea of my mother and being in such close proximity to her.

Jack steps next to me and shakes Mr. Klein's hand. "Nice to see you again, Rint."

He nods. "You too, Jack. You want to come to my office and talk, Terra? I have so many questions for you."

I shake my head. Jack helps me out.

"She has an appointment with medical first." Jack turns to Nell and Red. "Why don't I show you where you'll be living?"

"Mind if I come to medical with you, Terra? It's not anything involved, is it?" Mr. Klein looks a little embarrassed to be asking, but I'm sure he doesn't want to spend a minute away. Not with someone who's been to the Burn and back.

I don't mind at all. I'd rather have someone with me—someone I trust—than be in there alone while they try to solve my 'problem.'

Mr. Klein waits outside while the doctor performs a few last tests, and then he comes in and sits down in a chair. I'm glad I have Mr. Klein with me because my blood starts to boil as soon as the doctor says, "Voice box."

Mr. Klein stands beside me while the doctor returns with a device in his hands. It's a sleek silver card on a clear strip of plastic. It's a thousand times more sophisticated than the voice box I used in the labor camp, but it's still a voice box, and I want to fling the thing away from me. I scoot back on the exam table and hold my hand out to say, *Stop. Don't let it near me.*

Mr. Klein frowns. "What's wrong, Terra?"

I shake my head. I don't want to even touch the thing. I won't be reduced to a machine here in the colony, a place I used to call home.

"You don't want the voice box?" Mr. Klein asks, confusion wrinkling his forehead as he exchanges glances with the doctor.

No.

"Why?"

Oh the reasons would take far too long. I put my head in my hands. He pats my back awkwardly.

The doctor steps forward. "I can assure you it's perfectly harmless. It simply senses the vibrations in your throat and vocal chords—"

I know. Oh, heavens do I know. And I also know the way it makes me sound like an automaton.

"Then I don't understand the problem."

The doctor still has his hands extended toward me when the door slides open and Jack steps through. He takes one look at the doctor and what's in his hands and stops dead in his tracks. He laughs humorlessly.

"Are you serious?"

The doctor looks from me to Jack. "Well, yes, I'm serious. I thought Terra would like being able to communicate more efficiently and so thought the voice box would be an ideal solution. It's painless, easily put on and taken off, and weighs virtually nothing. She won't even notice it's there."

Jack puts a hand to the back of his neck, and his eyes linger on me. "They really are serious."

I nod. I'm glad he knows me so well.

"Dr. Keyes." I forget he must know him. He worked in medicine until he came back to me. "Here's the problem with the voice box. You may or may not know that Terra was imprisoned in a labor camp while she was on land." The doctor flinches when he says this. The people here really have no idea what life is like up there. People like my father have more than seen to that. "In this labor camp, just one of the humiliations Terra faced was to wear a voice box that made her sound like nothing more than a robot just so the people in charge could have the satisfaction of—"

The doctor holds up a perfectly manicured hand. "Say no more. The voice is of no concern. There are five voices you can choose from, and I'm certain one of them will be to your liking."

I roll my eyes and rip the voice box out of his hand. He's so clueless. I really can't blame him—he was raised to be clueless. I'll put the stupid thing on just so I don't have to deal with the doctor again. Then I'll slip it in my pocket as soon as I'm out of here.

"You don't have to," Jack says.

I know.

The doctor hovers over me, fussing with his hands in the air, as I attach it. He almost jumps in a few times to adjust it, but I lean away from him. Mr. Klein stands by Jack and watches the whole production with a raised eyebrow and a small smirk. Finally the doctor nods his head in satisfaction.

"Now to change the voice, simply press this button here." He guides my fingers until I find a small raised bump. "One press for each change. It will cycle through them. The voice box itself has speakers in it, which can be adjusted in volume. You may find if you turn it up too high, however, that the sound will distort."

My fingers slip away from the plastic and I nod. I admit it—it will be easier to actually talk to people instead of spelling everything out. Especially in my meeting with the council scheduled in two days. But I'm not going to do this in front of him. I'll test it out with Jack when we can find a quiet place in a corridor somewhere. It's too embarrassing trying on new voices in front of everyone.

I slip off the exam table and grab my clothes. Everyone is still hovering around the edges of the room, and I give Jack a pointed look.

"Oh, right. I'll meet you at the Juice Deck?"

I nod, and Dr. Keyes and Mr. Klein take the hint and leave the room with him. I remember the last time I was naked for a physical; when I needed to be hosed down and sanitized at the labor camp. My fingers brush along my colony clothes. They actually are mine—not ones assigned to me—and I wonder if the medical staff retrieved them from my quarters or if Jessa picked them out herself. The fabric is soft as I slip the dress over my head. It falls down to my knees. I look in the mirror hidden behind the door. The dress is robin-egg blue. If you had asked me a year ago what robin-egg blue actually looked like, I wouldn't have been able to tell you. But I've seen robins' eggs, and this color matches them exactly. I'd like to be able to tell Jessa that, but I'm not sure if she'd really get it.

I smooth my hair. I'm about to turn to the door when I stop and study the girl in the mirror again. The bruises on my face are just about gone after being tended to by Dr. Keyes; only the faintest green hue over my jawbone remains. My hair is shiny after my perfect diet of the past few days. I push my feet into my slippers and stare at myself. I look older than I did when I left the colony. Not like I have crow's feet or anything, but my eyes are older. I've seen and done more than I could possibly imagine. My jaw is sharper. My arms and legs are thinner, but they've also filled out with muscle. I'm not as soft as I used to be. No wonder Dad looked like he hardly knew me when I stepped off the sub.

I fiddle with the collar of my dress, arranging it so it hides most of the voice box. I'm stalling here, but I'm not sure entirely why. I know Jack waits for me outside, and I want to be wrapped up in his arms more than anything. It's everyone else I can't face. Everyone else and the questions that muddle their faces every time I walk by.

I take a deep breath and stand stock-still in front of the door until it slides open. Jack leans against the wall on the other side of the corridor. I'm not used to seeing him so relaxed, but he's a chameleon that way—he looks equally comfortable down here as he does up there. I wish I had that skill. He smiles and holds out a hand. I slip my fingers through his and he stands and leads the way down the hall.

Mr. Klein?

"He was called away—had an appointment with a student." Jack takes my hand. "You'd better talk to him soon, though. I don't think he can wait much longer."

I nod and run my fingers over the voice box, unable to leave it alone.

"Do you want to pick out a voice now, or put the voice box in a drawer and never look at it again?"

I smile up at him and all my hesitation melts away. How does he always know exactly what to say? I wrap my other hand around his arm and pull him against my side. We walk down the corridor that way until the next intersection. Then I take a right. This will lead to a small observation deck that hardly anyone ever uses—it's too out-of-the-way.

Now.

Jack sits down on a bench by a window. Through the black water I see the shimmering lights of another observation deck. I sigh and look up and find the watcher imbedded in the ceiling. Even when you think you're alone down here, you never are.

Jack follows my gaze and then presses his palm against my cheek to turn my face toward him. "Ignore it."

Right. There are eyes watching me wherever I go. I miss the forest where there's nothing but trees, animals, and my cabin. Then my heart catches as I think of the watchers and scanners installed so close to my home. There's nothing that's just mine anywhere now.

Jack's other hand finds my cheek, and he holds my face and looks at me. My skin warms under his touch. "You don't have to do this, you know. We can take the voice box back to medical and just tell them you won't use it."

I shake my head. It's never that easy. There's a whole political game you have to play, and I wouldn't be surprised if it was the council who orchestrated the whole voice-box thing just to feel like they were back in control again.

I'll do it. And even I have to admit, it will be easier. I trace my finger along the plastic until I find the button. I press it once and speak.

"How's this?" The voice is high-pitched and breathy.

Jack smiles at me. "Not quite you. Or was it? Somehow I can't imagine you sounding like that."

I laugh. *Definitely not.*

I press the button again, but this one is a low alto and I could almost be a guy. I press the button and it's more manageable, but too monotone. It's like the robot all over again. I press the button, and this time the voice is a tone or two lower than mine, but closer. The words come out just a little too husky, but it's much better.

"I like that one," Jack says, sitting back.

"Me too. I think it's about as close as we'll get."

Jack takes my hand. *You don't have to use it with me.*

I kiss him. *Thank you.*

SIXTEEN

Jack and I are staying with Jessa and Gram. The colony had tried to offer Jack his own quarters back, but Gram wouldn't hear of it. "He's practically family," she said. And he doesn't mind sleeping on the couch. It's a million times better than sleeping with a rock under your back. It's funny to think Gram used to be a speaker herself. I can't imagine my father letting someone sleep on a couch.

I put my hand to the door scanner, it glows green, and the door slides open. Gram gathers me into her arms. I breathe deeply, taking in the scent of freesia and nutritionally optimized bread slices. It sends a pang through my heart. Not everything in the colony is bad, and there are some things I really miss.

Gram runs her hands over my hair and then holds my face and just looks at me for several seconds. Then she breaks into a wide smile.

"It's so nice to see you again, Terra. You've been missed."

Not by everyone. But I don't say it or spell it; it would be too hurtful. That doesn't stop Gram from reading it in my expression, though. Her silver eyebrows knit together for a moment, and I can't bear the scrutiny of her gaze. I turn my head and her hands slip away from my cheeks.

Gram wipes her hands on her apron. "I was just getting dinner ready. Did you want to help, Jack?"

Jack steps from the doorway. "Yes, ma'am."

Gram beams at him. "You've been missed too." She leans to my ear. "I like Jack very much, you should know."

I raise an eyebrow. How much time did he and Gram spend together during those months we were apart?

Jack and Gram work in the kitchen, passing dishes to each other. Gram doesn't let me help. She shoos me to the table, fluttering her hands to get me to sit down. The screen in the front room shows images of the dinner prep step-by-step, and I watch the screen show cut vegetables, and then Gram cuts the vegetables and Jack browns the meat. Gram tries to make conversation.

"So how are you, Terra?"

"Good."

"Are you happy?"

Funny how the question makes me pause. When Mr. Klein talked about my happiness, I didn't think twice about it. I wonder if everyone else down here doubts such a thing as happiness is possible up there. I look at Jack, who stops stirring the meat to watch and listen.

"Yes. I am."

Gram pauses with the knife hovering over a mushroom. "I'm glad to hear that. I worried every day after you went. . . . After you left."

I look at my hands that have nothing to do. "I'm fine. You didn't have to worry."

The knife slams against the cutting board harder than strictly necessary for slicing mushrooms. But Gram's voice is calm. "Perhaps. But I didn't know that." Chop, chop, chop. "Neither did your father."

That statement hangs in the air for a good five minutes before any one of us speaks again.

"This isn't my home. Dad didn't help with that, you know."

Gram sighs then dumps the mushrooms into the pan. "You broke his heart, you know."

"My mom broke his heart."

Then Gram clamps her mouth tight shut and stirs the sizzling mushrooms around the pan and doesn't say another word about it for the rest of the night.

The next afternoon the Juice Deck is crowded; it takes me several moments to scan over the faces for the two I've come here to see. Jessa and Brant sit in our usual booth with a view of black water. Their heads are bowed close together and they haven't noticed me yet. As Jack and I cross the cavernous room, several people turn to look at me, hands covering their mouths. The room buzzes with conversation, but I can imagine what their whispers say: "Speakers's daughter . . . ran away . . . broke his heart . . . better off without her." Maybe even something like, "Traitor." I wouldn't put it past them with the way their eyes bore into my back like knives as I order a smoothie. I use the voice box, and the worker raises an eyebrow, but mercifully doesn't stare at the box strapped to my neck.

When I turn from the counter, Brant looks up. His eyes look past me for a moment before lighting up. He didn't recognize me right away either. Jessa laughs and waves us over.

"It took you forever!" Jessa says as she slides her empty cup out of the way.

I lean forward, wondering if the voice box picks up on whispers. "I was being fitted with my sexy voice."

Jessa guffaws. It's been a long time since I've heard her laugh like that, but she does it now and the sounds makes me not hate my voice box quite so much.

"That one was probably the best option, right?"

I sip my smoothie and nod. Cold. I haven't had anything cold for so long. The food at the settlement was always lukewarm or hot, the labor camp was more of the same, and quarantine was all soup and stew. They must have thought we were invalids or something. I relish the way the chill goes all the way from my mouth and down my throat and I can feel it for just a split second in my belly before it's gone.

"So did you have any of that sugar?" Brant asks.

I raise an eyebrow.

"You know, how the Burn has unnecessary sugar and they put it in their smoothies and they're infinitely better than ours?" Hostility lines the edges of his voice. That's unexpected.

My mind rolls back to the last conversation I had in the Juice Deck. Jessa and Brant had been there that day. I had talked about sugar. Brant knew how much the Burn intrigued me. Did he feel like I abandoned him for something better? Jessa puts a hand on his arm and shakes her head slightly. I look at my fingers wrapped around my cup.

"No, where I was there weren't many luxuries."

He must hear the seriousness in my tone and see the hollowness in my eyes. He relents. "That's too bad. I would have liked to hear about it."

Jessa's hand is on his arm, and he turns to her and touches her hair. They seem stuck in time, like the clock hasn't moved forward a single minute since I left.

"I missed you guys."

Brant shakes his head. "I missed you too, Terra." He looks down and purses his lips. "Jessa had it rough at first." He looks up at me and there's accusation on his face. "But then she said she understood why you left. I never got there."

"I don't know how to explain it."

"I figured you'd say that." He laughs, one corner of his mouth higher than the other, but his eyes aren't smiling. He shakes his head. "You were my best friend, you know. I just thought you'd tell me something like this was going on. I thought maybe you'd say good-bye to me."

I can't tell him that we hadn't really been best friends since he started dating Jessa. Relationships change all the time. "I didn't think you'd understand."

"You're right I didn't understand." His voice softens. "But you could have let me try."

Jack leans closer to me. He hasn't said a word, but I know he's trying to strengthen me.

"I never meant to hurt you, Brant. You or Jessa."

Brant shrugs. "I guess it doesn't really matter now. You're home." He cocks his head and narrows his eyes at me. "You're not going to stay, are you?"

I shake my head. "There's too much I need to do up there."

"What is so important up there that you can't stay here with your family?"

Brant knows about my family. We were friends for so long—he's lived it all with me. My voice drops to a whisper, and I'm thankful the voice box picks that up. "My family is up there now."

Jessa doesn't even blink—she knows what I mean by it, she knows how much I love her and she also knows that I belong up there. Brant on the other hand, can't help but flinch. The hurt returns to his face.

"The government up there, they're horrible and oppressive and cruel. They've made this loyalty serum. It makes the people think the government can't do anything wrong, and I've seen it, Brant. I've seen what it does to people—good people. I need to go up there and help them if I can."

He nods. "You're braver than I'll ever be. Crazier too. You never were any good at anything down here. Now you've found a vocation. Jack, did you know Terra tried medicine once?"

I grin, and Jack scoots forward, ready for a good story.

The doors of the Juice Deck slide open, I look up, and I can't stop the way my grin goes even wider.

Jessa leans in. "I hope you don't mind. I invited Kai, Jane, and Madge."

Of course I don't mind. I wondered when I'd see them here. Madge's red curls are cropped close to her head, and her face is more serene than I've ever seen it. Jane is hardly recognizable. Her limp blond hair is lustrous and wavy, her cheeks and lips are fuller. And then there's Kai. She has a baby on her hip, a dark-haired cherub that I just want to cuddle for a while.

"This is Terra," Kai says as they reach our booth and squeeze in next to us.

The baby looks at me and grins, and the pearl of two tiny teeth greets me.

"She's so beautiful," I say, reaching for her. Kai passes her to me, and baby Terra grins and touches my cheek. A thread of drool drops from her mouth onto my hand, and she laughs. Kai grabs a cloth and wipes it up. Mothering suits her; she looks so content.

"She's mine because of you, Terra. I could say it a million times over and it would still never be enough."

I blush and wave it off. I'm so used to saying things with gestures and few words, but here there are no words. I don't deserve Kai's praise.

Madge slurps a smoothie. "Your voice is pretty kooky. You know that, right?"

"I know." I draw the words out.

Jane laughs. Her hands rest on her arms folded on the table.

"What's your vocation?" I ask. I wonder how they put her nimble fingers to use.

"Textiles," she says.

I make a face.

"It's okay, really." She leans forward and her eyes light up. She's come alive down here. "They told me I could make new designs."

Jessa nods emphatically. "She's really good at it too. You know how boring those old clothes were getting. I have a dress she made, and it's incredible."

Brant glances up from his food. "The purple one?"

Jessa nods.

"Yup, definitely incredible. The way the skirt hangs . . ." He waggles his eyebrows and Jessa hits his arm.

Jane laughs. "It's nice being able to try new things and not be told to sew the same gray and yellow clothes over and over again."

The mention of the labor camp cuts through the happy mood like a razor, and Kai shifts Terra to sit on her other leg. Kai presses her lips to her cheek, and Terra squirms, grabbing for her mother's hair.

Madge clears her throat. "We don't talk about it much anymore. There's nothing to talk about really. It's over and done."

The weight on me hangs. It's not over and done, though, not for me. There's so much I still need to do. I feel Madge's eyes on me, the same intense stare I felt so many times in the camp.

"What are you planning? You going back?"

I can't meet their eyes. To them, I just got here. Jack runs a hand along my arm. His touch asks a question neither of us has had the courage to ask yet.

Jane finally breaks the silence. "It's okay, Terra. We figured you'd go back. We just didn't know when."

"I need to talk to my father first."

"Good luck," Jessa says. "He's different since you left."

"How much worse can it be?"

The way Jessa's eyes take me in and shine at me, I know I won't like what she'll say. She looks so tired.

"You know Gram and I moved out a month ago."

Everyone quiets around me, succumbing to fidgeting fingers, wandering eyes, worrying about food and that thread on her pants and that spot on his shirt. They've heard about all this, and I'm the last to know.

"Why?"

"He's harder to live with. I know that's hard to believe." She laughs but there's no trace of humor in it. "After you left he threw himself into his vocation and closed off to everything else. Including me and Gram."

"So you—what?—just left him?" I have no right to say it after what I did, but I can't imagine Jessa abandoning him like that.

She sighs and tucks her hair behind her ear. "You don't have to make me feel worse than I already do."

"I didn't mean that."

She puts a hand up. "It's okay. I ask myself the same thing every day. Sometimes I think he's better and worse alone. He doesn't worry about hurting anyone else this way. But he does get lonely. I wonder." She looks down and picks at her napkin. "I wonder if I should tell him about Gaea."

"What?"

She sighs and puts her napkin down. "I know, I know. It sounds like holding a bomb or something, just waiting for it to go off. But if he knew she was here, if he knew she's been watching this whole time—"

"Yeah, watching and not wanting to say a single word to him? I don't know if it's a good idea, Jess. I can barely talk to her."

"I've talked to her."

Jack's head has been whipping back and forth this whole time. "What does Gaea have to do with it?"

I look at him. "Jess never told you?"

"Told me what?"

I open my mouth, but the words stumble in my throat. You'd think they would spill out now that I can finally talk again, but they catch and I cough. I rub my eyes with the heels of my hands. Jack waits patiently.

"She's our mother."

His eyes widen.

"Your *mother*?" Madge whistles a long note. "The crazy lady from the sub? The one who cut out your tongue, right? She's your mom?"

What a tangled life I lead. I nod.

Jack's voice is quiet. "Wow, Terra. I thought you had told me everything."

I grab his hand, ready to explain, ready with the reasons why I won't ever hold anything back but why I hadn't told him this yet, when he shakes his head.

"No, no, I'm not upset that you didn't tell me. I just didn't realize it was so . . . messy."

I laugh like Jessa had. "Messy is putting it lightly."

"I knew your mom had left. I didn't realize who she became."

The conversation moves along without me. Jessa explains what happened all those years ago. She explains what price I paid to leave. She explains what Gaea has been doing to help. My head is so fogged over, I can barely follow the words as they circle around me. My brain catches on the one idea—that maybe Gaea and my dad should talk—and everything else fades to the background. She's already walked out once. What's the worse that could happen? No, wrong question. How much more can my dad take?

SEVENTEEN

"Next destination: the vocational quarter."

The transport slows to a stop and the doors hiss open. I thrum my fingers against my pants. Come on, come on, I will the doors. I've spent the entire ride from the Juice Deck trying to focus on Jack's face while feeling the stares on my back. While turning and saying, "Why yes, I'm the freak-show daughter of your beloved speaker. Want to line up and shake hands?" had a certain appeal to it (especially if I switched voices on the voice box), it wouldn't do me any favors. So Jack whispered nonsense to me, trying to make me laugh.

Jack holds my hand as we step out and head to Field #3.

I see a figure through the glass of the dome. He's crouched among the rows of strawberries, tending the plants. It's so familiar to the first work I ever did with him—pulling weeds in the oca fields—that I can't help but think of that day. I remember the smell of rain and green plants. I remember the way the sweat trickled down my back as we worked in the hazy summer sun. I think of the way Dave smiled at me and the way it was so easy to laugh with him. I haven't laughed as much lately. As crazy as it sounds, life was simpler then.

Jack touches a hand to my back. "I'll let you go talk to him alone. If he talks to you at all. Don't expect too much."

I nod and press my hand to the screen that opens the door. The light scans over my palm.

"Access denied."

My old field. The one vocation I might have stuck with—I tolerated it more than the others, even if I wasn't very good at it—and now I can't get in. I wonder how long it took security to remove my name from the access lists. My hand slips from the glass plate.

Jack clears his throat and steps beside me. "Let me try." His voice is hushed. He knows how awkward this is, to have him let me into my own home. The light scans his hand, turns green, and the door slides open.

He shrugs his shoulders and one side of his mouth turns up. "I have access to just about everywhere. A doctor needs to be able to get in to help people."

"I know." I almost make myself believe it, but my voice cracks. I really am a stranger here.

I step into the pod and take a radiation suit from its hook. My breath catches as I pull the zipper up to my chin. I've done so many things since that day months ago—months? It feels like years—when I zipped up my suit and tended corn for the last time with Jessa. I never expected to feel the same clench of claustrophobia in my chest with the suit on. I put the visor down and step into the field.

I never tended strawberries here or at the settlement. The rows and rows of short plants with white flowers stretch out. The soil is soft, and my feet leave prints behind me as I carefully tread down the rows. The suit's climate control kicks in and a breath of cool air travels down my limbs. I'm so used to sweating that this actually feels cold. I'm ten feet from Dave when he stops digging.

"I wondered when you'd come see me." His voice is hollow. He doesn't even look at me. He just says it, waits a beat, and then keeps raking through the row.

I stop dead in my tracks. I don't know what would be worse—Dave not speaking to me at all, or this.

I decide to use the voice box. Writing words and signing things would take far too long for the conversation we need to have. "I would have come sooner. I've been busy."

Dave snorts. "Doing what? Convincing those idiots that it's finally time to do something? Good luck." His tone is so sharp it could almost cut me. "Nice voice, by the way. Is that what you sounded like before?"

"No. This voice is much sexier."

He turns enough so that I can see his face through his visor. His lips turn up in a wry smile, but I can tell he doesn't find it very funny. He turns to the ground and pokes the dirt with his spade. "This place is unbelievable. No weeds. I barely have to do anything to make these grow."

I kneel beside him and touch one of the plants. "I wasn't very good at agriculture. I wasn't good at much of anything."

"So I've heard. Jessa visited me for a while after . . . " The sentence hangs between us, and I can fill it in by myself. *After Mary died.* Dave's eyes are clouded, but he shakes his head and the storm in his face clears. "Jessa told me how many vocations you burned through. Was that because everything down here just isn't *real*?" Dave sits back and lets his hands fall uselessly at his sides.

"What do you mean?"

"You know exactly what I mean. You've lived up there. You know how everything is sharper and more intense and makes your heart beat faster. Here I'm lucky if I even want to get out of bed in the morning. I feel like I'm walking around in a fog, and there's all these other people doing the same thing. The only difference between me and them is that I know I'm in a fog. I know what real life is like."

I pick up his spade and turn it over in my hands. "Do the others who come down here feel that way?"

"No." He snatches the spade from me and stabs it into the soil. "They think this is Neverland and they've never looked back."

"Neverland?"

"Never mind." He rocks back and lies down in the furrow, just like I did once. His hands are over his visor, and I can't see his face. "It's like they forgot what it means to really live." He's quiet for a moment, and all I can hear is the fan whirring in my suit. "I wonder if she would still be alive if we hadn't come down here. She wouldn't have liked it here anyway."

"Do you want to go back?"

His hands drop away and he looks at me more earnestly than he ever has—here or on the Burn. "Yes."

There's something in his eyes that bothers me. Some scorching hunger that looks like it could burn him to ash. "Why?"

He won't meet my gaze. "I feel useless here."

"But you're important here."

He snorts again. "You of all people shouldn't buy that crap about everyone's important. They tried to put three people on this field with me until I convinced them it only took one—"

"Yeah because heaven forbid you had someone else here to talk—"

"—So don't give me that spiel about how essential everyone is. They just say that so no one goes insane with nothing to do. Trust me."

I narrow my eyes at him. He looks a little unhinged—it could just be the reflection of the solar lamps on his visor—but I'm not entirely sure it's over not having enough to do. I want to choose my next words carefully, but there isn't a nice way to say it.

"How are you doing since Mary?"

And those words completely cut him off from me. His expression goes stony and he rolls back to his feet and walks down the row.

"Dave?" I get nothing but his back. "Dave!"

I jump up and run after him, the swish of the legs of my radiation suit rubbing together too loudly in my ears. I touch his shoulder, but he shrugs me off and keeps walking. I let him walk away. I want to cry, but with the air blowing in my suit, my eyes feel far too dry for that.

Does Dave blame me for her death? Well, of course he does. I still blame myself for her death, so why shouldn't he?

I want to rake my hands through my hair and scream a little, but my gloved hands find nothing but slippery fabric. I close my eyes to take a breath, to do anything to collect my thoughts, but when I close them all I see is Mary with her hand pressed to her stomach as blood like rubies drips between her fingers. I limp back to the pod.

"He talked to you?" Jack asks as I shrug out of the suit.

I nod. I won't use the voice box right now. I don't want to hear that phony voice with those words that drove Dave away.

"I told you he changed."

I just didn't realize how much. I turn to Jack, and my eyes well with tears.

"Oh, Terra." He takes me in his arms and I let him. I lean against him, burying my head in his chest, smelling the fabric, and his soap, and just him underneath it all. His heart beats out a gentle, lulling rhythm in my ears. "He's been that way ever since they took her body away. I'm amazed he even talked to you."

I trace my fingers against his shoulder. *He's so angry. It scared me.*

"I know. There's something boiling inside of him, and I'm worried one of these days he's going to explode."

What can we do?

Jack's shoulders shrug. "I don't know. He refuses to see his counselor. He refuses to talk to just about everyone. He works double shifts and lives by himself and never goes out."

Would he go with me when I go back?

Jack puts me at arms' length and searches my eyes. "You're going back for sure?"

And there's the conversation we've been avoiding for several days now. I nod. I can't stay here much longer with the recycled air and the ocean looming just through the window and the people running in circles around this place every day. Each day I'm here just reconfirms why I left in the first place. I look up at Jack, and I search his hazel eyes. His eyes burn back into mine.

"Yes, I think he'd come with us when *we* go back."

My tears spill over. Yes, Jack will come with me. My heart swells and feels like it might burst through my chest.

Thank you.

"I'm done leaving you."

I know. But it still surprises me.

"It shouldn't." He cups my face in his hands and leans his forehead against mine. "You should know how I feel by now."

I do. I just don't understand why.

Jack sighs and pulls me in against him again. Then he turns us and we step through the pod door. A few people walking by glance at us. Jack smiles and waves and holds me tighter.

"There are too many reasons to even begin. But one of the most important ones is because you are good."

I turn away from him, but he cups my chin and looks me in the eyes.

"You may not think so now. You've seen too many things. But I know you, Terra. I know your heart. And you are good. Come on, let's go back to our quarters." He takes my hand and leads me away from the field. As we step onto the transport, I look through the glass of the field and glimpse Dave at the opposite end, pounding the soil with every ounce of force he can muster.

EIGHTEEN

Things with Gram are better today. Gram actually smiles at me when Jack and I walk through the door. She's sitting on the couch in front of the screen, reviewing messages.

"Welcome back, Terra." She pats the cushion next to her and I sit down. "You'll be happy to know they've scheduled your meeting with the council for tomorrow at 0900."

My stomach clenches. So soon. It would have to be soon—I can't stay here for weeks procrastinating this—but I can't help the dread that fingers its way into my gut.

Gram studies my face. "I forget how different from your sister you are. Every day I look at Jessa—see her figuring out her vocation, see her with Brant, see her with her clothes strewn on the floor because she can't decide what to wear—and I see the seventeen-year-old girl there. You're different." Gram touches my cheek with her wrinkled, crepe fingers. Her hand is soft and warm as it trails down the side of my face. "You've done so much and helped so many people. But you're still just a seventeen-year-old girl."

I want to crawl onto her lap the way I did when I was little. I want her to wrap her arms around me and sing me lullabies and shush my worries away. I want her to hold my hand as we go into the council chamber and tell me it will be okay. But that would just make me look weak. I need to put on a brave front before the council. I need them to see the value of these people who come to them for refuge, and I need them to see the value of the people still left on the Burn. I need to be convincing, and a seventeen-year-old girl holding her grandmother's hand and shaking in her boots will not do the job.

"I wish it didn't have to be so hard," I say.

Gram laughs wryly. "The important things always are."

Jack squeezes my shoulder and goes into the kitchen to start making dinner.

"Did you want to read the message?" Gram asks.

"Might as well."

Gram uses the remote to open the message *Re: Council Meeting*.

Terra, the Council has agreed to offer you fifteen minutes during tomorrow's council meeting. Be prepared to discuss your business within that fifteen-minute time frame. Please arrive at 0900. Thank you, and we look forward to meeting with you.

Nice and impersonal. I sink deeper into the couch, letting my head fall back into the cushions.

The door hisses open.

"You look terrible," Jessa says as she plops on the couch by me and sinks in just about as low with a huge sigh of her own.

Her hand falls next to mine and I take it. I'm done with the voice box for today.

Rough day?

"The worst. I've been working on a new fertilizer for the fields, and the council rejected my latest proposal. Red tape to the max."

I smile.

"What?"

I don't miss much of this on the Burn. But I miss you.

She turns to look at me. "I miss you too, Terra. So much."

I turn away and stare at the screen with the time for my own meeting with the council blazing back at me.

"I don't know what I'm going to do when you're gone and I have to keep going with my life."

You'll manage.

"I'm serious." She's suddenly playing with her hands. She glances over her shoulder. Gram and Jack are busy with dinner. Jessa's voice drops. "Things like Brant and I talking about getting married in a few years. You're one of the only people that I care is there or not. And you won't be."

A pang goes through my heart. No, I won't be there. Or if they do get married and then they have kids, I won't see them either. I'll be Aunt Terra, the one who left for the Burn and will never come back. I frown. There will be so much I miss out on. But even as I think about all that, I can't imagine doing it differently.

Jessa touches my arm. There are tears in her eyes. "I didn't tell you that to give you a guilt trip. I told you that just so you know how much I miss you."

Miss you too.

Jessa swipes at her eyes and manages to eke out a smile. "Come on. Let's go have some dinner."

I share Jessa's bed. Jessa is already asleep—she was as soon as her head hit the pillow—and I'm staring at the black of the ocean through the small window on the opposite wall. The faint hum of the climate regulator and Jessa's soft breathing are the only sounds. I already long to sleep in the woods with the sounds of insects, the fall of rain, the whisper of wind, and the creak of tree branches. The whole world was alive up there. Down here, only the people are. It's only metal, plastic, and glass.

I turn on my side and close my eyes, trying to push all thoughts away, but my mind keeps veering back to the loyalty serum, the government, and my meeting with the council. It's going to be a long night.

"Relax."

Jessa's staring at me, her spoon half-raised to her mouth. I stop my fingers from thrumming on the table and take a bite of my oatmeal, but my stomach twists as soon as it hits my mouth. Jack watches me with the corners of his mouth turned down in concern, but he doesn't say anything. Gram bustles around the kitchen, and she looks at me out the corner of her eye now and then, but she doesn't slow down.

Jessa stands and slings her bag over her shoulder and swigs down her juice. She pecks Gram on the cheek. "I need to be going. I'm going to the lab to work on the new formula some more. Good luck, Terra."

I try to smile, but it comes out like a grimace. She sweeps me into a hug.

"It'll be okay. You'll be great."

She has so little idea what's at stake here. I feel like the whole world may very well be in my hands. I drop my head to the table. I'm going to be sick.

"She's right, Terra." Gram stands with her hand propped on one hip, clinging to a dishrag. "I think you of all people are the best choice to help those poor souls on the Burn. If anyone can get them some help, it's you."

I had no idea she even knew what was going on. But I should know better. Her intelligent eyes focus so intently on me that I want to turn aside.

"Now listen to me closely," she says as she pulls out a chair and sits down next to me. "Some of those council members make your father look like a teddy bear. Some of them are downright nasty. Not in a mean way, but they're prideful and can't imagine anything done differently than it has been for the past hundred years. Ignore them. Try to convince those that will listen. I know your father told you he wanted you to try public service as your next vocation before you left. You were angry about it, but there was a reason he said it. Look how good you are for people and how much you help people. You put those skills to work up on the Burn, and you would have also been brilliant at it here. Just do your best. Just help your people."

I hug her harder than I've ever hugged her in my life. Then I stand up and take a deep breath.

"Ready?" Jack asks. I nod.

I feel Gram's eyes on me as we step through the door.

Jack holds my hand as we walk down the corridor. His hand is the only thing keeping me steady. My heart races and my palms sweat. Jack laughs.

"Nervous?"

I nod. *How?*

"How could I tell?" He pulls his hand away from mine and wipes his palm on his pants. "You're a little slippery right now."

My cheeks redden. Jack laces his fingers into mine.

"Don't be embarrassed. I would start to worry if you *weren't* nervous."

We climb onto the transport, and I squeeze his hand harder. We're surrounded by people, and the murmur of voices and the glances at me press me into the corner. I look at my feet.

"Can you loosen it just a little?" Jack whispers.

I realize I've been crushing his hand. *Sorry.*

Jack kisses my forehead. "You'll be fine."

When we get off, a few public servants get off with us. I recognize most of them, and one of them even gives me a sympathetic smile. They'll all know why I'm getting off here. They might not know exactly why I'm talking to the council today, but the looks on their faces make me feel even more nervous. They look like I'm headed for the lions' den.

The double sliding doors that open into the council's chamber stand before us. The chrome gleams in the bright lights. I fasten the voice box to my throat. I have fifteen minutes with the council. There's no time for spelling things out. The council's aide stands up when he notices us. He's dressed in gray, just like all the other council members do. Its neutral color signifies that the council loses itself in the service of the colony.

"Welcome, Terra. I remember the last time you came to a council meeting." His voice is almost squeaky, and I can't suppress a smirk. Finally something I can smile about. "You were only this high." He holds his hand about two feet off the ground. His voice was just as squeaky back then as well.

"And you used to give me grapes."

He beams. "You remember. It's been a long time since you've been down this corridor. A shame you couldn't come back more."

If he only knew the half of it.

He shakes his head and puts on his official face. "The council is expecting you. If you'll wait just a moment while I record the details of your visit." He gestures to two seats beside the door. Jack sits down and pulls me down with him.

"Relax," he whispers.

Yeah, right.

The aide presses a few buttons on his tablet then looks up at us and smiles. His gray hair sticks up in every direction and the light illuminates it so it looks like a silver halo. With his wide smile, crinkly eyes, and squeaky voice, I can't help but like the guy.

A plaque on the wall reads *Vox Populi*.

"The voice of the people," Jack says.

I nod. *Learned that lesson when I was a toddler.*

Jack picks up on the sarcasm. "You don't believe it?"

You know how I feel.

211

He does. I've told him more in the past few weeks than I told him in months of roaming the forest together. Yes, it is the voice of the people—definitely more than the government on the Burn is ruled by the voice of the people. I just didn't want what the voice of the people wanted. That's what my dad had such a hard time understanding. If the voice of the people wants it, why shouldn't I want it too?

Jack squeezes my hand. "You can do this."

"All finished," the aide says, gesturing toward the door. I take a deep breath as the door slips open.

The council chamber is dominated by a huge circular table. Ten council members sit around it, and my dad sits on the far side—the spot reserved for the speaker. There are two empty seats at the table for visitors. My father's hands are folded together on the table, and he's watching me casually, his eyes guarded. Is he trying to appear impartial? The warmest greeting I get is a hint of a smile from a woman two seats down from my father whose daughter I played with when I was five. So much for not being nervous.

The council aide steps in behind us and guides us to the empty seats. My knees are shaking so badly I'm sure the council member next to me will give me a dirty look, but her eyes are trained straight on my father. I sit down.

My father looks at the tablet in front of him, clears his throat, and then looks up at me.

"The council acknowledges you, Terra, and you're invited to speak when you're ready."

No "Hi, honey." Of course I wasn't expecting something quite that personal from him, but I could be any other colonist sitting across from him. Equity for all, I guess. His motto.

"As you know, I've lived on the Burn for almost a year now." My eyes flick from council member to council member, but I can't bring myself to look at them for long. Why am I so intimidated by them? "You also know that I've been helping nomads—those who live outside the designated cities as a means of escaping the government—find their way to the colonies."

One of the council members clears his throat and raises his hand. The movement catches me off guard and I stutter. I thought I would have a few minutes at least to make my case until the questions started. Maybe not.

"Yes?"

"And how do you know these 'nomads' you bring here aren't spies for New America's government?"

His tone spikes my anger, and that cuts through my nervousness better than anything could. I take a breath. I'm ready to fling a response at him, but I pause. Something he said doesn't line up with everything I've been taught in the colony. My eyes narrow at him.

"And how do you know it's called New America up there?"

His face pales and his eyes flick to my father and back to me. My father nods almost imperceptibly. The council member steeples his hands, but doesn't speak anymore. I take that as a sign that I'm free to continue, and I'm guessing I won't have any more interruptions. But I file the past few seconds away to bring up later. Something's going on here.

"I've been bringing the nomads to the colonies to get them away from the government. You may or may not know that I was imprisoned in a labor camp while I was on the Burn, so I've seen firsthand some of the atrocities the government is capable of. I was imprisoned for nothing more than not being in a designated city. Many of the other inmates there were imprisoned for much less. They deserve a better government—one that will treat them like people.

"What I'm doing on the Burn is important to me, and it's making a difference in the lives of the nomads who come down here. They've become an essential part of colony life. They're happy and healthy." I eye the council member over medical affairs. "None of them have brought any diseases to the colony and have never posed a health risk." I turn back to the rest of the council. "And they all work very hard. But it's not enough. Up there, the government is working on a loyalty serum, a drug that alters people's brains. It's a way to force the citizens to become mindless drones. They'll never oppose the government, and they'll never have a voice again. As council members you all know how important it is that the people be heard. And the government is very close. I've come to ask the council to help me find a way to stop the production of the serum."

I sit down and the whispers begin. It starts low, the hum of bees, and then it rises until the council members are shouting at each other. My father's voice rises above it all.

"Quiet! Now is the time to voice your concerns."

Starting at my father's right, the council members speak.

"We can't make a decision of this magnitude in the time provided this morning. It will take careful consideration—"

"But there is no time!" I say. My father silences me with a look.

The council member continues without even acknowledging me. "We have a strict code not to get involved. It would be dangerous for us to even think about assisting them."

"Such an act would be a definitive acknowledgement of our existence. It would put us all in danger."

"If we come to their aid now, they would expect us to help them at every juncture. When will it end?"

I snort at this response. My father glares at me and I glare right back. I'm ready to interrupt the next council member when the doors open and Gaea whisks into the room, her curly hair and long dress billowing behind her.

My father's face warps from anger to confusion to sadness to shock and back through about five times. All the color has drained from his face and his mouth hangs open. Gaea comes to a stop right behind me and puts a hand on my shoulder.

The next council member in line flaps her mouth. "Who are you to barge in here like this? We are in the middle of an important meeting. There's a reason you need to schedule an appointment. Who are you anyway? Does anyone recognize this woman?" The council member sees my dad's face. "Mr. Speaker? Do you know her?"

It's all my father can do to speak. "Teresa?"

At the name, all the council members shift in their seats and the whispering behind hands begins. I can just imagine the wheels cranking. *Teresa? Wasn't that his wife's name? She disappeared years ago, not long after Terra and Jessa were born. Do you know why she left? No, I never heard. Just up and left him. I think it was another man. Well I think she couldn't live in his shadow, being the speaker of the colony. If it is her where has she been all these years? And* look *at her. Who knows where she's been hiding looking like that.*

My father is still paralyzed, so I stand up. She may not have been much of a mother to me, but she's helped me more in the past year than this entire colony has in my lifetime, and frankly

I'm tired of the pettiness running rampant through the council right now.

"That's enough!" I'm actually kind of impressed with the way the voice box carries my anger. "This is my mother, and you should show her the same respect you show any other member of this colony."

Gaea's hand trembles on my shoulder, and I raise one of my own to squeeze it. I feel Jack's warmth next to me, and I know that no matter what happens next, I can do this.

My father wobbles to his feet and takes one step around the table. "Teresa, where have you been?"

Gaea doesn't move an inch as she watches him approach. She grabs my hand with her other to keep from bolting.

"Say something," I whisper.

"I—" Her voice comes out in a creak and she clears her throat. "I've been in the trench."

My father steps back. "You didn't transfer to another colony?"

She raises an eyebrow. She's steadier now. "You would have known if I had. You tried to trace me."

"You left me. How could I not trace you?"

"I left because of what you did to my children." Her voice is soft, but there's so much venom in it that my father flinches back like he's been slapped.

The council member next to him looks defiantly at Gaea. "Mr. Speaker, what is this woman raving about?"

My father finally shakes the shock off. "This woman is my wife, council member. Her name is Teresa. She is not a raving mad woman. Please correct your tone."

The council member *hrmphs*, but sits back.

"And everything she says is true." My father's eyes fall to the floor. I've never seen him look so defeated.

The whispers start again, and my father raises his hands. "We don't have time to go into details now. This time was reserved for Terra. When she is dismissed, we will discuss this further. Please continue."

Gaea leans down to me. "Do you mind?"

I shake my head.

"I have access to the satellites orbiting the earth. You're not the only ones who can spy."

Two council members glare at her. Spying, huh? If the council members have the same access to the Burn as Gaea does, that would explain the council member's slip when he said New America. But why would the council lie so much about what they know?

"As such, and you may already know this depending on your dedication to the said spying, you know everything that Terra has presented is true."

A shrewish woman leans forward. "Regardless, it is not our concern."

"Silence!" My father glares at her. "This colony may have protocols regarding the Burn, but this council also has protocols regarding these proceedings. You'd do best to remember that."

The woman eyes him icily and leans back.

"My only question for the esteemed and wise council—" the sarcasm in her voice is unmistakable "—is what will you do when the mindless drones created by the loyalty serum are ordered to attack the colonies?"

I brace myself for more shouting, but the silence is deafening. I lean to Jack and smirk.

"A real stumper." I feel so relieved to have another ally that all I want to do is laugh, but Jack shakes his head. He's right. Now's not the time.

My father crosses his arms. "Did you have anything more to add, Terra?"

"I wish you would help the people of New America because you want to—because it's what's right. Not because you're worried about saving your own skins."

"It's not that easy, Terra. You've grown up here. You know how difficult the relationship we have with New America is."

I roll my eyes. "What relationship? You always told me contact was forbidden, and now I'm suddenly learning that you guys know just about everything that goes on up there."

Gaea leans forward. "If you would just give Terra the access she needs to their computer system, she could get to the government island, and—"

"And what?" A council member snorts. "Maneuver a sub right to their doorstep, sneak on board, and hijack them? They would know in an instant a nomad could never accomplish such a thing. Once again, it would confirm our existence."

Government island. It's what the physician's assistant said in the tunnels. It gives me hope. Surely it would be easier to reach an island than to penetrate a mountain fortress. My mind races.

"Just give me the resources I need. You don't even have to offer any more help than that. Just let me take a sub to this island, and I will do what I can."

One of the council members rolls his eyes, and that makes me seethe. I look to my father, wanting an ally somewhere, but he looks about helplessly. I can tell he's deciding exactly what to tell me. Finally he scrapes his hands down his face and speaks.

"The colonies kept an eye on the Burn from day one. There were a lot of reasons, but the two that were tossed around the most were to monitor military activity—for our own protection—and to see if there ever came a time when we would go back up."

Go back up? My heart dares to jump. Could the colonists abandon the underwater life and create a new one on land? My father holds out a hand.

"I see that look in your eyes. Don't get your hopes up. It would take a lot more than a loyalty serum to convince us to return. A loyalty serum could be enough to convince most colonists to never return. We don't have the resources to come charging out of the sea like a cleansing army. It doesn't work that way. And from what I have heard from the nomads, most citizens of New America despise colonists. I don't see how that would help us at all."

"They hate colonists because we abandoned them! But everyone I've met on the Burn gets over that pretty quick."

"Regardless, it's not in my power to simply command us all to migrate land-side."

"And it's also not in your power to at least help the people up there?"

Dad pinches the bridge of his nose. "We can't do anything, Terra. Not right away."

"There is no time. My friend Nell who came with me, she was under the effect of the loyalty serum, and it scared me to death. If they've made it work for one person, it won't take them long to get it to work for the whole population."

"Terra, the founders laid out rules and protocols for a reason, and I'm not going to disregard those at the first emergency that crops up."

"The first emergency? This is just one in a long string of emergencies. Have you heard anything about what the government is doing to its people? Did you hear anything I said about my time in the labor camp? Don't you understand? People are dying up there for this."

"And we're not to get involved without the consent of the council—not just this council, but the high council over all the colonies—and that takes time." Dad looks at me with narrowed eyes, and I'm reminded of the way he looked at me every time I failed at a vocation.

"Do I look like that same child to you? Do you think I'm still that same girl who left all those months ago? You think I'll be cowed just because you're glaring at me? I appreciate that you're in a tight spot right now, Dad, but it's not going to get any easier from here on out."

Dad's color is rising, and he makes a sound at the back of his throat like he's really trying to be civil, but it's not working out so well.

"You can talk with all the council members and spin in circles all you like. I'm leaving—going back to the Burn—" Dad's eyes nearly bug out of his head "—and doing something to help the people that you somehow feel no responsibility for."

Gaea sweeps away from me, and I jump to my feet. My chair falls over, and the clatter echoes around the room. Jack stands next to me, but he doesn't touch me. He lets me stand up to my father alone, to show him I don't need anyone else to do it. But I know he's there just an arm's length away, and I'm so grateful he's here with me especially with the eyes of all the council members on me, burrowing into my skin.

I stand as straight as I can and turn and leave the room.

NINETEEN

I sink to the floor. I'm not even sure where I am—a supply closet, maybe? As soon as I left the council chamber, I ran blindly down the corridors with Jack calling my name behind me. But I didn't slow down for him, not until my palm print opened a random door. When it closed behind me, all I could hear was my breath coming in gasps and my heart churning in my chest.

Now that I'm alone and it's dark and no one is watching, I cry. The feeling of being stared at like a specimen slowly fades, but not slowly enough. The looks of the council members remind me too much of the way the agents looked at me. I don't remember anyone ever looking at me that way before I left for the Burn. Did my time up there really make me so different from them? Can they not bear to think of me as one of them anymore? That I've somehow been tainted?

I lean back and find something soft to rest my head on. A mop, maybe. Right now I don't care if it's dirty. Knowing the hygiene protocols down here, it's probably as sterile as the medical area. I take a deep breath, and then there's a soft knock on the door. I fold my arms over my face.

"Go away," I say without even thinking. My fingers find the voice box. I sigh.

"Terra, can I come in?"

Jessa.

The door slides open and the light shines in my eyes. After I stop squinting at her, she smiles.

"How did you find me?"

"You don't know where you are?"

I shrug. "Supply closet. There's dozens of them around here."

She nudges me with the toe of her slipper. "Not just any supply closet. This is the same one you hid in after dad's big blow up the day you first asked him about the Burn."

"Really?" I look around. I remember that closet lurking over me like a huge mouth ready to swallow me. This supply closet just looks like a supply closet.

"I'm not surprised you found the same one. Jack told me what happened."

I'm all cried out and my eyes are too dry. I rub them hard. "I don't know why those people can't see past the ends of their noses."

Jessa laughs. "Well, for the evil witch—" I wonder if she means the shrew "—that would be pretty hard. Did you see how big her nose is?"

Oh, Jessa. I can't help but laugh, and Jessa smiles. Mission accomplished. She always knows just how to snap me out of it. She holds out a hand and helps me up.

We wander the corridors with no real direction and then take the transport to the vocational quarter. Our feet take one step and then another until we end up by the fields. I put a hand on the glass, and Jessa sits on the floor.

Jessa hugs her knees as she stares though the glass into the field. "We're seventeen, you know. I should be off with Brant right now, kissing on the Juice Deck. He's a good kisser, did you know that?"

I smirk. "Jess, how in the world would I know?"

"What? Oh, right. But that's why I decided to help you, to bring the sub every time."

I frown. "You bring the sub because Brant's a good kisser?"

She smiles, but there's no humor in it and her voice quavers when she speaks. "When you asked for a sub that first time, Mom told me what you were planning, so I went." I blink. When did Gaea become *Mom*? "And then I saw how you were helping, how what you were doing really mattered. I wanted that, too. I mean, sure growing food is important, but there are dozens of other people doing the same thing, and dozens more who could take my place. But what you were doing *mattered*. It changed lives, and you were the only one who could do it. I needed to help. I don't know why Dad couldn't see that."

"When did he find out you were taking the sub?"

"Not until I came back with your friends that first time. He flipped. First that I left without permission, second that I was going to the Burn, and third that there had to be someone else helping me, but I wouldn't tell him who. Terra, he almost had me turned in for illegal contact with the Burn. Me. His angel child."

224

She looks at her hands. I study the carefully manicured fingers and look at my own hands. The nails used to be rough and uneven, but now they're filed down just like hers.

I look in her eyes. They shine in the bright light. "He doesn't understand that we need to help because he doesn't want to see," I say. "That's a lot easier than dealing with the truth."

"All you asked the council for was some help."

I shake my head. "But to him—to them—it was so much more than that. If they agree to help, that would mean they admit that everything they ever told us was wrong."

"It's amazing how there is this whole world that exists that I didn't even know about."

"None of us did."

"That's not true, though. You listened to Mr. Klein. The rest of us heard it like it was a fairy tale, but you did something about it. You *knew*. I was happy just ignoring it." Her face scrunches up and finally a tear streaks down her cheek. She wipes it away and leans her head on her hands.

"But you're helping now."

"Sure. But am I doing enough?"

"It's never enough." I put my chin on my hands and look at the rows of strawberries. The field is empty, and I wonder why Dave isn't out there.

"I can't come with you to the Burn," Jessa says. "I can't do it. Piloting the sub, that's all I can do. I'm not brave like you."

I rest my head on her shoulder. "I never asked you to come with. You're doing more than I ever dreamed you would."

She laughs, and the sound is warped by tears. "I probably am, huh, when all I ever cared about before was dressing you up and coercing you to come to a dance with me."

My mind flashes back to a tall, gangly redhead boy. Funny how I haven't thought about him in months. Not since I started wandering with Jack. "Whatever happened to Matt anyway?"

Jessa shrugs. "Last I heard he transferred to another colony."

I stand up and brush off my pants and offer my hands to her. She grabs mine and stands up. We link arms and walk down the corridor. Funny how we never walked like this before I left. We're walking like old friends, equal partners, like sisters. Why didn't we do this before? I didn't love her any less back then.

"I feel like I'm finally starting to understand you, Terra." Jessa trails her other hand down the padded corridor wall. "I could never do what you're doing, but I finally get it."

Maybe that's the answer. She can look at me and not wonder *why?* anymore.

When we turn the corner, we almost run into Jack, and he's breathless.

"I've looked everywhere for you. Are you okay?"

I nod. "Jessa found me. Old hiding spot, I guess. I'm fine."

Jack swoops me into a hug and kisses me. "You were brilliant."

"I didn't feel brilliant."

"Maybe not, but you questioned them. From what your grandmother says, it's been a long time since anyone has. It's not something they're used to."

Jessa squeezes my hand. "I have to go back to work. We'll talk more tonight?"

I nod. "Thank you."

She beams. "Anytime." Then she disappears around a corridor corner.

"You missed her a lot while we were up there, didn't you?"

"Every day."

"You never told me about her until that night on the beach when the sub came, but I could tell there was something."

"She's the one thing that makes leaving hard."

"So when do we go back?"

That *we* in his sentence still thrills me, and I turn to him, wrap my arms around his neck, and kiss him hard.

We turn down the corridor to our living quarters. Jack's head is low to mine, and he's talking quickly, his hands moving with each word. We're going. Finally going. Gaea can point me in the direction of the government island, I'm sure, but once we're there, I don't know what I'm going to do. All I know is I've been down here in the cold water for too long. My muscles are aching to do *something*.

I look up and see a figure sitting on the floor, hunched against my door. His head hangs down between his shoulders, and his hands rake through his sandy blond hair. Dave looks up when he hears our footsteps. His face is pale and his eyes burn into mine.

"You're going back?" His voice shakes as he says it.

I nod and squeeze Jack's hand. "Why don't you go ahead. I'll be inside in a minute."

Jack pauses, sizing up Dave and his hands hanging uselessly off his knees. It doesn't take a doctor to know that Dave is sick, and not the kind that a bowl of chicken noodle soup can fix.

"Okay. Let me know if you need anything." He kisses my forehead and then holds his hand to be scanned and steps around Dave.

Dave stares at the floor until the door hisses closed. "Is Jack going with you?"

I slide down on the floor next to him. "Yes."

One corner of Dave's mouth turns up, but that half of his lips is the only part of his face that's smiling. "Of course he is. Mary would have done the same thing for me. I would have done the same thing for her." He turns his hands over and studies them. He closes them into fists so tight that his knuckles turn white. Then he stretches them open again.

"It's not your fault she died," I whisper.

He snorts. "Just like it's not your fault." He leans in. "But do you really believe that?"

I look at my own hands. "No. No, I don't."

He clamps down on my hands with one of his. "I need to go back with you."

I'm surprised at how strong his grip is. The way he's looked so withered down here, I expected something feebler from him. His eyes water as he looks at me. He's scaring me even more than when I saw him on the field.

"Why?"

His eyes are trained on mine, and the blue is icy in the fluorescent light. He doesn't answer me, and he doesn't need to. The hunger is looking back at me—the unnamed hunger I caught a glimpse of when I first talked to him on the field. Only the hunger has a name now. Revenge.

"I don't know, Dave." I pull back against his grip. "Can you let my hands go? You're hurting me."

He recoils and stares at his hand like it disgusts him. "I thought you would understand. After being in the camp and seeing what those people do, I thought you'd understand."

"I do understand why you want to go up there."

"There's nothing for me down here. Just meaningless jobs and the same people day in and day out who will never really know what it's like."

I shake my head. "Don't lie to me. Not now. Those are the same reasons I used when I left. That's not why you're leaving." I can see the blood in his eyes right now. The way he hungers for the blood of the agents and soldiers.

There's desperation in his voice. "I'm not lying, Terra, I—"

I hold my hand up. "I never said you couldn't come with us. Just that I know why you want to go, and I think it's a stupid reason."

He sits back against the wall like I've punched him. His voice is small. "You said you feel it too—the guilt. Every day."

"But that doesn't mean I'm going to the Burn to blow up every government official I come across. That's stupid."

"But you'll let me come?"

I let a breath out. "Yes. Jack's not going to like it. Don't think you're not as transparent to him as you are to me."

"He doesn't have to like it."

"You have to promise me something, though."

Dave looks up, and his eyes have finally overflowed. There's a trail of tears down his cheeks.

"You're not going to do anything reckless that puts Jack in danger."

Dave shakes his head.

"Promise me."

"I won't do anything to get you two in trouble. This is something I'll do by myself."

"What we're going up there to do is serious. We need to destroy the serum and give the people a chance to fight back. If you mess that up, I don't know what will happen to everyone up there." I lean my head back against the wall and watch one of the lights flicker in its fixture. I'm surprised there's not a maintenance crew tightening the blub right now. "Do you really think it will help?"

"What?"

"Hurting someone up there."

Dave looks startled. "Why wouldn't it?"

"You'll never find the soldier that pulled the trigger. Do you really think killing any number of them will help?"

Dave rakes his hands through his hair again. "Anything will make me feel better than I do now."

"Don't be so sure."

"Please just let me have this, Terra."

"We're leaving tomorrow." I stand up and go in my quarters. When I check the monitor an hour later, Dave is still sitting in the hall, his head in his hands.

TWENTY

"You told him he could come?" Jack's eyebrows are raised and his voice is incredulous.

Yes.

"He's going to get someone killed."

I know. That's the point.

Jack shakes his head. "I don't know if I can go along with it. Are you sure about this?" He puts another foil pouch of water in his pack.

Yes.

"I still don't think he should come."

I sigh and put down the emergency rations. We're in a large room lined with shelves of emergency supplies. Water, food, first-aid kits, clothes, fuel cells. We've been going through the supplies, deciding what to pack. The voice box sits silently next to my pack. When it's just me and Jack, I feel more like myself to communicate with him the way we always have—gestures, silent words, finger spellings.

He'll waste away here.

"That's probably true. But I know how you feel about everything else that's happened up till now. If anything happens to Dave up there, do you want to add that to your burden?"

It's my burden either way.

Jack stops my hand from sifting through flavors of energy bars. The foil package crinkles in my fist. I didn't realize I was squeezing it quite so tightly. I uncurl my fingers, and the bar falls to the floor.

"Dave's not the only one I worry about."

I turn my head. I look at the light above us and will myself to keep my throat from tightening.

"Ever since that meeting with the council, you've been different. I haven't been able to put my finger on it, but I can see you're planning something, Terra. I wish you would tell me. The way you kissed me after Jessa left us by the fields reminded me of something. It reminded me of that night I left for the colony and you kissed me while we were standing in the water." Jack looks down, and his face is puckered with the painful memory. "There aren't supposed to be any more secrets between us."

His words slice through my ribs right to my heart. No more secrets. He's right; I know he is. But there are some secrets that hurt more, aren't there? I close my eyes, and a traitor tear slips out. Jack's hand is still on my own, and his breath catches.

"Terra, what's wrong?"

I can't pull away from him. I feel like if he lets me go, I'll be blown away like a leaf in a storm and end up somewhere far, far away. I put my other hand to my face and lean against his chest. His arms wrap around me. I write the words on his sleeve.

I'm still going to stop the serum.

His face rests on my hair, and I feel his cheek turn up in a smile. "I know."

Don't know if I can come back from that.

"Because you don't want to or because they won't let you?"

Leave it to Jack to cut right to the heart of the matter.

Does it matter?

He pulls away and his eyes bore into mine. "It does to me."

The tears fall earnestly now, and once they've started, I find I don't want to stop them. *Sometimes I feel like giving myself up is the only way to make up for everything.*

"Like Mary's death?"

I nod. *And Dave. And everyone who's been punished because of me.*

"They made their choices, Terra, just like you made yours. Everyone needs to live with the consequences."

But no one should pay with their life.

"Tell that to the government. That wasn't you, Terra. It was them."

Some part of me knows he's right, but there's another part of me that feels like he's splitting hairs. Why do blame and guilt have to go along with every hard decision I've had to make?

"Just promise me something, Terra. You'll try your hardest to come back to me." He leans close so he's whispering in my ear, and his breath is hot. "I need you to come back to me. Do you hear me?"

I nod, and the tears fall even faster. He's one more person I'll feel guilty about if I don't come back. Can you even feel guilt after you die? I pull away and look at him—at the way his jaw flexes when he's being stubborn, at the flash of light in his eyes, at the freckles on his cheeks and nose, at the way his hair never wants to lay tamely. No, he's right. I don't want to leave him. I don't want to leave these arms around me, and his voice in my ear, and his kiss still warm on my cheek. I'm so torn between staying with what I love and doing what is right.

"I'm going to tell you again. I'm coming with you."

I laugh. *I never doubted.*

He smiles and puts a package of bandages in his pack. "Not since I first caught a glimpse of you. You looked like a drowned rat, by the way."

Thanks.

"Well, you did. Sleeping outside all night in the rain and all."

Once again, thanks.

He smiles. "My pleasure."

Our sub is scheduled to leave tomorrow morning at 0600. After our packs are ready, we slowly make our way down the corridors to our quarters. Kai, Madge, and Jane wanted to see us one last time, but I can't bring myself to do it. It's just like the first time I left the colony: the fewer the good-byes, the better. Jack and Jessa go to the Juice Deck with them, though, and now I'm sitting on the couch by myself.

The clang of pots and the whoosh of water into the sink comes from the kitchen. Gram is busy cleaning up. She wouldn't hear of me doing something as mundane as the dishes on my last night in the colony, and now all I can do is sit and stare at my hands. Finally the water shuts off, and Gram pokes her head out the door. She takes one look at me, throws her dishtowel down and starts rummaging through a box in a niche on the wall.

"It's in here somewhere," she murmurs.

I start to stand up—please give me something, anything to do—but Gram waves me down.

"I'll find it in a minute. You just wait right there. Aha!" She pulls a photo from the box, replaces all the other contents in a neat stack, and then sits down next to me.

It's a picture of me and Jessa with Gaea. No, that's not quite right. It's a picture of me and Jessa with our mother, the way she used to be. Her curly hair descends in shiny ringlets, and her green eyes are bright. Jessa and I are a few months old, and our gummy grins light up the whole picture. Her arms surround us and she holds us tightly to her, like there's nothing in the world more important. The picture breaks my heart.

"She loves you so much, you know. Leaving just about killed her."

I look up then, and my eyes sharpen.

Gram sighs and removes her glasses. "Yes, your mother and I remained in contact after she was gone. And no, your father never knew. The poor thing was desperate for news about you and your sister." Gram stops for a long moment.

I put a hand on her arm. There are so many questions I have for her. Why did it all happen—everything—is at the top of the list.

"She doesn't know how to be a mother now. In so many ways, her heart has broken and as it broke, everything else did too." Her eyes are wet when she looks up at me. "She also told me that you wanted to leave the colony. I knew you were leaving that night—the night of the dance."

She knew and didn't stop me. Suddenly my heart is full to bursting for her. I wrap my arms around her. Her shoulders shudder.

"I never understood, Terra. But I let you go because I love you. I raised you and your sister and then I had to let you go. I have to let you go now. I'm showing you this picture just so you know that she was the first one to ever let you go, and it's haunted her entire life. She's loved you more than you'll ever know. I don't agree with everything that's happened, but despite all that, she loves you. She's been so lonely for you, and she loves you. I don't know what you're going to do once you get back to the Burn, but I hope that knowing how many people down here love you might help you just a little."

I open her hand and touch the soft skin. *It does. Thank you.*

When I fall into bed after Jessa and Jack get back from the Juice Deck, I sleep better than I have in months.

0600 comes way too early.

I'm bleary eyed and stumbling as I make my way to the sub dock. Jack and Jessa walk on either side of me, and Dave lurks behind us. I don't look at him. His face is too stormy. My pack is slung over my shoulders, and Jack's fingers are woven with my own. Whenever we go somewhere together, we're touching. Part of me is afraid I'll lose him forever if I let go.

As we near the sub, a shadow separates from the wall, and Gaea steps into the corridor. I narrow my eyes to ask what she's doing here.

"I'm coming with you," she whispers.

Did you know? I ask Jessa.

She nods. "She asked me not to tell you. She thought you'd tell her to go back."

She's right. Why do I have to feel responsible for so many people?

"I'm just coming in the sub, Terra. I just want to be with you again."

Fine. That word sounds so much harsher than it is. I lower my eyes. Gaea puts out a hand as if she wants to touch me, but doesn't bridge the last few inches between us.

"Thank you. And I can help you. I have the coordinates for the government island."

The sub nudges the side of the dock, the rhythmic thumping beating along with my heart. The hatch is open, and the sub techs scurry about making sure the oxygen levels are adjusted and the computer systems are working.

I take a deep breath. This is it. I'm going back and I'm going to do something. No more trickling the nomads down to the colonies—that would have never solved anything. Now I'm going to destroy the serum. My resolution solidifies and helps ease the knot in my stomach. I'm doing something, I repeat to myself.

Jessa, Jack, and Dave go down the hatch, and I'm left on the platform with Gaea, my hands holding the straps of my pack. I close my eyes and breathe. I'm stepping into the hatch when he calls me.

"Terra?"

My father.

His voice is uncertain, filled with the doubt that has pulled us apart more times than I can count. I turn back to him.

"Teresa," he says.

My mother nods and then she turns and goes down the hatch.

I raise my hands to ask, *What?*

His eyes find mine for a moment and then he drops them to the floor. He looks different, and it takes me a second to realize why. He's not wearing his speaker's sash. Could he really be coming to me just as my father?

"Terra, I . . ." He doesn't say anything more.

I cross my arms.

"I resigned as Speaker. The elections will be next week."

That startles me. Being speaker was the most important thing in his life. Then I notice he's holding a drive case in one hand. I point to it.

He looks at it like it could reach out and bite him. Then he sighs, long and drawn-out. "I should have done this the second you asked me for help. I should have said yes as soon as I saw you. There are so many things I should have done." He runs his hand over his face, and I notice how tired his eyes are.

What is it?

He holds it out to me. "One of the security techs put this together for me. A special request and thankfully he didn't ask too many questions. It's part of why I resigned. As speaker, I never could have condoned this action. But as your father—something I should have been more concerned about from the beginning—there was never a question. I tried to see if we could establish a link to their servers remotely, but it can't be done. The code on this drive will hack in. If you can install this on their main server, we can link to it, and then we can wipe out all their data."

I raise an eyebrow and shake my head. Sure that would be an inconvenience, but it wouldn't be the end of the regime, right? I'm ready to wave off this offering that feels like too little too late, but my father speaks.

"We can destroy all their data about the serum."

Tears prick my eyes and my throat is thick. Finally, after all this time, my dad is helping me. I swing my legs out of the hatch and throw my arms around him. His hands hesitate in the air, but then he presses them against my back and hugs me more tightly than he ever has before.

"I'm sorry. I'll spend the rest of my life saying I'm sorry."

He leans his head against mine, and I close my eyes. This is what it should have been like the past seventeen years. This is what it should have felt like to have a father.

"This isn't enough—I know it's not—but it's all I could do with such little time. I don't know exactly what their technology is like to know how you'll install it." Dad smiles ruefully. "I'll leave that to your ingenuity."

I smile at him—maybe the first genuine smile I've offered him in years—and he puts a hand on my cheek. Worry knits his brow and his lips turn down.

"Please be careful. What I'm giving you is so dangerous that I don't know why I'm even doing it. They won't forgive this. You know that, right?"

I nod, turning the small device over in my hands. This small scrap of metal and plastic might just save all of the citizens of New America. I will never be forgiven if the government finds me.

Dad holds me for a moment more before his hands let me go and he steps back. His eyes are wet, but he doesn't turn away.

"I love you, Terra."

I love you too, I mouth. It's true.

TWENTY-ONE

Jessa is masterful at maneuvering the sub. We've all been raised doing it, so I'm not too shabby, but she glides smooth as silk from the sub dock and away from the colony. The lights burn brightly, cutting through the dark water. I'm trained on them until they're no more than pinpricks and then they're gone, swallowed up in blackness as if they were never there at all.

Leaving the colony the first time was terrifying but liberating. I left everything I had ever known and loved, but I escaped the monotony and the life that felt like a prison to me. All for a whim, a fleeting dream. Now I'm leaving the colony with the drive clutched in my fist and a seed of dread planted in my heart because I know what I need to do and I know what the consequences will be if I'm discovered.

Jack sits beside me but says nothing. There's nothing more to say. I don't know if I'll ever come back again.

I could have refused the drive. I could have told my father no. But that would mean abandoning the citizens of New America—people who have become my friends, people who I love—to the government that wants nothing more than to have absolute control over their lives. There never really was a choice for me. I had known it the second my father offered his last gift. This chance to free them is something only I can offer them. I just hope they'll use this chance to break free. Erasing the data of the serum won't erase the serum from their lives forever. There are scientists who will recreate it, but if the people—my people—fight back first, the serum will never take control of them again.

Jessa's fingers run over the control panel, entering coordinates and programs for the sub to follow as it slips through the Pacific Ocean for the government island.

I turn away from the window. It's been ten minutes since the lights of the colony faded, and my eyes are dry from straining through the darkness. I'm ready to stand. I need to move my legs, I need to pace, I need to keep my brain away from the drive in my hand, but Jack tucks me against his side.

"You're amazing," he whispers, kissing my forehead.

I don't feel amazing right now. There's a pit starting to gnaw at my stomach, and its root is what I know I have to do in a matter of days.

"I'm coming with you. All the way to the end." He takes my hand and uncurls my fingers from the drive.

I take his other hand. *Remember what you said after I left the settlement?*

He smiles. "I'll go with you. I may not be what you're looking for right now, but you'll need a friend. I'll come with you."

Word for word.

"I'll never forget it. Because that wasn't what I really wanted to say."

What?

"Don't worry, I meant every word of that." He strokes his fingers down each one of mine and turns my hand over and over in his, like he's memorizing every line. "I just couldn't say the whole truth. You would have kept running from me."

The pit is gnawing, but I can't help smiling in spite of it. *What did you want to say?*

"I'd follow you anywhere."

I look at his face, and he stares back earnestly. I shake my head and take his hand to write on it, but he stops me.

"That's the whole truth. That's what I've tried to show you. And I'll follow you to the end of this." He nods at the drive. "So don't try to talk me out of it. I know you'll try. I know you, Terra. But it won't work, because I'm coming with you. Do you understand me?"

I look at his hands that have healed me in so many ways. His hands are strong and gentle. They should never be used for this kind of work. A part of me wishes he would stay as far away from me as he could. Where I'm going there's nothing but blood. But there's another part of me—the selfish part—that won't let him out of my sight again.

I understand.

I feel eyes on me, and I look up to find Dave staring at us with a longing look on his face. I clear my throat. I can see it in his eyes—he's thinking about Mary, and it's probably killing him to watch us be like this when he should be the same way with her. I train my eyes on my hands until I feel his gaze finally relent.

Jessa gets the sub on course and then pulls out our breakfast rations and sits with us.

"Two days," she says between mouthfuls of oatmeal.

I close my eyes. Two days. It's such a short amount of time.

"Want to play checkers?"

I laugh, but then see she's serious.

"I brought Dad's old set. Remember how we used to play when we were little?"

You made up the rules.

"And I won every time."

Let's play.

So we pass the next two days talking and playing games. Gaea sits on the periphery, not saying anything, but always there, just where I can feel her presence. I feel like we're all making up for lost time—for the days we spent not understanding each other. It's refreshing to be completely myself with everyone here.

The guidance system beeps at us.

"Destination is five miles away."

Jessa flips on the view screen, and we get a glimpse of the government island looming on the water. Island is a little generous. Island implies trees and sand and bugs and life in general. This is nothing more than an oversized barge with office space—even from this distance it puts a shiver through me with its cold looming. It still looks imposing, though, as it cuts a jagged shape on the horizon. The government was smart about this. There's no way any citizens could mount a decent attack, and the barge can sail anywhere along the coast it wants to.

"Destination is four miles away."

I look over Jessa's shoulder. The lowest access doors are along a corridor ten feet above the water. There are more levels above that, and the barge is topped with several turrets. I can see the faint shapes of soldiers in them, and mounted guns aim away from us.

"Destination is three miles away."

I want to turn the blasted computer off. I know how far we are, and I don't need a reminder. I squeeze the drive that's burning a hole in my pocket. It's such a little thing; how can it scare me so badly?

"Destination is two miles away."

We're too far away for them to see, and they're looking in the wrong direction anyway. They scan the coast—not the water—for threats.

Jessa stares at the barge on the view screen, her mouth hanging open. "Are you sure about this?"

No.

Jessa grips my arm and turns to me. Her eyes are wide and panicked. "Then don't do it. I know why you want to, and I understand that. But there are other ways you can help. Other things you can do. I feel like if you leave this sub I'm never going to see you again."

"Destination is one mile away."

I gently pry her hand off my arm. I have a rock in my gut, and Jessa's words aren't helping at all. I have to peel her hand open to write on the palm.

If I don't go now, I never will. I need to do this.

She turns her head and a hand sweeps in front of her cheeks. She puts it back down on the controls, and her fingers are wet.

"Then please just be careful. Promise me."

My eyes flick back at the screen—at the image of the hulking metal on the ocean. The knot in my stomach tightens.

Promise.

The beeping stops and the sub slows to a crawl. Jessa drops her head in her hands for a moment and then pulls her hair away from her face. "Okay, here's what we're going to do. It looks like this side of the island—" she points to the far side "—isn't as well guarded. They're not expecting someone to come from below the water. I'll let you out there. It looks like this door may put you in the right direction."

Dave scoots in closer, studying the screen with a feverish intensity. I want to ease him back, but I know I'll never be able to. He's here for one purpose alone. He wants blood to avenge the stains he still carries from Mary's death. Jack, though, is determined to keep him in check. He claps a hand on Dave's shoulder.

"Come on, Dave. Let's grab our packs."

Dave shrugs him off. "We need packs? It's not like we're going camping."

Jack hesitates, his hands hovering in the air, unsure whether to bring Dave with him or let him go.

"He's right," Gaea says. "No matter what happens in there, you're not staying long. And if they do capture you, your packs will only raise more questions."

"About the colonies, you mean?" Jack says.

Gaea nods. "After what happened to Terra in the labor camp, I don't believe it would be prudent to give them any more clues about the colonies."

Jack raises his hands. "Fine. Just ourselves then."

Dave shakes his head. "We'll get some guns from the first soldiers we come across."

I close my eyes and try to stop a shudder. Not more guns.

"Don't worry, Terra," Jack says. "You don't have to use one."

Gaea hands me a knife instead. It's like the knife she gave me when I first left for the Burn. Her fingers are tremulous as I pull the sheath from them.

"I'm proud of you." Her eyes shine as they look at me full on. They're blazing and honest, and she's not hiding anything from me now. "I don't know if you can ever forgive me, but I'm proud of what you've done and what you're doing now. You're my brave, selfless girl. I wish I were more like you."

She reaches out her hand to a lock of my hair that's fallen toward my eyes. She silently asks my permission, a begging look in her face. I nod. She caresses the hair back and her breath hitches. She's waited years to touch me like this. All the gentle touches a mother should share with her daughter were forfeited the day she left, and I can tell she's been starved for them. She closes her eyes.

"Thank you," she whispers. She turns from me and tucks her arm against her side before I can say anything or touch her hand in passing. She whisks away to the opposite end of the sub. I'm surprised at the sudden ache in my heart. My throat is thick and I try to clear it. People are all around me, but I feel so alone right now as I watch the mother I should have had disappear out of my reach. I want to say something—anything—but the voice box is back in the colony.

I croak.

Gaea looks up.

Thank you, I mouth.

She smiles at me. I can tell from the serenity that washes over her that my gratitude is more than she ever hoped for.

TWENTY-TWO

When the hatch opens, we're as low as Jessa can get us in the water without swamping the sub. Still, water sloshes in as we bump against the side of the barge.

"Careful!" Dave hisses to her.

Her teeth are gritted as she moves her fingers along the controls. "I'm working on it. Do you want to have a go at it?"

"You bang a drum too long and someone's going to come looking."

"That's enough," Jack says, looking up the hatch at the circle of daylight above us. "Jessa's doing her best. Let's get out of here."

Dave scurries up the ladder before I can even blink. Jack shakes his head.

"It was a mistake bringing him. He's going to get one of us killed."

I nod. *I couldn't stop him.*

"I know. He needed to come. Whatever comes from it, he needed to. I just hope we don't have more blood on our hands after this."

I gaze at the circle of light above me until dark spots float before my eyes. Where did Dave go? Before I even step onto the first ladder rung, I hear a muffled cry, the thud of a punch landing, and a grunt.

"Not yet," Jack mutters as he flies up the ladder.

I follow behind him and when I peer over the lip of the hatch, a soldier lies sprawled out on the walkway. Dave stands over him, shaking his hand out. There's a glint in his eye that terrifies me.

"That one hurt," he says. His voice twitches at the end, like he's fighting to keep it under a whisper.

Jack takes a small step toward him. "Are you okay?"

Dave smiles, but his lips look like they're stretched too tight. "I'm starting to be."

Dave leans over the soldier and pulls the gun from his hands. Jack motions for it.

"Do you want me to take it?"

Dave shakes his head. "Why would I want you to do that?"

Jack looks at me sideways, and I know what he's thinking. Dave is walking a very thin line here, and everything is about ready to slip out from under him. Only we're the ones who can see it; Dave has no clue.

"No reason," Jack says.

"Well then, let's go." Dave motions for the door a few yards down.

We've come off the sub onto a narrow walkway with a railing. The sub slides beneath the water. Jessa will be waiting for us. I hope she doesn't have to wait too long.

I peer down the walkway. This side of the barge is quiet. I look up along the metal face and squint. At the very top I can make out the back of another soldier who's facing landward. He's the only person I see. A shriek nearly sends me out of my skin, and I whip around. Just a gull hovering in the breeze. Nothing but this barge and a few sea birds for miles. I have to hand it to the government—they know how to protect themselves. They're either very smart or just very cowardly. Maybe a bit of both.

There are portholes in the wall, and we creep along with hunched backs as we make for the door. The gray paint is peeling and rust eats at the metal underneath. A layer of crusted sea salt ices the wall. Dave puts a hand on the door, and when voices float down to us, he instantly bristles.

"What about the camp in Washington? What about the escape there?"

"Not my concern. Besides, that was months ago."

"That was the first in this long string. There hadn't been any attempt for over ten years, and then suddenly they're popping up everywhere. You think that's a coincidence?"

"And what if it is?"

"You'd better hope it isn't related."

"It doesn't matter because we're almost there. Just a few more tests and there won't be anyone left to fight." The voice laughs—a squeaky sound that reminds me of wet shoes on tile—and then clears his throat.

"I thought that was confidential."

"Then how come everyone already knows?"

"Hey, what's that?"

We press ourselves against the wall. I can barely make two heads craning out over the wall above us.

"What?"

One of them points to the water. "That right there."

My heart stops. Does he see the sub? Go lower, I think. Before they see you.

"Dunno. Could be some garbage. Could be a fish. I don't know."

"Should we report it?"

"And what? Have one of *them* yell at us for a false alarm? No thanks."

Huh. Could it be the soldiers hate the agents too? Maybe not as much as we do, but do they dislike them nonetheless?

"Ignore it. It'll probably be gone in a minute."

"Whatever."

Then their heads disappear back over the wall and their voices fade away on the wind.

Jack squeezes my hand. "You were right to come as soon as we did. It sounds like they almost have the serum ready."

"Just hope that little drive from your dad is all it's cracked up to be." Dave's fingers tighten over the gun. His jaw clenches. "Ready?"

I nod. As ready as I'll ever be, which is not very. I put my hand over my pocket and feel the small square that my father promised would help. Please let it help.

Dave creeps to the door and taps on it. I hold my breath, expecting it to swing open and see soldiers pour out of it, but nothing happens. The water laps against the barge and the gulls cry, but everything else is calm.

"No one's home." Dave grabs the handle and slowly pries the door open.

Jack's hand finds mine again as Dave steps into the darkness of the doorway. My heart clenches.

"Dave?" Jack whispers. Nothing.

I look back and Jack shakes his head.

"Dave?"

Then Dave's head pops out of the doorway. "We're in luck. No one's around."

I let my breath out and I step over the threshold. The room is littered in junk: papers tossed in the corners, old folding chairs strewn in heaps, and the acrid smell of gasoline twists my nose.

Dave shoves a box out of the way with the toe of his boot. "A bunch of slobs, aren't they?"

Jack puts his hand on the back of his neck. "You would think the government would take a little better care of itself."

"Could just be a junk room. Everybody needs a place to dump their old stuff."

I signal Jack over and take his hand. *Why not reclamation?*

He glances from pile to pile and his expression is puzzled. "I don't know. The whole barge seems kind of dingy and run-down."

Dave shrugs. "Could just be for show. It looks pathetic, so why would anyone think twice about it?"

My brain is processing the clues—the need for a loyalty serum, the barge that is the capital of the tyrannical government but looks like it could fall to pieces if a wave hit it just right, the deprivation forced on the citizens.

I look into Jack's eyes just as he figures it out too.

"They need the loyalty serum because they're about ready to fall."

I nod. *Can't sustain themselves.*

"Right. So they need the people for their slave labor."

"So who's in charge of this upside-down regime?" Dave asks, stepping over a crate on his way to the door at the other side of the room.

"A president. That's all we've heard."

I nod. There are agents and soldiers and people like Dr. Benedict, but the only thing I've heard about this president has been the few whispers and rumors—and no one seems to like her.

"Doesn't matter now," Dave says as he peers through the small window on the door. The light on the other side flickers.

"Is anyone out there?" Jack says.

Dave cranes his head to peer down the hall. "Can't see anyone."

"The lights keep shutting off. Do you think that's normal?"

Dave laughs. "It is if they can't pay the power bill."

But I don't feel like laughing. I feel sick. The mildewy smell and the dust and the humidity are all pressing down on me, and I want to get this over with.

Dave checks the window one more time then spins the wheel and opens the door. We stand on either side, but there are no footsteps and no shouts. We all peek through.

Metal corridors streaked with rust stretch out before us, the smell of seawater and old food is even stronger, and the lights burn for another moment then flick off again. The sunlight from the outside door sends a long sliver down the hall, and we follow it to a corridor. When the lights flick on again, I have stars in my eyes.

"Maybe they have most of the power going to the parts of the barge they use most," Jack says, peering through the small windows as he passes each door. "There's no one in any of these rooms. They all look like they're used for storage."

Maybe further up? I write. I point upward for Dave's sake.

"Could be. That's where all the soldiers were."

"Where are the stairs?" Jack asks.

"Got to be around here somewhere." Dave opens a door. "Keep looking."

We check every door and finally find one marked *Stairs*. Jack and Dave have to both put their full weight against it to get it to open. It opens with a snarling creak, and I freeze, expecting to have soldiers flying out from every nook and cranny. But once again, they never come.

"How far up?" Jack asks as we enter the stairwell. White stairs and white railings spiral around above us as far as I can see.

The main server is probably heavily guarded.

Dave nods. "We go wherever the soldiers are thickest."

Jack regards him. "That would be convenient for you with this death mission you're on. But if Terra and I just go storming through, we'll both be killed and then where will we be? That drive from her father won't be much good then, will it?"

Dave shrugs. "I never said I was in it for the serum."

Jack shakes his head. "What happened to you? You used to care about so much more than just yourself."

Dave's eyes blaze at him. "Don't ever ask me that again." He thunders up the stairs.

"This was a mistake," Jack murmurs as he follows after. I feel it in my gut, too. Dave is a cannonball, and in just a matter of time, he's going to come crashing down.

We race after him, and I take two steps at a time, but it's barely enough. He skims above the stairs, his footsteps echoing on the metal steps and the gun swinging back and forth in front of him. I don't even have time to blink before we're up four levels, the door onto the landing opens, and two soldiers step through.

Dave charges at them, crunching the butt of the gun into one of their faces and roaring savagely at the other. He doesn't even get his gun raised before Dave tackles him and pummels him in the face. After five blows, he stops moving. We reach the landing and Jack grabs Dave's shirt to pull him off the soldier. Dave rips away.

"Don't touch me!" he hisses. Then he's gone through the open door.

Do we follow?

"I don't know if we have a choice." Jack cranes his neck and peers down the corridor. "This might be the right place."

Jack takes a gun from one of the soldiers and hefts it to his shoulder, and he's just about to lead us from the stairwell when he pauses and turns back.

"Wait." He eyes the soldiers. "That one looks small enough for you to manage. Let's put on their gear."

We strip their uniforms and masks off. The smaller one is still three sizes too big, but if I roll the sleeves and stuff the extra into my boots, it might pass if no one looks too closely. But who am I kidding? No one's going to believe that I'm a soldier. I'm too small.

I'm pulling the mask over my head when the *pop pop pop* of shots fired echoes down the corridor. I grab Jack's arm. Not Dave, I tell myself. Please not Dave. We race down the hall. I gasp when we come to the first intersection.

Four soldiers lie dead on the floor. The mask of one of them is cracked down the center, and the other three are riddled with bullet holes. I look over. All I see is the mask of a soldier staring back at me, and even though I know Jack is in there, it gives me chills.

"Let's go." His voice is grim.

We follow the path of carnage down the hall and to a short flight of stairs. At the top a sign on the wall points to the Kitchen and Dining Hall to the left and the Command Center to the right.

Command Center?

"Looks promising. Even if the main server isn't there, it should be close."

Down the right hallway, another soldier lies face down. *Dave came this way.*

"He doesn't care about the serum, but he's certainly clearing a path for us." Jack shakes his head.

We follow the corridor and are about to turn down another path when there's a scream that's suddenly cut off. Dave. I race ahead.

"Terra! Come back!"

I ignore Jack and try to run faster, but the extra weight of the soldier's uniform makes my legs sluggish. I'm about to race around a corner, when the stamp of boots cuts me off. Two soldiers trot around the corner. I stop and do my best to stand at attention and look taller. Jack skids to a halt beside me.

"We just found a nomad on board."

I nod. I hope they don't expect me to say anything.

"His body is outside the server room." I try not to cry. If he's just a body, he's dead. "We're going to report to command. Watch this area and make sure there are no others."

"Yes, sir." Jack says as he turns on his heel and turns the corner. I follow him.

Dave slumps against the wall, the gun on the other side of the corridor, and his hands limp on his lap. I race to him. His chest rises and falls. He's still alive, but judging by the pool of blood spreading out to his right, he won't be for much longer.

I fall to his side, and he cringes away from me. His face is ashen and he can barely open his eyes. I rip off the mask, and when he sees me, his shoulders slump again.

"You know, I don't feel any better," he gasps out. I put a hand over his mouth.

Just then a yellow light above our heads starts flashing and an alarm sounds.

"There's going to be a search now," Jack says. "If they thought one nomad was on board, they're going to look for others. We don't have much time."

"I found the server room for you," Dave whispers, as the hints of a smile appear. "I do feel better about that." He reaches for my face, and his fingers barely skim my cheek.

I close my eyes. I remember the first time he touched me. It seems like ages ago. Now I feel so sad for him that my heart just might break. Then his fingers fall away from my skin, I open my eyes, and his eyes are closed and his chest is still. My head falls.

Then there's the click of a gun ready to fire.

"Don't move."

I look up, and a soldier stands at the end of the corridor, and he and Jack stand square, their guns trained at each other. Just to my right is the door to the server room, and it's been wedged open. I smile through the tears that I can't let fall yet. Dave did help us, after all. Jack half-steps back and catches my eye. I nod without taking my eyes off the soldier.

"Don't move!" he yells, and then we dive through the open door.

Jack yanks away the gun that propped open the door and it creaks closed behind us. I whip my head around. The room is full of blinking machines, computers, and monitors. Which one do I use?

Jack pulls his mask off and stalks down the aisles until he finds a computer at the end. "Try this one."

I'm at his side in a flash and dig under the soldier's uniform to find the drive in my pocket. I insert the drive into the port and look at the display. The words *Upload File?* appear on the screen. I press *Yes*. Impossibly slow, a progress bar begins filling from left to right. I tap the computer with the side of my thumb, slowly at first, then faster and faster. This is taking too long. Jack puts a hand on my shoulder and squeezes gently. I give him an apologetic smile when there's a crash against the door and a muffled shout.

I whirl around and see a face pressed up against the glass. The soldier stands there, his mask hiding the eyes I'm sure that grow wide at the sight of us. Then he disappears. Another crash against the door sounds.

"I don't know how long it will hold," Jack whispers.

Long enough. The upload is halfway done.

Then I hear the *rat-tat-tat* of the soldier's gun, and my hands fly to my face as bullets pepper the door handle. The sound of shots ring through the facility and pound into my brain, leaving my ears humming. Jack and I drop to the floor. The door swings open, creaking on its rusty hinges, and the soldier creeps in, his rifle to his shoulder, his sight down the barrel as he peers around the room. Jack and I huddle closer to the floor. His breath stops as we watch below the desks and see the soldier's feet step closer.

Jack crawls two feet from me, cringing as his knees scuff, scuff against the floor. The soldier whips around. Jack hides beneath a desk and waves me to another one. I curl myself tight as a moth in a cocoon. The soldier's boots scrape on the metal floor, and he steps down the aisle of desks we had just been crouched in. My lungs ache from holding my breath.

The soldier steps next to me. I can see his shadow. He's turning side-to-side, surveying the room along the barrel of his gun, ready to fire. He walks right by me, and I'm sure my heart is hammering so loudly that he could hear it if he knew what to listen for. He walks right by the computer and doesn't even look at the progress bar that shows three-quarters done.

Then the computer lets out a slow, steady pulse. I look up. *Thirty more seconds until upload complete.*

A lot can happen in thirty seconds.

It takes one second for the soldier to whirl back toward the computer and curse. Then another second for him to grab his walkie-talkie.

"Don't know what's going on in here, sir. They're doing something to the computer."

"Can you tell what?"

"They're uploading something, sir. Not sure what."

"Are they logged in to the server?"

"No idea, sir."

"Well get over to the computer and figure it out."

"Yes, sir."

The walkie-talkie hisses as he thumps past me, and he slings his rifle over his shoulder and bends down over the computer. His hands hover uselessly over the keyboard and he taps a random key.

Nothing happens.

I finally let my breath go, and it whooshes out of me. I close my eyes and clap a hand over my mouth.

Then the soldier sees the drive and lowers his hand to grab it.

Jack is past me in a blur. Despite all our months of running the woods together, I had no idea he could move so fast.

He grapples the soldier around the waist, wrenching him away from the computer console. The soldier grabs for his gun, but it swings out of his reach. His elbow finds Jack's ribs, and Jack whistles a sharp breath and clenches his teeth, and I'm out from under the desk too, scrabbling along the ground in my too-big uniform until I can grab the soldier's feet and the three of us fall to the floor with a clang. My elbows hit and the soldier's heavy boots come down hard on my right leg, and I feel the tears spring to my eyes, but there's no time to think about all that now. I'm grabbing at his mask, his sleeves, the strap of his gun—anything I can get my hands on to keep him away from the computer and the drive.

Ten more seconds until upload complete.

The soldier is big and powerful. He rips himself free from both of us and lurches toward the computer. I dig into his left boot and throw my body to the side, twisting his ankle until he screams. He shakes his leg, trying to get rid of me, but I cling to him. He takes another tripping step toward the console. Jack grabs his arm and pulls him back. The soldier takes another step. He's almost to the computer. I seize his leg in both hands, finding the spot where there is no armor on the back of his knee. I sink my teeth into his pants, biting until I feel the flesh beneath the fabric.

The soldier yells. Jack shouts something back at me, but the blood pulses in my ears so loudly that I can't understand either one of them. I don't understand that Jack is saying the word "Knife!" until I see the sharp metal point flashing in the soldier's hand. The world shudders to a halt around me as the blade slices into my shirt and then my skin. I gasp.

"Terra!"

I understand perfectly what Jack is saying.

I also understand that the computer is no longer beeping. The soldier stumbles off of me and curses, pounding at the keyboard.

Upload complete.

Jack roars. I've never heard such a savage sound come from him. He picks up the soldier's gun—it must have come off him at some point during the fight—and, holding it by the barrel, cracks it against the soldier's helmet as hard as he can. The soldier sways for a moment and then falls to the floor. Then Jack scrambles toward me, and there's fear and desperation written so clearly on his face, I blink. Why is he so scared? We did it. We uploaded my father's program. Right now, my father should be miles below the ocean, working with the tech crew to set up the link to the server. If it works, then we will have given the citizens of New America a fighting chance. I watch the screens, waiting to see if something happens, but Jack steps into my line of sight.

"Oh, Terra."

I look around him just in time to see all the monitors go black. I smile. We did it. I turn back to Jack, expecting to see his exultant face, but instead his hands flutter over me, and I find that for some reason I have no more strength. As I collapse back into his arms, the knife twists inside of me. Oh, the knife.

"Try not to move."

Jack is using his doctor's voice—the calm but determined voice he always uses when tending to someone. But his voice is a shade different this time. It's tremulous.

His hands stroke the air over me, and I've never seen him more uncertain. Finally he brings his fingers down close to where the knife juts out. I glance at it once and see the blood well up around the steel. I look away.

"Just look at me, Terra." Jack's gentle hands find my cheek and turn my face to his. His eyes are dewy and wide, but his gaze doesn't falter. "Just always look at me. I have to get you out of here."

I nod. If he gets me away from here, if he can get me to the sub, then we'll both be okay. Jack yanks off his jacket and carefully wraps it around the knife and my torso.

The soldier's walkie-talkie crackles. "Report on the computer."

The soldier's unconscious body lies in a heap. If he doesn't answer, more will descend on us in a matter of moments.

"Lieutenant are you there? Report."

"Let's go," Jack says. He helps me wrap my arm around his neck, and then he carefully puts his arms behind my back and under my knees. The knife bites at me and I whistle a breath.

"I'm sorry, Terra. I'm so sorry. This is going to hurt. Just be brave for me. One last time."

I nod and grit my teeth as he hefts me up. The pain radiates from my ribs, touching every nerve and setting my body ablaze. Jack stumbles between the desks and over the soldier's body, but he makes it to the door. He steps past Dave's body, and I clench my eyes closed. Then he turns down the corridor the way we came. In the distance, I hear shouting and the thump of footsteps against metal. They're coming for us—I'm not sure where they are, but they're coming and we have to hurry. I cling more tightly to Jack's neck.

"I know. I just can't go too quickly or I'll make it worse."

I don't have to ask what will be worse, and I'm glad he doesn't say it. If he had said "It'll make your probably fatal knife wound worse," I would have made him drop me on the spot and run for the sub alone. Then I would know he'd be able to get away. We're too slow together, but I'm grateful he holds me to him. With my head resting against his chest, I can hear his heart beating out the rhythm that drives his legs and will get us out of here.

We turn a corner and sunlight pierces the dim corridor.

"Almost there," Jack pants, sidestepping the debris and crates littering the storage room. He pokes his head through the door to the outside and peers left and right, but there's no one. Of course there's no one. They're all headed to the server room where they think we still are. This half-forgotten part of the barge will stay that way. Half-forgotten. At least something can make me smile over the throbbing in my ribs.

The sub lurks at the side of the barge. An inch or two of water covers the hatch, and Jack steps to the very edge and stomps on the top of the hatch. His fingers tighten around me, and he doesn't dare to let me go. Thank heaven for that. He's holding me together again, the way he always has.

The sub rises up and the water drains off. After a moment the hatch hisses and then swings open. Jessa takes one look at Jack holding me and all the color fades from her cheeks.

"Oh no."

"Help me get her down. Carefully."

Jessa reaches for me, trailing her hands along my arms as she tries to shift me into position to lower me down the hatch. Her hands are so warm, almost fiery. I don't remember her ever feeling quite that way. Am I really so cold?

"Terra, can you hear me?"

I think I'm nodding to her but my head feels heavy, and the worry in her eyes haunts her face.

"Mom!" she shouts. I hear footsteps below. "Please hold on for another minute. The sub is equipped with a med kit. Just hang on and Jack will patch you up in no time." She squeezes my hand so hard I flinch.

Of course. I can hang on for another minute. What's a mere sixty seconds?

Jack grips me under my armpits and lowers me down while Jessa guides my legs. Shouts rain down on us. I guess that half-forgotten part of the barge was remembered after all. Then guns fire and the water bubbles around the sub.

I gurgle at them. Who cares about me? If anything happens to Jack or Jessa, I'll never forgive myself. They should never have come on this errand.

"Hurry," Jessa says, her voice desperate.

"As fast as I can. I can't risk hurting her more."

Then Jack has to let go of me and Jessa supports all my weight down the last two rungs of the ladder, and I scream as I fall into her and the knife twists in my side. I feel warm liquid splash onto me, and I think it's just more blood until I open my eyes and see that Jessa is crying freely and she's trying to stop, but she can't.

"I'm sorry," she says, covering her mouth with her hand.

Then Jack jumps down next to us and cradles my head in his hands. "Where's the med kit?"

"Here." Gaea kneels down and opens the kit, pulling bandages and sutures and antiseptic out into neat piles.

Jessa races away. "I need to put the sub down before those idiots blow a hole in the hull."

"Hurry."

The sub vibrates underneath me and I hear the splash as it slips beneath the water. A few taps echo in my ears, but we're too far below the surface for the bullets to harm us now.

The tap of Jessa's feet along the floor reaches me, and I feel like the sub—too far below the surface, and all the sounds around me are dull and waterlogged.

Jessa kneels beside Gaea.

"Hold her head," Jack says.

Jessa moves my head onto her lap so carefully her hands feel like butterfly wings. Gaea hands Jack scissors, and his tired eyes follow the line of the soldier's uniform. I try to keep my eyes focused on him, to think about anything else but the pain in my stomach that has the weird tendency to fade to almost nothing and then coming ripping back at me. Why would it do that? My eyelids are leaden, but I use all I have to keep them open.

Then Jack removes the jacket from my side and snips through my shirt to expose the wound. When he pulls away, the scissors shake in his hand.

"Oh, Terra."

"What?" Jessa's voice cracks on the word. "Why did you say it like that?"

Jack flings the scissors away and rakes a hand through his hair. "I just . . . . I don't know if . . ."

Jessa grabs his arm. "Stop it," she hisses. "Don't say anything like that again. Help her. You understand me? Help her."

Jack's eyes are rimmed red and he wipes the back of his hand across his nose, but he nods. "Okay." He touches his palm to the side of my face. "I need to take the knife out, Terra."

He's telling me with his hand, his eyes, and his face that this will hurt. But it couldn't be worse than going in, right? I try to nod, but my chin just quivers.

"I'll need your help, Gaea. Take that compress. As soon as the knife is out, you press down with that on her as hard as you can. Even if the blood soaks it through, you keep pressing."

I hear her breath catch, but Gaea nods.

Jack leans over me and kisses my forehead. "I love you, Terra."

I close my eyes. When Jack's hand grips the knife, the flames come roaring back as the pain sears through me. Then it slides free. I want to gasp but my body won't let me; at the same time I feel so much freer without that steel wedged into me. Then Gaea clamps down on me with the compress and it feels like my ribs are going to crack. I moan. Jessa is crying again.

"Are we going home?" Jack asks. His voice is hoarse and dry.

Jessa doesn't look away from my face. "Yes, the sub is programmed to take us there. Two days."

Jack leans over the med kit and threads a suture through the needle. "That's too long."

Gaea's eyes narrow. "What do you mean?"

Jack's voice lowers to a scarce whisper, but I can still hear him, and he can barely get the words out. "She's lost too much blood."

Jessa blanches. "I told you not to say that."

"I wish I didn't have to." His soft fingertips roughly wipe a tear from his face.

I look up into Jack's eyes, and the greens and browns there glow as I blink the tears from my eyes. He bows his head toward mine, and a salty drop splashes across my cheek. But it's not my tear—it's his. Gaea's hand that has been pressed so hard against my ribs now gentles against me, and I suck in a breath as the pain bounces around my chest.

"I love you, Terra. I always will." His forehead touches mine, and his skin feels so warm.

"Jack . . ." Jessa turns away.

I smile. My lips form the words, *I know*. It's so inadequate for this man I could spend the rest of my life loving. *I love you too.*

His body shudders with a sob, and he pulls me against his chest. My wound throbs, but this time I don't mind. I'm with him. My eyes want to drag closed, but I fight the heaviness, and I memorize him, satisfied that he'll be the last thing I see when I close my eyes.

TWENTY-THREE

"Wait, Jack!"

At the sound of my name, I turn back and peer through the trees, watching for the girl.

"Terra!" I hear Kai's voice calling in the distance.

A small, dark-haired girl ambles between the slender trees. She waves when she sees me, her face lighting up at the sight of me, Jessa, and Jane standing here in the undergrowth next to the cabin.

"Where's your mother?"

Terra points behind her. Terra's cheeks are flushed and her breath is short. We're all winded from climbing through the forest to this spot. Terra reaches for me, and I swing her up in my arms and onto my shoulders.

"You're going to be too big for this soon."

Terra laughs and hangs on to my ears.

Kai appears from between the trees. Her radiant smile lights the entire clearing.

"This place is more beautiful than you described it, Jack." She rests a hand on the hewn logs of the cabin.

Our cabin. Mine and Terra's.

Jane nods. "This was a good idea. It feels right."

"This was her favorite place. This was her safe place for a long time." I glance around at the watchers lurking in the trees. It's been two years since a scanner or a watcher has made any noise in New America. When Terra shut down the network, all of these shut down too. Most of the others have been destroyed, but no one has come through this way for a long time. It's almost exactly the way she left it.

"Can you reach that one?" I point to one two feet above my head.

Terra stretches both arms up and yanks the small black lens out of the tree. She turns it over and over in her hands.

"What do I do?"

"Here, give it to me," Jane says.

Terra gives the watcher to Jane, and she puts it in her pack. Already the clearing looks more peaceful. But one person doesn't notice.

Jessa hasn't said a word since we drew near to the cabin. She talked almost without taking a breath the moment she stepped from the sub to land for the very first time—she was so nervous I almost checked my back out of habit. She touched one foot to the sand like it might be red hot. Then she got her footing and she rambled on about the weather, about the trees, about life in the colony, about what that animal over there was. Anything to keep her mind off of Terra. Now her lips are trembling and her cheeks are tear-stained.

I can't blame her. I do pretty well most days, but every once in a while, something will remind me of her, and I have to tell myself to hold it together.

I understand Dave better now than I ever did.

I hoist Terra off my shoulders and swing her over to Kai. Then I unzip my pack and ease out the small urn. I hate to part with it, but this is as she would like it. After all, she was mine, but she wasn't *mine*. She was all of ours and she was the Burn's, and she belongs in these woods. I never saw her more truly free, more magnificent, than when we were running through these woods together.

When I close my eyes, I can see our time spent in this cabin the day we found the old sleeping bags. That was before the labor camp and her hair was longer then. Her bright eyes drank in everything. I never realized it was because she was seeing so many things for the first time. Her eyes drank in everything, and I drank in her.

She would want to be here. I can feel it in the marrow of my bones.

Kai clears her throat. "Should we say a few words?"

Jessa laughs, and the sound is strangled in her throat. "She wouldn't have wanted us to *say* anything."

"What do you mean?" My hands clench too tightly around the beautiful jar Gaea gave me.

"Hold out your hand."

Jessa turns my hand over with her delicate fingers. Then she tentatively touches my palm. Kai, Terra, and Jane all lean in to see what she's doing.

She writes.

Terra was brave.

Kai smiles and finds my hand. *Kind.*

Jane's nimble fingers hesitate over my palm. Her eyes shine. *Loyal.*

Their gazes settle on me. I find a stick and sweep my foot over the leaves to clear a spot of ground. I trace the words in the earth. It feels more permanent that way.

The best of us all.

Then I open the jar. A breeze threads through the trees and I slowly overturn the blue glass, and the last physical reminder I have of her whisks away, here and there, spreading across this small piece of land that will forever be hers now.

I'm sad she didn't get to see what I have over the past two years—to see her father smile again, to see her mother return to the colony, to see a few dozen colonists venture to the surface, to see the scanners and watchers come down, to see the people she grew to love take back their liberty after the government was finally vulnerable.

But I think she knows.

I can almost feel her touch on my arm, on my hand, as the wind dances past me and continues on through the woods toward the sea.

ACKNOWLEDGEMENTS

I'm indebted to so many people who have helped me see this trilogy through from start to finish. The biggest thank you goes to my Heavenly Father for blessing me with my husband and my beautiful girls who gave me the time to write and all the love I could ask for.

Then of course, thanks are due to Maggie and Dave, beta readers extraordinaire; to all my family who cheered me on; to Danica for intellectual debates over comma use; to Maurianne for reminding me about lay and lie; to Renée for creating covers that still wow me; to the book bloggers who helped spread the word; and to my readers, without you the last two volumes never would have been told—thank you for the adventure.

Lastly, a debt of gratitude to Hans Christian Andersen, whose "A Little Mermaid" laid the groundwork for *The Burn*. You never know where inspiration may lurk.

Away from her writing, Annie is the mother of the awesomest girls in the world, has the best husband in the world, and lives in one of the prettiest places in the world (the Wasatch mountains are breathtaking!). She loves to cook, sing, pretend she's artistic, play the piano, and participate in community theater.

Find out more at annieoldham.com

Made in United States
Troutdale, OR
03/12/2025